Brenda Little was born in Engla...
by contributing humorous articl...
antiques, running a health-food...
being a slave to a 200-year-old ... ...aged to cram in being a newspaper columnist — local history regularly — Pet's Corner and Gardening when there was a crisis in the office. When she broke her foot and had to stay in one place she wrote a novel and it was published. The habit caught on; she wrote three more and they all did quite well. Once in Australia she went back to journalism and wrote for *Vogue, Vogue Living, Cleo,* was a book reviewer for the *Australian* and had a long stint as a writer for a soapie. There have also been books on art, the consumer society, herbs, organic gardening and three ghost-written stories for survivors of the Holocaust, along with a great deal of editing. *Knowing Sophie* is her first novel for some years. Brenda says she had a ball writing it and the habit has returned. Her next novel *Dear Henry* will be published by HarperCollins in 2001.

KNOWING SOPHIE

BRENDA LITTLE
KNOWING SOPHIE

HarperCollinsPublishers

HarperCollins*Publishers*

First published in Australia in 2000
by HarperCollins*Publishers* Pty Limited
ACN 009 913 517
A member of HarperCollins*Publishers* (Australia) Pty Limited Group
http://www.harpercollins.com.au

Copyright © Brenda Little 2000

This book is copyright.
Apart from any fair dealing for the purposes of private study, research, criticism or review, as permitted under the Copyright Act, no part may be reproduced by any process without written permission.
Inquiries should be addressed to the publishers.

HarperCollins*Publishers*
25 Ryde Road, Pymble, Sydney, NSW 2073, Australia
31 View Road, Glenfield, Auckland 10, New Zealand
77–85 Fulham Palace Road, London W6 8JB, United Kingdom
Hazelton Lanes, 55 Avenue Road, Suite 2900, Toronto, Ontario M5R 3L2
and 1995 Markham Road, Scarborough, Ontario M1B 5M8, Canada
10 East 53rd Street, New York NY 10022, USA

National Library of Australia Cataloguing-in-Publication data:

Little, Brenda.
  Knowing Sophie.
  ISBN 0 7322 6491 X.
  I. Title.
A823.4

Cover photograph: Australian Picture Library/Picture Book
Printed in Australia by Griffin Press Pty Ltd on 70gsm Ensobelle

5 4 3 2 1
03 02 01 00

For Surya and Lotus, with love.

CAROLINE

My friend Sophie was small and merry; all the lines of her face ran upward. She had the wholesomeness of warm, fresh bread, and even the most unexpected people became hungry for her. A Lovely Person, was the chorus. And she was. It was no surprise when she married early. David was a catch — in everybody's view but mine. She soon produced two sturdy and beautiful children and was held up as an example to us all. Nobody minded. I can't remember anyone bitching about Sophie — until she slit her wrists.

It *can't* be true, people said. When they found that indeed it was, shock turned to outrage. How *could* she?

All pity was reserved for themselves who, they considered, had been far less well treated by life than had Sophie Martin. For weeks they dined out on their suppositions.

At least, they had the good sense to stay clear of me.

It was the sort of funeral that paralyses the life of a town. Even the policeman who had nicked her for double-parking was there. He looked large, heavy and very uncomfortable. I could have laughed, if only she had been there to laugh with. Her boys were not there either. Somebody had obviously decided it was not in their interest to be exposed to the terrible words of the funeral service. I hope whoever it was got it right. Someday those kids may say, "I wasn't even allowed to see my mother buried".

David didn't look at me once, not in the church and not over the yellow clay gash of the grave. I didn't go back to the house with the mourning party; there were plenty of other people to see him through the ritual of the ham and sherry.

"Drive me home," I said to the most promising man there.

We screwed the rest of the day away.

"Somehow, I can never regard it as a *pastime*," she once said.

Odd that Sophie, who never felt the need to kill time, should have been under the imperative to kill herself.

Before he left, he tucked the sheet around me and smoothed my hair.

"Don't take it so hard," he said.

Strangers should never have the gall to offer pity. I turned away from the offensive gentleness.

"Just go."

I felt him hovering. "Poor lovely Caro."

"Go!"

My name is Caroline and nobody, *nobody* but Sophie has ever dared to call me "Caro".

It was a week before David telephoned. Even then it was too soon. "How are you?"

One stupid question begets another. "How are *you*?"

It was the shortest conversation we had ever had.

After I put the receiver down, I vomited, but that was hardly new. Whoever said that brandy was medicinal should get their facts right. Even now I retch when I see the familiar label.

He didn't come round, of course. Nobody did. Grief frightens people off. Sophie would have been round with the speed of light. She would have got rid of the bottles, cleaned me up and soon had me believing that none of it could possibly have been my fault. She would probably have quoted her old pal, St. Augustine, at me: "I say there is no sin where there is no personal will to sin."

He never did much for me. Unfortunately, I am not the type to take the soft option.

I was back in a loose version of my right mind when Nell, David's mother, telephoned me. "Do you know when David plans to fetch the boys home?"

"No."

She did her parrot-click of the tongue. "They were supposed to stay here for three weeks, and then Sophie was coming down to collect them."

"Well, that's out, isn't it?" We had never got on; we recognised each other. "Why are you asking me? Why not speak to David?"

"I — well —"

For such a famous actress, she was making a real job of fluffing her lines.

"If you are sick of having them, put them on a plane and send them back. They are old enough."

"Nobody has thought fit to tell me why they were sent here in the first place."

"I understood you complained that you didn't see enough of them."

"I had been complaining for years. I don't imagine my wishes had anything to do with it."

Our mutual dislike was such that another minute would have us in it up to our elbows. I did not reply and let the silence drag.

"How is he?" she said at last.

"I don't know. I haven't seen him."

She made a vulgar sound of disbelief.

"I was *Sophie's* friend."

"You mean she was yours."

We both knew the value of the dramatic pause. We had been taught to count it in heartbeats. Her training was better than mine. "I have to go," I said.

"The question I ask myself is — *Where?*"

I put the receiver down on her. I had suspected she knew, but it hadn't bothered me. She was worldly. She was fond of Sophie, fond enough not to trouble her with her suspicions. But she was not the sort of woman to understand that though I could share David's bed while Sophie's place in it was warm, there was no way in the world I could now that it was cold.

I did not go back to the bottle. Talking to Nell had made me aware that it was time I pulled my wits together.

If I had not been born so comfortably off, I might have made a better fist of things. I do have talents, but well-heeled girls can sidestep discipline and are accustomed to having what they want when they want it. I had never learned how to wait, and failure was unthinkable. My assurance fascinated Sophie and made her laugh.

"Aren't you *marvellous!*" she used to say.

She liked me. She knew all my faults, poked loving fun at them and never wavered in her affection. When I was with Sophie, I was at peace not only with myself but with the world.

We met when we were in our teens and students at the same small drama school in Sydney.

Nell, no doubt recognising that she was slipping and wanting to cash in on her name and her glamour, had ceremoniously renounced acting and taken up the teaching of dramatic art. Even now I meet people who say mistily, "You were with Nell Martin, too, weren't you?" as though we should dab our eyes in memory of that magical time. The old fraud. She could con anybody. For a time she even conned me.

I went to her in a state of irritation because, on a recent trip to Europe, too many amused English voices had said, "Ah! An *Australian!*" Sophie was there because she loved acting and needed the opportunity to use the beautiful cello voice nature had given her.

When we read Shakespeare in class, Nell always cast her as Lady Macbeth or Gertrude but, when the plays were produced, other girls played the roles. We moved on to Shaw and, though she broke our hearts when she read St. Joan, one look at her said that this Maid was too cosy for any soldier to be willing to follow.

"Short-thighed girls with round faces have narrow perimeters," Sophie said.

I am tall. Make-up can do wonders with deep eye-sockets and high cheekbones, and Nell had, at least, been able to make my voice carry well.

She never forgave me for the mess I made of her production. I never forgave her for being stupid enough to push me into it. It didn't occur to Sophie that she had anything to forgive.

The school only lasted four years. Nell had had enough of it by then. But at least it gave me Sophie.

Somebody once said "You two! Between you, you've got it all!"

And we had. We were the two parts of a whole. God knows I took her for granted and made no effort to please. It was enough to feel dependence without having to show it. Anyway, she *knew*.

She never did become an actress. She became a public relations girl. I spent Father's money and cultivated my persona.

Then she met Nell's son, David.

If ever there was an unmaternal woman, it was Nell but, so the story goes, like many another who has shunned motherhood and been sickenly bored by other people's children, once overtaken by conception, she behaved as though it were the first time it had happened in the history of the world. David's father appears to have protected himself by dying soon after the birth. The stepfather who followed knew his place.

Actually, as I understand things, she was a sensible parent. She offered him challenge, she never guaranteed his safety and she made him fight to win her approval. Small wonder, though, that he fell so deeply in love with Sophie.

To my amazement, Nell didn't seem to mind. I had expected her to be territorial and do everything she could to put the mockers on. I had *counted* on it. Now I had to face the fact that it was no longer Sophie-and-Caroline but Sophie-and-David.

I took him to my bed when Sophie was in hospital having the twins. Even decent men in love with their wives are easy to seduce. I didn't particularly want him — then — but at least it meant I couldn't be left out any longer.

He would have preferred it to be a one-night stand. He thought we could both claim the emotional stress of concern for Sophie as the catalyst for such frantic coupling, and he was sophisticated enough to be able to forgive himself one lapse, even though I was Sophie's best friend. He didn't know me as well then as he does now. Nobody makes use of *me*.

He showed brief alarm to find me still around when Sophie brought the babies home, but the situation soon settled when he found I posed no threat to his marriage. All men like their cake and half-penny, too, and I took care to be a half-penny worth having.

I gathered from conversations with both her and David that Sophie was the loving, giving partner to whom the missionary position is the whole story. I am told that girls in love find the greatest exaltation when taken flat on the back. I was not in love but I like sex, which I regard as an inventive art. David is an attractive man and an adept lover. I grew to like him. But I loved Sophie. I never felt closer to her than when I was in his arms. Naturally, I did not tell him that.

Did she find out about us? It all comes back to that.

If she did, she should have come to me. I would have been able to make her understand. There was nothing in David's relationship with me to make her feel life was not worth living.

And what do I do now?

DAVID

I have to fly down and collect the boys tomorrow. I would have thought that even she could have held her hand a little longer.

"It is more than three weeks," her cross voice said.

"I was hoping —"

"You must remember that Henry is an old man. They disrupt his way of life." She had never had any hesitation in disrupting it herself, but there was nothing to be gained by pointing *that* out.

"All right, all right. Just let me know which plane to meet."

"Do you imagine I would allow two small boys to fly by themselves?"

She had allowed me to fly by myself often enough when I was their age.

"You expect me to collect them?"

"Naturally."

She made no mention of Sophie. She did not ask me how I was. God knows why I thought she might.

"How are they?"

"Bored. Adelaide is wasted on them. They have no more cultural interest than you had."

Poor little devils. I could imagine what she had been putting them through. "I'll come tomorrow," I said. "As early as I can. Just have them ready."

"For what? You will obviously stay a few days."

"Just have them ready."

"Do you realise how long it is since I have seen you?"

"Nell," I said, "just have them ready."

"I would have thought you would *want* to stay."

I felt my hands begin to shake. "Why?" I said. "Just tell me bloody why." I put the receiver down and turned to tell Sophie.

It seems that the funeral was not the worst of it.

I flew down — and stayed, of course. Once we were face to face, I was no more proof against her certainties than I had ever been.

A man may have more than one wife, his mistresses may be legion, but he has only one mother. It doesn't seem to matter if there is neither love nor liking in the relationship, it is inescapable. Need is established early. God knows what it is I wanted from Nell, but I never got it. Resentment that, against my will, I remained the eternal supplicant clouded all my dealings with her.

"So ...", she said, holding me off and submitting me to scrutiny before permitting the salutatory embrace.

She seemed satisfied by what she saw. "You look dreadful," she said.

She was looking rather more splendid than usual. Her hair, piled high, was all one colour.

There was no sign of the boys.

"I sent them out with Henry — to bring in things for lunch."

So she was still God's gift to the delicatessen. The food she provided often flew small flags proclaiming its identity and usually tasted a great deal less appetising than one was led to expect.

"Come and see what I have done," she said, leading me to the room which was the core of the house.

It was all windows, stark white walls and great loops of curtain. And mirrors.

"Be careful," she said, as I sank into one of the deep couches, "there are pins."

She had achieved one of her tatty triumphs. Colour blazed against colour, was heaped, strewn, reflected. Texture challenged texture and made unexpected and satisfying marriage. Green plants ran riot. Some were in need of water. The effect was startling, but what could one *do* in such a room — except protect oneself against the pins?

"Why are you laughing?" she demanded.

"Nell — oh, Nell —!" Once begun, the laughter would not stop.

"Pull yourself together!" she said sharply. "Don't think you can become hysterical on *me*! You need a drink, but I don't suppose you have brought any."

I indicated the brown paper parcel. One knew better than to visit Nell without an accompanying bottle.

"Whisky," she said with disapproval.

She slopped too much, too carelessly into a champagne glass.

"That material cost the earth," she said, "don't spill —"

I had already done so.

"Nell," I said, as she swooped the glass away from me, "Sophie's dead."

I thought I knew every expression of her marvellously expressive face. No Nell I had seen before now stared at me.

"Do you think you have to tell me that?" she said, and hit me. Her rings split my lip.

She was quite matter-of-fact when she saw the blood and offered me her handkerchief.

"Don't think I'm sorry," she said. "You should not have had the effrontery to *whine*."

We lied to Henry and the boys about my swollen lip. Sophie was not mentioned. The boys squinted at me under their eyebrows, indicating their desperation to get away. Henry would clearly be grateful to be rid of the lot of us; the situation taxed even his exquisite manners.

I like old Henry. Devoted to Nell as he is, he still remains his own man. He gives her rope, but the length is of his choosing.

"I hope you admired her room," he said. "She did it all in one day — just because you were coming."

"Do *you* like it?"

"My boy!" he said, and Nell, at her most expressive, never endowed two words with such a wealth of meaning.

It was a fraught two days. Caroline had always said that Nell knew about us; now it was clear that she had been right, I waited for the accusations. None came and I did not dare invite them. I stood in need of absolution, not blame.

"The boys must go to boarding school," she said. "You are quite unfit to bring them up."

"We'll see."

"What else do you suggest? The surrogate mother?"

It was imperative to get away.

"Goodbye, Grandma," Ben said as we prepared to leave.

She kissed Tom firmly, preventing speech.

"Thank your grandmother for having you," I said.

She flashed me a sharp look, cut short their mumbles and shooed us towards the waiting taxi. As I turned for the mandatory farewell, she lifted her arms with theatrical grace. Her lips on mine were soft and warm, as yielding as those of a young girl, and then I felt the blood beginning to race through them. For a moment . . .

"Goodbye," I said, hurriedly disengaging myself and taking my sons by the hand.

She stood by Henry's side, waving us away. I wish I did not remember her slanted smile.

The familiar road to the airport peeled by.

Tom sagged at my side. "Boy," he said, "am I glad that's over!"

I put my arm round him.

"Dad," said Tom, butting at my other side, "about boarding school —"

"Hush," I said, "that was only your grandmother talking."

"But if we did go, we'd go to the same one, wouldn't we?"

"Of course."

It was a small enough certainty to offer them in their new uncertain world.

From the moment I arrived, we had been wary of one another. God knows what Nell had said to them or what they had overheard — she was a careless talker. They had not asked a single question about their mother. I had been unable to mention her name.

When I had made the difficult telephone call to Nell, I could not face speaking to them.

"Leave that to me," she had said. And, later, "You must let them stay here until it is all over."

She had never considered coming to the funeral herself. "I never go to them," she had said. It had made things easier at the time, but how about now?

During the flight back, I worried about the state of the house. I had been unable to bring myself to get rid of Sophie's things.

Her books, her clothes, her painting and sewing gear, tapes and records were where they had always been. I could no more rid myself of them than I could be rid of her by the gesture she had made. Now I agonised over what home — so much the same and yet so different — would mean to the boys when we got there.

"There'll be time for a swim when we get back, won't there, Dad?" Tom asked.

"Loads of it, old son."

"Do you know if she — is my surfboard mended?"

"Good as new," I said.

They were, after all, only nine years old. They still had the wide, rock-strewn beach. They still had the sea and the sun.

"Make your own beds, put your clothes away and I'll keep the place tidy and do you one meal a day. How's that?" Sophie's cleaning lady had said.

I had agreed that it would do very well.

"Any fool can use a washing machine. How about ironing?"

As a bachelor I had been devoted to the drip-dry.

"Stick with it," she said.

It sounded easy; the difficulty was in remembering what to do when. I always seemed to be shouting at the boys.

We did not like the type of food she left for us. We shovelled it into the garbage bin and ate out, mostly Chinese. Before long we knew the menus of every eating place in the area. I brought food in. *Takeaway* soon became a dirty word. There were months to go before the beginning of the new term when I could send the boys away to school. Sophie had chosen a very inconvenient time of year in which to die.

The first time the thought came, I felt ashamed, but the pressures and irritation of the scramble to get through the days soon overcame that. I am a solicitor and deal with fraught people during my working hours; I need to come home to peace and not the piddling problems of shopping and the frantic search for clean underpants.

I bought time by sending the boys on an Outward Bound course. Ben came home with a sprained ankle and Tom with bowels set in concrete. They grizzled about their mosquito bites and scratched them until they festered. "For God's sake, stop whining!" I bawled at them and was immediately sickened by the memory of Nell's face when she had said much the same thing to me in the incredible moment when she struck me. I knew her looks of anger and distaste but not the one of maddened grief which had blazed so suddenly. I can forget it no more easily than I can the small, shut face of the little body on the slab.

"Yes, that is my wife," I had said.

I wish someone else could have done the identification. That is not how I wish to remember her.

I can't bring Caroline's face to mind at all. Probably defence mechanism — the thought of actually seeing her again fills me with dread. I have always thought of myself as a decent man; she is the continual reminder that I am not. To be forced to live with self-dislike is not pleasant.

But then ... Sophie's smiling trust in me was absolute; she made betrayal far too easy. I don't forgive her for that. There are sins of omission as well as commission. If blame is to be laid, I cannot allow it to rest solely on my shoulders.

HENRY

They left this morning looking dispirited and bedraggled. As I knew it would, Nell's panache disappeared with them. I am her only audience now. As we turned back to the house after watching their taxi disappear, she reached for my hand. I helped her back into the house, where we were confronted by the wild extravagance of the room she had created.

"Let's get the bloody stuff down," she said.

"I'll do it."

I gave her a pain-killer, took her teeth out and put her to bed. She looked at me with pure dislike. "You think you've won, don't you?"

"Bloody Henry," she said, and then the drug began to take over. I sat and watched her fall into sleep and wiped the saliva from her slack lips. When I was certain she was deep under, I left her to rest.

It was easy to take the curtains down and strip the material from the couches. I put the pins in a magnetised container; she might need them again. I watered all the plants. It was good to see the room become bare and quiet again, window and wall simple and honest. I plumped up the soiled and comfortable cushions of the couches.

She called out several times in her sleep, but I am used to that. Sometimes she cries for David, sometimes for me; today it was for Sophie.

I cooked scallops in cream and white wine for our meal, and then I sat by her bed and read. I get through a lot of Dickens this way. I am glad I did not read him when I was young. He is a man for the time when the heart remains strong but the juices run thin. Nell has no time for him. Too many words, she says. I draw his words over me like a blanket.

They should be home by now.

Nell is right; David is quite unfitted to bring up those two boys, but then he was unfitted for marriage, too. In fact, the word that springs to mind when thinking of him in any other area but his work is "unfitted". It would be easy to dismiss him as of little account, but I remember the early days when I took him on. I plead guilty to the sin of selfishness. I watched things going wrong for him, but there was no way in the world I was going to queer my pitch with Nell by fighting with her over the upbringing of a child for whose birth I was not responsible. If his own father had lived ... fruitless to wonder; anyway Nell would still have been his mother.

"You really think the meek inherit the earth, don't you?" she once asked me, fixing me with her basilisk stare, and then laughed. Take it on, you tender-hearted fool, had been her unspoken challenge. What she does not realise is that I can.

I watch her in her drug-induced sleep and think of her death, which cannot be far away. Much of what I am will go with her when she dies, but she has never been able to rob me, as she robbed her son, of personal validity.

"Sophie," she calls. Her eyes are rolled back so that only the white is showing.

I too grieve over Sophie's death. I loved that warm and easy girl, but she disappointed me. I thought there was too much humour in her for her ever to be unamused enough to take her own life. The human animal is ridiculous. We can only hope to cope with ourselves by keeping irony and affection in effective balance. To expect too much of ourselves — or of anybody else — is a recipe for disaster. I do not like to think that the ally I believed she was allowed her expectations to run too high, and forgot to smile. She leaves me lonely.

The telephone is ringing.

"We are safely home," David says.

"Oh —"

"I thought you would like to know."

"She is asleep."

"At this time of day?"

He had noticed so little he is capable of surprise. The familiar irritation I feel with him precludes further speech.

"Well, tell her, will you? When she wakes."

"Of course."

"Well..." he says again.

I do not help him.

"Thank you for everything," he says when the silence becomes too long.

"Think nothing of it."

"But I do." His tone is sharper.

I can hear a dog barking and the sound of a sudden yell.

"Have to go," he says.

I will be glad to be rid of him. There are too many problems here.

"Ask her to ring me, will you? When she feels like it," he says before I can put the receiver down.

"I'll do my best."

We both know her attitude to the cost of long-distance telephone calls.

"Thank you, Henry. You're a good man."

The conversation leaves me in a state of irritation. "Good" men are too often patronised and shown scant deference. It is time for

17

me to be less "good" than I have been in the past, but patterns of behaviour seldom change. I will have to rely on endurance.

I have long thought "endurance" to be one of the most satisfying words in the language. I place it beside "tranquil", "abiding" and "charity" as a word which carries its own blessing. Nell says I am pedantic. She is loose in her choice of words. She has also accused me of being epicurean, and has been wrong again. One may know what one is *not*, the difficulty is to know what one *is*. I read Dickens to try and find out — and to pass the time when she lies silent. I am glad he was such a prolific writer.

DAVID

I can put it off no longer. I must deal with Sophie's things.

The boys, thankfully, are away for the weekend. People are being surprisingly kind.

A woman I barely know appeared at the door. "A beach barbecue and your kids can stay over?" she asked.

The boys looked at me with urgent appeal. I hope it was not too plain that I was as grateful to be rid of them as they were to go. After they left I realised I had not reminded them to take comb and toothbrush, nor had I given them any money — in case.

There are so many clothes. And shoes. She cannot have worn half of them. Taking the silky stuff and cottons from the hangers and pressing them into a suitcase has released the scent of her trapped in the fabric. I can smell her as surely as though she were standing at my side. My warm, brown girl.

There are gilt sandals and shoes which are nothing but straps of leather and tall heels. Caroline-type things. Soph usually wore flat little kung-fu shoes or went barefoot. Her feet were small and splayed with comically prehensile big toes. She ran and climbed better than I can.

Her wardrobe is tidy, and she was never tidy. She left clothes where they fell, books open at the page she had reached, wool and tapestry where they could be picked up and worked on again at a moment's notice. There were little pools of Sophie all over the house. Every now and then she displayed wrathful energy and got everything put away and in order, only to begin to undermine her efforts almost at once.

All the drawers are tidy too. We had three each. Mine always were tidy. She placed my shirts in neat piles, after folding them with precision. I could always depend on there being clean socks and underwear. She had to burrow into her own in search of elusive garments. I once gave her a St. Anthony medal as a joke. Now they are all tidy and sorted. There are flimsy scraps of nylon and lace, but no sign of the little cotton panties she used to wear. She slept naked. If it was cold, she would slip into one of my old cotton shirts. I never remember her wearing any of the beautiful and expensive nightgowns which lie here. I have to close the drawer. I am looking at orchestrated and premeditated death.

Not that I need further proof of premeditation; there is no possibility of accident or miscalculation when the hand draws the razor across the vein. Her suicide was no cry for help, but a statement of intent. And she went without a word to any of us.

Her silence is a terrible thing, for when else did we know her silent? She talked to people next to her in shops, to the men who came to fix the drains, the woman who collects the envelope for the Spastics and the scruffy kids the boys bring home. She talked to Nell, and Nell, smoothed and easy, talked to her, and not only about their boring and abiding passion, the theatre. When I came into the room, their lively conversation would stop.

It stopped because Sophie was glad to see me, and all her attention had become mine; Nell made it clear that my appearance spoiled things.

"What do *you* want?" she once said, and was taken aback by Sophie's sudden, uncharacteristic anger.

"NOT to be spoken to like that, for one thing!" she had said, "and I hope that another is to pour us all a drink. I have been in need for some time."

I expected outrage and umbrage, but Nell had only looked amused. "So . . . our puss can spit," she said.

She gathered up her bag and gloves, and I had thought we were in for one of her dramatic exits, but she had leaned over and, with more affection than I have known her to show, ruffled Sophie's short curls.

"You should do that more often," she said. "Try it on your friends."

She refused the drink I proffered, kissed Sophie and left.

When I came back from seeing her out, Sophie sank down among the cushions of the couch and blew out her cheeks. Her lips were pale.

"You do need this," I said, handing her the glass Nell had refused.

As she took it from me, she looked up into my face. "She has never liked Caroline," she said.

It was then I began to worry.

I have filled all the available cases. Shoes are unwieldy. Now there is the question of what to do with her winter slacks and woollies.

"Why *do* moths always go for the crotch?" she once asked.

There are lavender bags and sprigs of fennel lying among the wool. The fennel is still green and only just beginning to shrivel. What does one do with the detritus of another's life? There are garbage bags in the kitchen cupboard, but I cannot bring myself to use those.

The jewellery, at least, poses no problems. Most of it is inherited and must be saved for the boys to give to their wives. She seldom wore any of it. The wide gold rings with the splendid stones were too heavy for her small hands.

"I do damage every time I wear this damn thing," she complained of the handsome bracelet of gold links weighted with many expensive "charms".

There are two cheap brooches, one of butterflies, the other of bluebirds, and six tinny apostle spoons. I think they were presents from the boys. Her wedding ring and the solitaire diamond I gave her are still in the cellophane bag the undertaker brought to me after the funeral. I had intended they should stay with her.

"Must be worth a packet," he had said, handing me the transparent little bag. He obviously expected thanks for his honesty and thoughtfulness and was bewildered by my hostility. She had grown plumper over the years and had difficulty when trying to take them off. He must have had to twist and wrench her finger. What, in God's name, do I do with them now?

Caroline loves old jewellery. She forages in antique shops looking for garnets, rubies and cornelians, but diamonds, set deep in the old-fashioned style, are her particular pleasure.

I have always admired the beauty of her hands and the unusual rings she has been clever enough to find. Now I do not know how she can bear to wear them.

Does she not realise how much they once meant to other people and that they carry meanings at which she cannot guess?

No-one else will ever wear Sophie's rings. As faithfulness goes, that may not be much to offer, but with all my heart, I will keep that promise. I cannot bear to take them out of the bag and actually touch them, but cellophane seems such a sterile and unnatural housing for anything that was hers. This is the first time I have really wept for her.

It has been a bad weekend.

The woman brought the boys home about an hour ago.

"I wonder," I said, taking her to where some of Sophie's things were laid out on the bed, "would these be of any use to you?"

She had pale eyes in a plain face. Her hair was spiked with salt and sand.

"No, thank you," she said carefully, "I don't care to scavenge and I wouldn't have thought you would have enjoyed seeing me wearing her clothes".

My stomach lurched. "I'm *sorry*," I said. "I didn't mean —"

"I don't much care what you mean," she said. "Now, the boys are fed —"

"I'm truly sorry," I said again, "and thank you for having them, Mrs —"

"Savage", she said, turning her pale eyes full on me, "by name — and quite often by nature".

I remembered her then. She is Dan Savage's wife. He is the speech therapist to whom Sophie took the boys when their early stammer showed no sign of disappearing. They live in the sprawling house under the pines down by the beach.

"A-aach!" She said, making a noise like a small, touchy dog. "Don't take any notice of my tongue — nobody else does. Send the boys down any time you like. I'm always at home."

"I'm very grateful to you."

"No need to be. Just look at it as bread coming home on the waters."

She is the sort of firecracker person with whom I am always at a loss.

"For heaven's sake," she said, impatient with my obvious bewilderment, "after all Sophie did for me —"

I hadn't a clue what she meant.

The boys were pleased with themselves and a great deal too boisterous.

"Shower and bed," I said.

I have yet to study the notes on the appointments made for tomorrow. A charming woman with whom I would have trusted my last penny has been charged with embezzlement. She is far less disturbed than she should be, because I doubt if she can be saved from imprisonment. On our first brief meeting, I became aware that she was being less than frank with me. I have to know more before I can advise her. It looks as though Kate Hamilton could be a problem.

There is a crash from upstairs and a wild burst of giggling. Storming up, I meet the boys, naked, on their way to the bathroom.

I can only tell them apart when they stand together; meeting one or the other around the house I can be fooled. People find this hard to believe; they seem to think that the loving eye should be able to distinguish between even the most identical of twins, and Sophie certainly seemed able to do so, but when they wished, they could trick even her.

As much for my own convenience as in the belief that it is important for them to establish their separate identities, I had refused to allow them to be dressed alike. Now the colour of the towels they carry — blue for Ben and tan for Tom — does not help. In their present mood, they could have made a switch.

"Knock it off and get showered!"

They remain cheerful. It seems a long time since I have seen them grin.

"We can go again next week, can't we, Dad? We can, can't we?"

"I'll see."

"Aw, come on!"

"I've told you. I'll see."

"Aw —!"

Their grins turn ingratiating.

"Come on, Dad," Tom says, "it will be OK. Mum doesn't mind."

The lunatic use of the present tense enrages me.

"Well, she doesn't. Does she, Ben?" he says, turning sulky.

I look from one to the other. Steady-eyed, they stare back.

"Now look here ...," I say as carefully as I can.

"All right! Don't believe me! Ask her then!"

I cannot read their faces. "I don't get you," I say slowly. "How could I possibly ask her?"

Ben's sigh is deep and gusty. "When she comes, of course," he says with exasperated patience.

I have enough to cope with without this. I bundle them into the bathroom, bumping and stumbling. "You've got ten minutes — and don't let me hear any more of this nonsense!"

I seem to have alarmed them as much as they have alarmed me.

Back downstairs I listen to the hammer of water through the pipes. "Our vocal plumbing," Sophie called it. Above the sound I can hear them beginning to laugh again.

If they are trying it on with me, they are being diabolical.

At last the bathroom door opens and I hear them crashing along the landing.

"Night, Dad," they call.

After the slam of their bedroom door, I strain my ears. They make no sound. I had not realised how silence can throb.

I take the notes from my briefcase and attempt to settle down to considering them, but how the hell can I focus my mind now? All my worries come flooding in.

How am I to run my working days in the future? What will the boys do if I cannot always get home on time? Can they be trusted to swim only between the flags? Will they stuff themselves with trash food from the kiosk and then have no appetite for anything decent when I get home? I have seen too much of what happens to children deprived of certainty and routine.

"It surprises me that people actually *choose* you to be their solicitor," Nell once said, as though commiserating with my clients.

She would have even less regard for my abilities if she could see into my mind now.

Funny, no matter how little a problem may have to do with Nell in the first place, she always comes into it somewhere.

I wonder if there is any point in asking her advice about this problem with the boys. I believe she flirts with what she calls "the spirits".

But the whole thing is absurd. It is on a par with that nonsense about the "playmate" the boys claimed to have had. One of my few disagreements with Sophie was about the way she allowed them to get away with such idiocy, even going to the extent of laying an extra place at the table.

"Does Zak like beans?" she once asked.

But she had the sense to abandon such stupidities. We heard no more of Zak after that particular upset.

Kate Hamilton. I must get my mind back to Kate Hamilton.

She irritates me. From our brief meeting, I get the impression she is looking forward to punishment. It seems to be her easy way out. No matter where I look, there are no easy ways out for me.

THE SAVAGES

Nin Savage stopped flailing the eggs with her old-fashioned eggwhisk.

"If you're going anywhere near the Martin's place, you might like to drop off the clothes the boys left behind."

Her husband gave her a look over his paper. "I suppose there's no getting out of it?"

Nin resumed her assault on the eggs. The whites rose and stood, stiff-peaked.

"While you're there, you might as well ask him to dinner."

Dan cast his paper aside. "Here we go!" he said. "Can I never teach you to stay out of things!"

They regarded each other in affectionate dismay.

"We have to do *something* about him," she said. "You should have heard me! I was awful."

"So what's new? You're an awful girl."

Her smile died. "Don't tease," she said. "It's bad enough about Sophie..."

"Hey," he said, and was across the kitchen and had her in his arms.

She sagged against him. "I get up with it and I go to bed with it. It gets worse all the time. Why did she do it, Dan?"

"Stop it, love."

"I can't."

Impeded by the eggwhisk, they rocked together.

"I'm afraid," she said. "There's no safety anymore. When a thing like this happens, anything can."

The kitchen was pale and cool, all bleached wood and smooth marble surfaces. Beyond the louvred doors, the huge windowed wall of the next room framed a picture of sand, sea and sky as primary in colour as a child's painting. The room itself retreated from the window; low Swedish chairs, pale nubbed linen and a carpet as neutral as bone made an instant peace. Nin was a girl from the Northern Hemisphere and dealt firmly with Nature's extravagance; the only disturbance permitted came from the jagged leaves of huge plants which threw dramatic shadows against the walls. Nin's home always came as a surprise to people; it did not go with her rasping truculence. She was not being truculent now.

"We can afford to be decent to him, can't we?"

"I'll enjoy watching you at it."

They began to laugh again.

"Let's have a drink," he said, "the pavlova can wait".

He led her through to the peaceful room and settled her in a chair. There was more gin than tonic in the glass he brought to her.

"The worst thing is to know that I could have —"

"No you couldn't."

"But, Dan, she used to talk to me — that's what I don't understand. What was it she couldn't say?"

He waited for the gin to begin to anaesthetise, but his luck was out.

"Do you think she'd discovered she was sick, something terminal?" Nin went on.

"No! She was a healthy little thing. In all the years we've known her, when did she ever take to her bed, except for that time when the boys were about three months old and she found she was pregnant again?"

28

"What? I never knew that!"

Dan avoided the blazing accusation of her eyes.

"You knew! You didn't tell me! Look at me, damn you!"

"I thought it was her own business," he said awkwardly. "I met her walking on the beach and she was upset. I ask you! They'd only been married a year and already they were a family of four. David wasn't coping too well. She was afraid she might have twins again."

"So you told her what to do?"

"I told her whom to go and see."

"Jesus!"

Shock had stripped the colour from her face. When he reached out to comfort her, she struck him off.

"Don't make so much of it, Nin! She didn't. It was a great relief — she said so — and it was all a long time ago."

"How long is long? Oh God, Soph . . ."

He captured her flailing arms and anchored her to his chest. "Stop it! I was fond of her, too, you know. She'd never rest if she thought she'd caused trouble between us."

She shoved him away. "You think she's resting?"

"She's dead, darling. That's the way she wanted it."

Her deep grunt of laughter surprised him. "Have it your way," she said.

In their clumsy groping, she had slopped her gin; his shirt was damp with it. He took the half-empty glass from her and went to refill it. When he brought it back to her she swilled the liquid around and stared down into it.

"It's like when you throw a stone into a pond, isn't it?" she said. "The ripples. If I'd have thrown that stone, I'd want to know how far the ripples spread. I'd stick around."

"Stop it!" he said. "There's a good girl. Stop it!"

They were on the edge of entering an area where disagreement was basic. He took the glass away from her with decision.

29

"I mean it," he said. "That poor sod is coming to dinner, so no nonsense, please!"

"What do you take me for? I won't even mention Sophie. Don't worry. David has nothing to fear from me. It's Kate Hamilton he has to watch out for."

She took her glass back from him.

"You'll see," she said. "Just sit back and watch the ripples widen."

DAVID

That Savage woman is incredible; I can't imagine how Sophie could have made a friend of her and am far from sure I have now done the right thing.

Yesterday, as I drove up the incline towards the house, I saw her walking ahead of me. Some women don't have the sense to know they should never wear trousers. She was waiting by the garage door as I drew up.

"Hell of a pull up here," she said, jerking her head towards the bends which wind down the hill between our house and their sprawling monstrosity on the beach. She hardly gave me a chance to struggle out of the car, clutching briefcase and a pile of papers.

"The boys are at our place," she said. "They get on with ours and we don't mind them being around, so how about letting them stay with us until the end of the holidays?"

"Just a minute —"

"I haven't got a minute. I should be at home cooking. Just tell me. Is it OK?"

How does one deal with a pushy woman, particularly when mutual dislike is so palpable? And when the mind leaps ahead and sees the advantage in what is so gracelessly offered?

"I can hardly presume..." I said, spreading my hands unwisely. The papers slipped to the ground and began to scatter in the light wind.

She was as loud a tongue-clicker as Nell, but at least she helped me to gather them up, which was more than Nell would have done.

"Think about it," she said, handing the last of them to me. "Then come down to dinner with us. If you're agreeable, bring all their things."

It didn't take much thinking about: to have them off my hands would be an enormous relief. It would be possible to have a civilised meal in the city at the end of the day, instead of rushing home to face the squalid food provided by the cleaning lady or the dubious nourishment of takeaways. And not only that, the elder Savage boy is a lifeguard and a hero to the lads who frequent the beach, so I wouldn't have to worry about them drowning.

I collected together what I hope will pass as "all their things". I had packed away Sophie's in every available case and now had to fall back on garbage bags. I had barely begun packing when I heard them storming into the house.

"We can, can't we, Dad? You're not going to say no, are you? Are you?"

Their faces were eager and alive, the dull sullenness which was beginning to worry me quite wiped away.

"Yes, of course you can go. Now find Pluto and feed him while I get your stuff together."

Pluto is our old tomcat and aptly named. His nature is as black as his coat. We have had him ever since Sophie brought him home, all skin and bone, and distrustful claws. It took time for love to mellow him. Now he arches and purrs and demands in the calm certainty that all his needs will be met. If they are not, his displeasure is loud. We've heard a lot of it lately.

He is nowhere to be found. I remember, with guilt, that he was not around this morning and that I forgot to leave any food out for him. Such is the power of his personality that we all know we cannot leave the house until he has been found and fed. "Pluto, Pluto," they call in anxious, penetrating trebles.

I prefer to forget the next hour.

Temper was not improved when I returned from a fruitless search among the scratchy shrubs of the lower garden, to find the boys watching television and Pluto stretched, replete, on the carpet.

"Why didn't you call me?"

"We had to feed him and answer the phone. You said to take all messages carefully and write them down straight away."

I didn't like the whine in the voice.

"And did you?"

"No, she put the phone down on me."

No need, then, to wonder who it could have been. Caroline wouldn't have spoken to the boys.

"It wasn't Mrs Hamilton. It wasn't Mrs Savage —"

Mrs Savage! All thought of Caroline was immediately stripped from the mind. Mrs Savage was not the sort of woman to be patient with tardy guests.

"Come on! Get all these bags together! We've got to be off!"

Dan Savage, fortunately, is not the least like his wife. God knows how he puts up with her. I suppose his professional training must come in handy. He had a glass of whisky in my hand as soon as we were through the door, and I have to admit that the house looks a damn sight better on the inside than it does from the outside. It was something of a jolt, though, to see one of the huge tapestries Sophie used to take such joy in doing, hanging on their wall. He saw me register it, and we both looked away.

The meal was good. At least the woman can cook.

The boys, in their dressing-gowns, hair slicked after their shower, ate with devotion. I could have wished their appreciation had not been so evident. It was clear that they had developed acute

33

hero-worship for the Savage boys, who are large and fair and given to wisecracks. After eating everything within sight, the four of them escaped from the table with indecent haste.

"Don't worry," Dan said encouragingly, "they'll be fine."

Part of my worry was that I knew they would be. I could imagine what Nell would have to say about the situation.

"Thank you so much," I said when the woman got up, saying "Coffee?"

"I won't stay, if you don't mind. Work has banked up. I really must get down to it."

She appears to be called "Nin", a name as unprepossessing as she is.

"I put everything I could think of in those bags," I said. "If anything has been forgotten, they can collect it."

"Ben will do that tomorrow," she said. "He noticed that Zak's things had been left behind."

"Zak?"

The stupid name they gave to that damned "playmate" they claimed to have.

"Yes," she said, with offensive patience. She always seems to be accusing me of something.

Dan gave me two slow comforting pats on the shoulder. "Nothing to worry about, old man, nothing at all." His calm assurance was welcome, but he needn't have sounded so damn British about it. I was glad to get out of the place.

The light had almost gone when I drove back up the hill. It seemed so strange to come home to a darkened house. I didn't like it and, reminded as I was of our disagreement about the boys and their unhealthy imagination, I felt a flicker of resentment against Sophie. I switched on every lamp as I passed through. For the first time, I wished we had chosen overhead lights — at least they throw no shadows on the walls.

CAROLINE

I bought a new car today; I had to do something to lift the gloom. I bought unwisely, but when a sleek young know-all looks you up and down and says, "I know just what Madam wants", and then leads you to what he calls "a nice little economical car for shopping …"

The manager didn't make the same mistake. I hope he sacks that stupid oaf. The Mercedes is pale blue. Heads turned as I drove down the High Street with the hood down. I waved to the butcher, the baker, the candlestick maker.

But where will I go?

It is twenty-seven days since we buried Sophie, and there has been no word from David. There should have been. I remember Sophie once saying, with her indulgent smile, "The thing to remember about David is that the poor love just doesn't realise — then the rest comes easy".

It doesn't come easy to me. When she was alive, I had only to snap my fingers for him to come running. It is time to snap them again.

I rang him when I knew the boys should be in bed and, if he is the father he claims to be, he should be at home.

There was a blare of television music and gunshot when the phone was picked up.

"Hello."

I thought it sounded like Tom, the most ebullient of the twins.

Nell's training comes in useful sometimes. I knew he would not recognise the voice in which I said, "I wish to speak to Mr David Martin".

"Is that you, Mrs Savage? We won't be long. Dad's out looking for Pluto. He's come back — Pluto, that is — but I don't know where Dad is."

That dreadful old tomcat. As far as I am concerned, once out, the beast should never be let in again.

"Tell him —"

"Oh, it's Mrs Hamilton then. Sorry. I've got a pencil. I can write down a message."

I hung up. Bloody David. Mrs Savage? Mrs Hamilton? What about *me*?

Sophie was always amused by the swiftness with which I lose my temper and she never took what she called my "right royal rages" seriously.

"You have a lovely time working up all that adrenalin," she would say.

I was not having a lovely time now. Anger, I find, is not in the least like temper. Temper is quick and flashy, an easy release, but anger runs cold and deep and offers no catharsis. I am very, very angry with David.

How dare he behave as though I no longer exist? Since that unspeakably offensive secretary of his is familiar with my voice, he must be aware that I have made several attempts to contact him. Or is she playing her own game?

As soon as I saw her, I was on to her. Funny how intelligent women fail to realise that the unfettered bust is only acceptable if it is small and high. God knows what makes her think she has any chance with David.

I dialled his office number and there she was.

"Yes, Mr Martin is in, but I cannot disturb him. He is with a client," the self-important voice said.

"I don't care if he is being visited by the Holy Ghost. Get him."

The quick indrawn breath told me she knew who was calling. "I can't do that — Madam."

"Oh yes, you can," I said, "for this telephone will ring until you do. And don't be stupid enough to think leaving it off the hook will do you any good."

She made a mewing sound of protest, but I knew it was only a matter of seconds before David would be lifting the receiver. Australia is supposed to be a classless society, but show me a girl from the western suburbs who can hold her own against the assurance given by wealth and privilege.

DAVID

Once life gets the boot in, it seems to develop a taste for it; problem is now piling on problem.

I overslept badly, no doubt due to relief at getting the boys off my hands, and, when I arrived at the office, my secretary informed me frigidly that Mrs Hamilton was waiting and had already been given two cups of coffee. She employed the tone of voice in which she recently told me that a person who refused to give either her name or telephone number had called — twice. A Rude Person, she, of course, knew it was Caroline.

Bianca (I had found her name as hard to resist as her credentials) is a feisty, intelligent girl who showed signs of what Caroline called "yearnings" early in her employment with me. I cut them down as gently as I could, for she is far too good at her job for me to allow her usefulness to be compromised. She seems now to have appointed herself guardian of my morals.

I found Kate Hamilton at ease on the big couch under the window. I knew little about the woman except that she had been the wife of an architect reverentially regarded locally, whose early death had been widely mourned in the national newspapers. Among regrets for the public loss, there had been commiserations for his widow, but the ripple of interest soon flattened and Bianca had had to remind me who she was. Now I was aware she had what Caroline would call the "right sort" of looks: the careless shabbiness of her corduroy slacks and woollen jumper did nothing to detract from the impression of what I could only register hazily as "quality". I am used to assurance in women — Nell and Caroline both have it in spades — but this peaceful ease had me baffled. She made it hard to believe she was aware the law was breathing down her neck and that she was under censure from the society into which she had hitherto fitted comfortably and unobtrusively. She made me feel uncomfortable.

"Sorry to have kept you waiting," I said.

"My own fault," she said peacefully. "I was early. I need to talk to you."

"And I to you!" I said, sounding falsely hearty. "There's a lot to discuss before we can decide what to do."

"Oh!" She was not afraid of eye contact. Her gaze was direct and steady. "I don't want you to *do* anything. I will defend myself."

I sank down into the chair behind my desk. The woman was out of her mind.

"Do you know what you're saying? I can't let you do that!"

"Don't look so worried," she said, "it's all quite simple".

I closed my eyes in exasperation; anyone stupid enough to think involvement with the law was simple was blundering into a minefield.

"You don't know what is involved!" I said impatiently.

"No," she agreed, "that is what I want to ask you about. Will you please explain the procedures and tell me how I have to address the different officials?"

Patience slipped away. The conversation was becoming ludicrous. "Mrs Hamilton," I said carefully, "you are accused of stealing over a quarter of a million dollars of your employer's money. There is a very angry man out there who wants his money back and can afford to engage a top-ranking barrister. The best defence lawyer you can find will have difficulty saving you from a prison term."

39

"I know that. And I will plead 'Not guilty'. I didn't *steal* the money. You know that. I just redistributed it."

"WHAT?"

For the first time, she looked uncertain. "I'm sorry. Don't you know? I thought Sophie would have explained it to you."

Now patience was entirely gone. "What the hell has my wife to do with it?"

"Oh dear," she said.

I had the sick feeling we were heading for deep waters.

We were.

I had to listen, hardly believing, as she spelled it out: "That man is a monster. We couldn't believe anybody could be so corrupt and heartless. We couldn't let him get away with it. Sophie said you would understand."

"You mean she took part in this?"

"Not directly. I didn't tell her how I did it, but we were agreed it had to be done. All those little people, desperate, all their money gone — and he congratulated himself. 'Good business!' he said. 'Clever!'"

She was actually smiling mischievously. "But I saw they got it all back. Now let us see how clever he can be!"

I was robbed of speech.

"Don't you see?" she went on eagerly. "When I defend myself, I will be able to stand up and tell the jury the sort of man he is and show the wickedness of what he was doing, so they will understand I just had to do what I did. It will all be out in the open. All of it."

"And you think that will save you from prison?"

"It might. I have to take my chance."

I had never heard such dangerous nonsense.

She looked at me apologetically. "I didn't ask Sophie to stand bail for me, you know, she just did it."

"*Sophie* stood bail?!"

I felt my stomach clench. Was there no end to all this?

Before I could stop myself, I had blurted out "How much?"

"Rather a lot, I'm afraid, but she knew I would never let her down. There was no need to worry."

No need to worry! The police would know my wife had stood bail for a self-confessed criminal! What the hell would that do for my professional standing? "I was lucky," she said, "that other people took over when she — when . . ."

I swung my chair around so that I need not look at her. Her soft voice pursued me. "I am so sorry — at such a time — but from what she said, I quite thought she had told you."

"Sophie told me nothing."

Neither of us could find anything else to say. The sudden ring of the telephone was a relief. As we were attempting to collect ourselves, my office door burst open, and Bianca, against all precedent, interrupted us. Her face was tight with temper. "You'll have to handle this," she said, without ceremony. "I told the woman you were with a client, but she doesn't seem to think that matters, so *you* tell her!"

Kate Hamilton rose from the couch. "I think it's time for me to go," she said.

It was, of course, Caroline. "I want to see you," she said, without preamble, "and don't say you can't make it. I know the boys are with the Savages. Eat before you come. I presume you still have your key. I will expect you."

Words said so often before, but everything was different now.

CAROLINE

He looked exactly as usual — smooth, clean, stylish — and had not the wit to conceal that he found I was not looking "usual" at all.

"I haven't eaten," he said. "There wasn't time."

I was damned if I would cook for him.

"You must at least have cheese," he said, "a tin of soup?"

I followed him through to the kitchen. He knew where the cupboards were. He found a tin of Baxter's Game Soup which I had been intending to throw away because of the date on the label and a half-pot of dried Stilton. I allowed him to make free with my tin-opener, saucepan, stove, milk and port wine. Watching him at work, I took particular notice of his hands, the knowledgeable fingers with the unerring touch.

I leaned against the doorjamb and considered him while he ate. He tidied up competently.

"Now I want a drink," he said.

I indicated the port. "That's all there is." It was too. I never thought the day would come when alcohol would be repellent to me. Me, with all the makings of a lush! How that would have amused Sophie! The look he flashed at me was all hostility. He filled a glass with the rest of the port and brushed past me into the sitting room.

"I take it you want to see me about something specific?" he said, prowling around and ignoring my indication to him to sit down.

"If you consider Sophie specific, yes."

His face closed like a fist. "I don't want to talk about her."

"I see. A case of that-was-our-Sophie-that-was."

"Don't be obscene!" The port splashed as he slammed the glass down on the sandstone mantelpiece. I watched it soak into the porous brick. It would leave a stain like blood. He might look unchanged, but his behaviour was unlike that of the David I knew. For the first time ever, I would have to be cautious with him. I stayed quiet and watched his face.

"How did you know the boys are at the Savages?" he said at last.

"Your cleaning woman told me." She had told me other things too. David was clearly not her flavour of the month. "He's packed them off already," she had said, "even before they're due to go to that school. Next thing you know, he'll be selling this place out from under them."

I knew then I had to see him. The house left to Sophie by her parents had been more home than home to me. If he had the nerve to consider selling it, there was only one person to whom he could be allowed to dispose of it. But there was no point in raising that subject now.

"Why do you want to see me?" he asked, sounding weary.

"More to the point, why don't you want to see me?"

As we stared at each other, his face changed; irritability and hostility were wiped away, and I saw instead the same guilt, fear and confusion as was bedevilling my own life.

"Oh God, David! Do you think she knew?"

"I'm not sure. I never have been."

"And you never warned me!"

"*I* warn *you*? You were always telling me you knew her better than I did."

And of course I did. In many ways, I was far closer to Sophie than any man could ever be. I searched my mind. Never, by so much as an inflection or a single unguarded word, had she ever shown the slightest hint of suspicion.

"She couldn't have," I said positively.

"You want to believe that. I can't."

His face was the colour of putty.

"I can't come to terms with the way she did it," he said, and I felt my stomach lurch.

"Think about it, Caroline." His eyes fastened on mine. "Why was she so insistent the boys should go to stay with Nell? They didn't want to.

"And then ..." his voice shook. "Why did she do it that way? She thought I would be the one to find her. It was the purest fluke I was not."

The window-cleaner, working late, had climbed his ladder, looked in through the bathroom window and had called the police. David, also working late, against expectation, had been spared the initial shock. The detail was something against which I had to close my mind. Some things cannot be faced.

"She could have taken pills," he went on. "She would have just looked as though she were asleep, but this way ... She knew I can't stand blood."

He was unbelievable. Even now, all he could think of was himself!

He seemed to read my mind and shook his head.

"You don't understand. This wasn't like Sophie. Have *you* ever known anyone so considerate of people's feelings? But she had no intention of sparing mine. The worst thing now is feeling I can never really have known her. Neither of us did."

"Don't be ridiculous! I certainly did."

"Did you?" His crooked smile had a touch of pity. "Then tell me about Kate Hamilton."

"Who?"

"A friend of Sophie's."

"Never heard of her."

"See?" He was gaining control of himself. "I'm afraid there is a great deal neither of us knew about Sophie."

There was no point in his staying longer; we were neither of us in a state to make sense of anything. When he reached the door, he turned, and his farewell look was almost kind.

"Leave me for a while," he said, "I'll be in touch, sometime. I promise."

I didn't care whether I saw him again or not. My mind was in a turmoil. Kate Hamilton? A friend of Sophie's? But I knew all her friends. Well, whoever she was, she would not long remain concealed from me.

"You should have told me about her," I said to the presence never far from my mind. "What were you thinking of, Soph? You should have told me about her."

HENRY

"Did you take my white suit to the cleaners?" Nell asked.
"Yes."
"And when will it be ready?"
"This weekend."
"Good. I will need it when we go to see David."

My heart sank. I had thought I had managed to head her off the idea.

"Nell," I said, "are you really sure you feel well enough to make the journey?"

"Of course I am."

Then why, I wondered, is the blue line around your lips so noticeable, and why does the smallest effort make you so short of breath? But these were not things to say to her.

"Why not leave it a bit longer? Can't you imagine the chaos there? I doubt if he will be in a fit state to cope with guests."

"I am not a guest! I am his mother! And why are you grinning?"

I was remembering Sophie's comical dismay on the eve of one of Nell's visits to them: "When she says she's coming to stay, she makes me think of the panic those poor courtiers of Liz the First must have felt when she announced a Royal Progress."

But I did not tell her that. It was dangerous to mention Sophie.

"What about your hair, then?"

It had grown thin and no longer took dye well. Her efforts to deal with it were intermittent and the results, on anyone but Nell, would have seemed ridiculous. The occasional visits to the hairdresser were occasions of high drama. I had suggested a nice wig, but she had scorned that on the grounds of discomfort and the encouragement of head-lice. "I know about such things", she had said grandly, refusing to believe that wig-making could have moved with the times.

"I will wear my Haroun al Raschid."

This is an ornate and multi-coloured turban which, though it suits her proud features, draws attention to the eccentricity which is becoming increasingly tatty.

I said nothing. That problem could be faced later.

"I have to see him," she said, "I have waited long enough for answers". I had refused to allow her to question him when he came down to collect the boys. I can be adamant when I feel it necessary. The poor fellow had endured enough agonies in having to face the inquest, the autopsy and all the searching questions, without the added one of being grilled by Nell.

"And I have to see that woman. That Caroline."

Another good reason this visit should be delayed or, better still, prevented altogether.

I took out my diary.

"What are you doing?"

"Looking to see when I have to have my next lot of shots."

Nell does not have the monopoly on ill health. Were it not for the chemicals they regularly pump into me, I doubt if I would be alive.

"Not for another ten days," I said. "We couldn't go before then."

"You are an old nuisance," she said, but without petulance. "I suppose we'll have to leave it for now." It was the nearest she could come to showing affection and concern.

So what do I do now? Warn David of her intention? I do not like to think of him at bay under her relentless questioning, for relentless she will be. Nell does not easily part with things she cares about, and she cared for Sophie a very great deal. One of the most selfless things I have known her to do was to keep her emotion under control when the news came through.

"They are too young for this," she had said fiercely, and remained calm in front of the boys.

I could see she was having difficulty when David came to take them home, so there was little hope of her control lasting much longer.

She said a very curious thing recently: "Sophie was a forgiving little soul. I wonder if there are things she would *not* forgive."

Nell is not a worrier. She considers it weak-minded and fruitless, so why was her face clouded so, and the crease between her eyebrows so deep?

"*Somebody* is responsible for —" her voice shook — "what happened to Sophie. I won't rest until I know ..."

"Stop it!" I said, knowing how her blood pressure flares when she becomes agitated. "No good will come of your getting upset."

Her mouth began to twitch in the way I dreaded to see. "Upset!" she said thickly. "Is that what you call it? Bloody Henry!" She turned the words she uses as a comical endearment into an indictment. "Don't you understand anything? What if it were my fault? Have you never thought of that?"

"No," I said, "and I will not think of it now."

Enough is enough, even for me.

I have recently discovered that being old and tired makes one selfish. Much as I loved Sophie, I resent the problems she has created. The time left to Nell and to me is short, and we have enough to face on our own account. The young have no right to burden the old with their problems.

"Henry! Don't dare walk away from me!" Nell was saying.

I kept right on.

NIN SAVAGE

"Dan," said Nin, pausing when about to pour his breakfast coffee, "that friend of Sophie's — you know the rich bitch — rang me yesterday."

"So?"

"She wanted to know if Kate Hamilton was a friend of mine — and of Sophie's."

"So?"

"I don't know what to make of it."

"Neither do I. Please pour the coffee."

"Then," she said, ignoring his request, "I saw her driving up the road. Flashy car, hair and scarf flying — all Isadora Duncan ..."

"I don't care if she was on a broomstick."

"She must have been heading for Sophie's. Or was she? Kate lives in that cul-de-sac at the top of the cliff."

"Nin," Dan said, sounding dangerous, "the coffee!" He shook out his paper, which cracked like a pistol shot, and retired behind it.

Without another word, Nin filled his cup. She recognised the futility of trying to come between a man and his morning fix of the world's news.

She went to the foot of the stairs. "Come and get it!" she bawled, her voice louder than the boisterous ones behind the bathroom doors. The morning was early, but already the house carried the tang of salt water and was gritty with sand.

Where does it all *go*? She wondered, when the bright faces were assembled round the table and she watched the rapid disappearance of muesli, toast and the croissants she had been hoping to sample herself.

She poured four large glasses of soya milk.

"This is the brand Mum gets," Ben said, "It's the one with the most potassium." He drank deeply.

Lifting his glass, Tom said, "Is there anything you want us to do, Mrs Savage? We're supposed to ask."

"No," she said, "No. Truly. Nothing."

She was grateful when her own boys rose from the table, nodded at her briefly, their minds obviously running ahead, back to the beach.

"See you," they said.

Emptied of man and boys, the house settled around her, calm and cool. These were the moments she called "my time". All demands had been met, and there was the silken certainty that no more would be made for a while. She drifted over to the great window and stared out over the quiet sea. Not a wave lapped. The boys won't like that, she thought, but turned her mind away from their displeasure. She was displeased enough with herself.

Why do I let her get to me? she thought. Caroline's crisp voice was still sharp in her mind. What is she after? She didn't ring me for pleasure, that's for sure. Swords had been crossed as soon as we met. Designer clothes and jewellery are not my thing and our meetings at Sophie's hardly led to harmony among the teacups. Sophie was amused by my obvious dislike.

"You just need to *know* her," she said.

She probably said the same about me.

Anyway it was a need unlikely to keep me awake at night, and I certainly had not given her my telephone number. What had induced her to consult the telephone directory? And what does she want with Kate?

More to the point, what would Kate want with her? She has enough on her plate without having to try to cope with that one too. I have to warn her.

"It was very good of you to suggest our meeting," said Kate Hamilton, rising from her chair at the back of the dimly lit café. "Not many people are willing to be seen with me these days."

"*Nobody* will see us here!" said Nin, brushing aside the fronds of a plastic palm and looking with revulsion at the heavily frilled lampshade. She saw, with a pang, that both chairs at the table faced the wall.

"People give me the shits," she said roughly and twirled one of the chairs so that it faced out into the room. "How are you? Don't tell me — even in this gloom I can see ..."

Nin cast down her handbag and sprawled uncomfortably into the chair shaped to accommodate upright eaters.

"And do sit down, I'm not visiting royalty and, for God's sake, turn your chair round. Only a determined masochist would be willing to face such wallpaper." Without a word, Kate did as she was told.

Settled, she let mischief tweak at her pale lips. "Why do I find you so restful?" she asked.

There had been ease between them from the moment they had met, almost as though they had simultaneously tested the rungs of a ladder and found it safe. Kate's face was looking paler and more worn than when they had last met.

"I shouldn't have left it so long," Nin said, making no attempt to disguise the fact that her probing stare was finding much that did not please her.

51

"So much has been going on."

"Yes."

For a moment Sophie's presence was so potent she might have been sitting at the table with them.

A waitress, with pad and pencil, loomed.

"I would have preferred strong drink," Nin said, two foaming cups of brown liquid later. "In vino I find my veritas; in coffee, heartburn and floating specks before the eyes. What do you know about Caroline Evans?"

"Who?"

"A friend of Sophie's, remarkable for her legs and being loaded, and not much else."

"I don't know anything about her."

"Well, she's very curious about you."

"There's a lot of it about," Kate said wryly.

"I don't get the feeling it was to do with *that*," Nin said, "but with Sophie."

Kate looked into her coffee cup. "What did she ask you?"

"Who you were, where you live and what was the connection between you and Soph."

"And what did you tell her?"

"That I hadn't a clue, and good morning." She looked anxiously at Kate. "Did I do right? Yes? No? I let my prejudices get the better of me as usual. I can't stand her, so I thought you wouldn't be able to either."

Kate was frowning. "A *good* friend of Sophie's?"

Nin snorted. "*Good* is not a word that leaps to mind when Caroline is mentioned! Close they certainly were. Could be irritating. Touch of the Siamese about it."

"Sophie would confide in her?"

"I dunno. I thought she confided in me, but how wrong

can you get? Come to think of it, though, Soph never talked much about herself. When you were with her, you talked about *you*."

The familiar wave of sickness came over her. The hours she had spent with Sophie, the time when there had been only one place to go.

And still is, she thought. Where else can I take my guilt with any hope of finding comfort? The wild clamour in the mind, the witless disbelief, the hard truth that waited to make its presence known when sleep came, and reared up again, remorseless, each morning, now had to be faced in silence. Sophie, the listener, was gone.

She shifted suddenly, impatient with the discomfort of the wretched chair, and her uncontrolled movement sent the little glass vase, resplendent with a single rose and a frill of maidenhair fern, reeling across the table. Water spilled and piddled through the check gingham cloth, which concealed the open-work of the plastic table beneath, and dripped on to her trousered leg.

"Whoops!" Kate said, making an efficient grab for the vase, rescuing the rose and setting it in place again.

"Death to décor, I am," Nin said, her flicker of a grin unable to conceal that distress had come upon her.

Kate looked at her curiously and, as Nin stared back, she was suddenly and irrationally annoyed to see that Kate's worn, pleasant face, full of concern, was more worn than she felt it had any right to be. She thinks she's got troubles, she thought savagely. I'd trade mine for hers any day!

Before she could stop herself, it was out. The leper's bell that rang so constantly in her mind demanded to be heard.

"I killed a child," she said suddenly, low and vehement. "Did you know that, Kate? Was that why you chose such a grotty place for us to meet? Didn't you want to be seen with *me*?"

How could I *do* it? She reproached herself, back at home and it still not lunchtime. She went round the windows, dropping the shutters against the sun and the brilliant sparkle of the sea, and played it over in her mind.

That poor woman, shocked and not knowing where to look or what to say!

"I thought Sophie might have told you."

And then she had pulled herself round and said — and I'll always love her for it — "I think *you* should. I don't imagine it was murder."

And so it all came out, the tale too often told. How she came out from behind a parked car, straight under my wheels. "It was so quick I had no hope of avoiding her. She was six. I knew her mother. She brings her other child down to the beach and sits by the rocks, staring at our house. It was *not* my fault. I was *not* blamed by the police, by anybody, but not being blamed doesn't seem to matter. I still feel the thump of the car hitting her. I can't get away from it. I am the one who took her life."

"Hush," Kate had said and took my hands.

"I don't know what I would have done without Sophie. Kinder than God she was, and more than that, *safer* than God. I knew she was always there."

"And Dan?" Kate said, with a touch of admonition.

"Dan held me. Holds me. No words. Just arms."

And what was I doing saying *that* to someone who has no arms to hold her?

It was then I looked up and saw Caroline, elegant in cream silk and a hat, weaving her way through the tables towards us. She was carrying an excessively splendid pink potted begonia and, upset though I was, I was delighted to see that it had been over-watered and brown stains were marring the cream silk. "Ha!" she had said, planting the pot on the table among the coffee cups, and glaring at me. "You are willing to talk to some people, are you? I couldn't get a word out of you this morning. Excuse me" she had said, turning to Kate, with one of her social smiles, "I really need to have a word with your friend. Do you mind?"

CAROLINE

Bloody woman, thought Caroline, fanning her fury with recollection of Nin's obdurate face.

Plain as a toad and oblivious to the fact that, no matter how expensive, a thong is still a thong and that, after the age of eighteen, it is wise to keep the human toe concealed. How can anyone bear to look like that? Not even a gun to the temples would force me to cross the threshold wearing such clothes. Shoestring straps, a neckline plummeting rather than plunging, and danger of full exposure of armpits should she lift her arms! True, what there was to see was brown and burnished and made clear that here was a healthy body, but how blatant can you get? Didn't she know that health and sweat often go together and that it was a hot day? And what is the betting that she is the type that considers deodorants unnatural?

She can't stand me any more than I can stand her, but she could have shown some manners. That nice-looking woman she was with had perfect manners.

"Then I won't intrude," she had said, picking up her bag. Gucci, it was, I could see. She had smiled down at that Nin and touched her on the shoulder. "We can talk later."

I liked her voice; it had none of the plummy English of that plain creature.

When she had gone, it was a case of let-battle-commence. Nobody gives *me* the brush-off.

"I asked you a civil question," I said. "Is it beyond you to give a civil answer?"

It obviously was.

"You asked me a lot of questions," she said, "and none of them civil. I could hear the thumbscrews clicking." She looked offensively amused. "How did you run me down?"

How indeed! We all know that dreadful old station wagon of hers. Always crammed with boys and surfboards. When I came out of the florists, there it was in the square, badly parked. I went into each nearby shop until I found her.

Now I fixed her with one of my looks.

"Why are you being so cagey?"

"Why are you being so inquisitive?"

"I am not!"

How dare she speak as though I were a common snooper! But I was trapped. I could hardly tell her of the challenging way David had thrown the wretched woman's name at me. I controlled my voice. "I was told she was a friend of Sophie's and naturally I felt —"

"Inquisitive."

"Perplexed. Sophie had never told me about her."

"Was she required to? Did she have to present all her friends to you for vetting?"

"Hardly," I said, with heavy emphasis, looking at her with distaste and making sure that rippling between us went the knowledge that if there had been any vetting, she would never have got to first base.

"Hasn't it occurred to you," the bloody woman asked clearly, determined to be offensive, "that Sophie might not have wanted you to know her? Or, to be more accurate, for her to have to know you?"

I can usually think fast, but rage and bewilderment do not help the mental processes. I badly wanted to hit her. As I rose from my seat, the table lurched and my potted plant keeled over. We both reached out instinctively to save it, and my hands touched her bare flesh. As we both recoiled in revulsion, the pot toppled to the floor and smashed into pieces.

Had it been a reputable restaurant, there would have been carpet on the floor, but, in this tacky place, they had gone for the vinyl tile, presumably because it makes for easy sweeping. There was plenty of sweeping to do now.

"The poor plant," she said.

Poor plant! What about the pot? The plant could be retrieved and re-potted but the pot, which was an original and exactly what I wanted for the place in which I wanted it to stand, was lost for ever.

There was a great fuss, of course. We were not the clients of the day. I had taken no coffee, but I paid the bill for the two others, silenced the waitress with a sizeable tip and left them to it. The last I saw of them they were making play with a large plastic bag and dustpan.

I came straight up here to Sophie's garden.

I came here yesterday, too. If David has selling the house in mind, I need to look at it carefully. He cannot be allowed to think that because I want the place rather more than most prospective buyers, I will turn a blind eye to defective gutters or other signs of structural deterioration. There are plenty of them! If he employs an estate agent to sell it, I will make sure these points are noted.

But today, sitting here under the tangle of roses where I so often sat with her, and faced with the sprawl of the catmint I knew she had been intending to cut back, all I could think of was Sophie. I could not, I would not, let her go. We had unfinished business.

I was unprepared for the sudden screech of wheels on the gravel. A young man was emerging from a small white truck, which was festooned with collapsible ladders. He saw me as he was about to unload them.

"Oh," he said, and stared.

He was young and carroty, blotchy with freckles, and with a gap between the front teeth. One could not help registering his engaging look of naivety. "The windows," he said. "I have come to clean the windows. Is it all right?"

I spread my hands. "Nothing to do with me," I said. "Suit yourself."

He left the truck and started to sidle towards me. "Actually," he said, "it doesn't suit me at all, but she always paid in advance. I owe this one."

It came to me then. A window-cleaner had given the alarm about Sophie. He saw my sharpened interest and turned his face away. "Don't start," he said. "Everybody keeps asking."

He was safe from me. I would never ask, for fear of what he might tell me. But there were other things he might divulge. "Do you clean windows for a Mrs Kate Hamilton?" I asked.

Relief flooded his face. "In the Crescent, you mean? There's a Mrs Hamilton there, but I don't know her first name."

It was all I wanted to know.

"I'm not doing these windows anymore," he said. "I'm leaving a note ..."

"Don't bother," I said, "I'll tell Mr Martin."

Surprisingly, it had turned out to be quite a successful morning.

DAVID

It has been a quiet week, and one is grateful for small mercies. I have spoken to the boys most evenings and they seem happy enough, and the Savages show no signs of strain in coping with them. The office is running well. Bianca, in spite of Caroline's suspicion of her tendencies, is mainly devoted to her work, for which she shows a real aptitude, and we have gone a long way towards clearing up the backlog that had accumulated. We share a professional pleasure in this. If it were not for the nagging worry over what Kate Hamilton might disclose, I could feel a slight lightening of the spirit.

This is not to say that I do not wake to sick incredulity each morning, but the shock is becoming less, and one becomes accustomed. I am going to have to learn how to walk with a stone in my shoe for the rest of my life, as Nell would describe it. We have heard enough of the stones in hers and her fortitude in withstanding the pain, but I doubt if she has had to face anything as crippling as this. She has remained mercifully silent for some time now, but I know I cannot expect peace for much longer.

Henry is a considerate man. His letter gave me fair warning that there could be disturbance ahead. I marvel both at his loyalty to Nell and at his adeptness in protecting others from her. I always felt that the move to Adelaide was as much on my account as on his and admired the way he steered Nell into accepting it with grace, if not enthusiasm. The family home he had inherited could not be deserted, he had said. One has loyalty to tradition. It has been waiting for you, he had said — the old slyboots.

I had been waiting for Nell to get off my back for years. If I had thought to evade her by marrying Sophie, I was wrong. My son, she continued to say. Sophie always said "David", not "my husband". It was Nell's "my Sophie" that really got to me. As though my function had been to go forth and bring back to her the daughter she would have preferred to have had. I heard a lot about that preference. I also heard a great deal more than was comfortable for a son to hear about Nell's pregnancy and accouchement. Once, when I demurred about the profusion of detail, she hissed, "For God's sake! You were *there*, weren't you?" As so often with her, I couldn't find an answer to that one.

She never left me in any doubt that I was HERS; neither did she conceal her irritation that I had devoured her time and destroyed her sleep, and that as I grew older, I did not turn out as she had a right to expect.

Once, when I asked her what my father was like, she bent down, cupped my chin in her hand and gave me a great kiss. "Good-looking", she said, "like you". I noticed that other mothers kissed their children on the top of the head, the cheek or the forehead. Nell always kissed full on the lips.

Being the child of a famous parent inhibits judgement; one grows up with the godhead established. Her values, her attitudes of mind, her behaviour were the creeds by which I lived. I see now that Henry wished it could have been otherwise, but he was left in no doubt that he was stepfather, not father, and so withdrew. Not, however, without making me aware that there was something he was withdrawing *from*. It is a pity I did not get Henry into focus in those days. He was just a background blur.

Sophie was quite different.

I was familiar with her voice before we met. Nell, finding that leading roles and long runs had become exhausting and quite unable to settle for anything less, had given up her stage career and opened a small, exclusive drama school. She charged an arm and a leg, rejected applicants ruthlessly if they did not meet her standards, and so ensured that students fought to get in. She is a businesswoman to her fingertips. To be fair, I think she gave good value. Anyway, I don't remember anybody complaining.

She used to bring home tapes of run-throughs and auditions, and play them while she and Henry sat taking their supper from a tray.

On my way up to my room one night, I was halted by the cajolery, impatience and longing in a voice saying, "West wind! West wind on the silver Loire!" and recognised it as one of Nell's set pieces. The young page Dunois, in Shaw's "St. Joan" is waiting on the banks of the river for the wind to change so that the banners can be lifted and the attack take life. The tape raced forward and the same voice cried in exaltation, "You dared me to follow! Dare you lead?"

I went slowly back down the stairs and stood listening. The young eager voice was suddenly cut off as Nell changed the tape. "Now listen to this," she said to Henry.

The same voice, but lighter now, cried in incredulous despair. "You promised my life! But you lied! You think life is nothing but not being stone dead!"

I am not an overly imaginative man, and my emotions are not easily roused. I stood and listened to the famous speech as Joan confronts her inquisitors and hardly breathed.

"Wonderful!" Henry said when the tape ended.

"Yes, but —"

I did not wait to hear Nell's "but". I stole up to my room and closed the door. I just wanted to be alone with the voice in my head.

When I first saw her, she was bending to help Nell out of her car. She was all bare brown legs and small bottom. As she straightened up and turned and I saw her face, I felt the rich warmth of a shock of pleasure. What a lovely little thing! I thought. And then the voice that spelled magic for me said in clear ringing tones, "Are you David? Then, for God's sake, give me a hand!"

We laughed about it afterwards.

"Those bloody oysters." Nell kept saying as we struggled to keep her upright and get her into the house. Sophie held her head as she vomited all over the black-and-white tiles of the hall floor. I did the cleaning up. By the time we had Nell in bed and the pails and disinfectant put away and were sitting down to a drink, the die was cast. We smiled at each other in love and recognition. Nothing was ever quicker, simpler or more inevitable.

My love for her was the one certitude in my life, and I thought hers for me was as unshakeable. That is why I cannot come to terms with either her death or the manner of it. I cannot think of anything, anything at all, which could have made me willing to cut myself off from her in so final a fashion.

Caroline. She is the last person I want to think about, but she is the first problem I must face. I cannot excuse myself by saying the relationship was not of my choosing and became something I could not escape. Once I knew she intended no harm to my marriage, I was happy enough and had no wish to escape it. Caroline is most physically attractive, she makes no bones about knowing it and taking pleasure in it. Once I got over the shock of what I originally thought of as my betrayal of Sophie, I took pleasure in it, too. Love was never mentioned. It never existed between us and we both knew it and, somehow, that made things all right. Or so I told myself.

I wonder how Caroline spends her time these days. Unlike most of us, she always had plenty to spare and required the emptiness filled — a matter of annoyance to me, as her open demands on Sophie and covert ones on me were inescapable. Not that Soph seemed to feel the need to escape, she liked having Caroline around. I could never understand why. Caroline made no effort to help with the house or the boys, but just followed Soph around, talking all the time. "She is my diversion," Sophie said. They certainly laughed a lot.

Happiness grew to be coming home to find the drive empty of Caroline's car.

This however, did not prevent me from inventing clients who had to be seen out of working hours — I even gave them names — so that I could visit Caroline. Often, when I had left her bed and gone home, Sophie's joyful greeting and peaceful, unquestioning trust, roused such an agony of love for her that nothing would do but the taking of that familiar little body in passionate proof of how much I cared for her.

It is strange how facts say one thing but the truth lies elsewhere. In my heart I was never more faithful to my wife than when I was deceiving her.

There is still the problem of what to do with her clothes.

"I must have the tapestry," Caroline had said.

The half-finished work, needle dangling and bag of wools spilling, still stands by Sophie's chair in the sitting room. I had the frame made for her and adjusted to her height. Caroline is tall. I told her she would find working on the tapestry uncomfortable.

"You think I would *work* on it?" she said in bitter scorn.

Dare I ask her help with the clothes? Or, and this is probably a better idea, should I ask Kate Hamilton for her advice? It might be well to retain contact with her so that I know what she is doing and can, perhaps, deflect her if I find she intends to make disclosures I would prefer her not to make.

These are problems to sleep on. I can relax now that the boys are with the Savages. I was able to eat in town in civilised fashion. A strong drink and early bed are all I need. Halfway up the stairs, I hear the telephone begin to ring. It continues to ring as I go to the bathroom. Through the sound of the running water, I hear it still. I close the door.

Not now, whoever you are, not now.

Showered and in my bed, I hear it begin to ring again. I am not even curious. There will be problems at the other end of the wire, and that is where they must stay. I am tired of problems. I am tired of other people. I am tired of myself and, surprisingly and sickenly, I am desperately tired of thinking about Sophie.

HENRY

I can smile now when I think of yesterday, but it wasn't funny at the time. Nell had decided that nothing would stop her from visiting David.

"Today is Friday," she said. "We will go next Wednesday."

I pointed out that our arrival mid-week might inconvenience him as he has his profession to consider.

"You expect me to travel at the weekend?" she said. "Among the *hordes*? And I doubt whether the legal world will suffer if he takes time off."

"How long do you propose we stay?"

"As long as it takes," she said darkly, and that gave me no ease of mind at all.

Nell, on the telephone, is at her most regal.

She required the airline to tell her whether they had a flight at a time at which she was prepared to travel and then to give her the number of the seats on the aircraft which had the most leg-room and were near both the emergency exit and the lavatories.

Nell's enunciation is perfect. She gives each syllable clear and full expression. After hearing her say "lavatories" one knows why "toilets" is so displeasing. "Economy or business class?" she was asked.

"Business class — naturally," she replied, with ringing hauteur.

At one time I used to be embarrassed by her high-handedness;

now I am grateful for it. It shows she is undiminished by age and ill health.

She hates to feel she is subject to either, and I can understand why hate for me sometimes surfaces. I see what she does not wish to be seen. Bloody Henry. I am also the Henry who is always there, the one presence on which she can rely. Does she ever, I wonder, wake in the night and listen, with anxiety, to see if I am still breathing? My illness moves slowly. The tremor of the hands, the dragging of feet increase at a snail's pace. I do not yet slur my words. I take my pills and keep going. My case is mild.

"Think of your age," my doctor said. "You could die of natural causes before the disease becomes acute."

I did not tell Nell that. Concern for others is not one of her strong points. Her antennae — if she has them — are poor receptors; straws in the wind mean nothing to her. As long as I am upright and breathing, she will notice nothing. She does not allow herself to be weighted down by sensitivity. She used to tell her pupils that a brilliant actress should be able to convey emotion without being overtaken by it. A leading role is physically taxing, strong emotion is exhausting. "If you allow yourselves to feel too much, you will be lying in a heap when the curtain comes down," she told them.

I have wondered if her training *not* to feel has spilled over into real life. If it has, it is highly selective. There is no restraint on the passion with which she feels for herself.

It seems to me — and how fortunate it is that thoughts can remain hidden — that though she was a brilliant actress, she is unlikely to be remembered as "great". And, one is forced to ask, how long will her name be remembered at all? I find it endearing that she does not give a toss. "What good would after-life bootlicking do me?" she asks pragmatically and demands due recognition while she can be sure of it.

Once the travel arrangements were dealt with, David had to be alerted to expect us. She would not telephone him during office hours, not because she was chary of disturbing him at work, but because of her well-known refusal to pay daytime rates. It was ten in the evening before she dialled his number. There was no reply. She rang again. And again. Still no answer.

She slammed the receiver down in temper.

"He is out with that woman! That Caroline!"

I had known of her suspicions and had downplayed them, not only for Sophie's sake, but for hers. We have been warned that stress can be dangerous.

"I will ring her up!" she now said.

"But you don't know her number."

"Fool," she said, "have you never heard of directory assistance?"

Ten minutes later, she shot me a triumphant, malevolent glance. Caroline Evan's number was ringing. Nell motioned to me to share the earpiece with her.

She cut short the answering voice. "This is Nell Martin," she said. "Is David there?"

There was a brief silence. Then: "Mrs Martin! Good evening! What a surprise! How are you?" The voice was silken with insolent politeness. Then, without waiting for an answer, the tone changed abruptly. "No. He is not here."

"Then where is he? He is not at home!"

"For heaven sake, woman, how should I know? He has probably gone out to dinner."

I waited, cringing, for the outburst. But Nell surprised me.

"Where are the boys?" she asked, tight and controlled.

"I can tell you that! No trouble at all! They are with some people called Savage. I will give you their number." She sounded more than pleased to be asked.

I wrote it down as she spelled it out.

"Be sure to ask for *Mrs* Savage," she said, and I'd vow there was an amused malice in her voice. Now what is David up to? I thought.

Nell had obviously reacted in the same way. With tight lips she dialled the number given to us.

"Dan Savage," a pleasant voice said.

"This is Nell Martin. Are my grandchildren with you?"

"Oh, well yes, indeed. David's mother is it?" Wits were obviously being collected. "How nice of you to call. I don't think we've met —"

"I'd like to speak to your wife," Nell interrupted.

"Nin? Sorry, she's out. Is it about the boys? They're in bed, but I could get them up — though it is rather late ..."

Nell took hold of herself. "No, of course not. It is David I want to contact. He isn't at home."

"No? He spoke to the boys earlier this evening ..."

The conversation faltered.

"He's probably out to dinner," Nell said and waited. The question "Who with?" was waving in the air like a banner, but he did not appear to notice. She changed her tack.

"Why are the boys with you and not at home?"

The man made a deprecatory sound. "Well, you know, good neighbours and all that. David has a lot on his plate. We thought it might help him out, poor chap. Terrible thing to have to face. Sophie was a good friend of ours."

Mention of Sophie quietened Nell. "Ah," she said, "I see."

She moistened her lips. I could tell she was preparing to put on her charm. She puts it on with the care and attention she gives to putting on her most beautiful and expensive earrings.

"We must meet," she said. "I must thank you properly. I am coming to see David next week — let us make it then. Do give my regards to your wife and tell her that I *particularly* look forward to meeting her."

She sat looking thoughtful after she put the receiver down.

"What do we have here?" she said at last. "Why did that woman tell me to speak to *Mrs* Savage? Don't tell me David has —"

"I don't. I don't tell you anything of the kind." Her use of the single pronoun had annoyed me. '*I* am coming' — indeed. I disliked her version of the royal plural.

"But he is out," she persisted, "and that man says his wife is out ..."

"He didn't say they were together!"

"He probably doesn't know."

I had had enough. I do not nettle easily, but nettled I had become.

"I am going to bed," I said, and left her to secure the doors and windows and turn the lights out; a small enough way in which to show displeasure one might think, but to Nell, accustomed to having everything done for her as she is, I knew it would signify much.

I heard her fiddling around for some time and muttering expletives, but, give her her due, she did not call for my help. She managed. As she climbed into bed beside me and pulled the covers over us both, she tweaked my ear. "Bloody Henry," she said.

NIN

Nin stood, throat thick with tears, studying the plant which stood in a pot in the kitchen sink. She had rescued it from the café floor and brought it home in a plastic bag. Re-potted, watered and given time for convalescence in the dark, it had now been brought out to face the light. She winced for it. The leaves hung limp and the heavy, beautiful flower head drooped.

Dan, coming into the kitchen, saw her standing immobile and came up behind her. He put his arms round her waist, dropped his head to her shoulder and stared where she was staring.

"That is one battered plant," he said.

"I know how it feels," Nin replied, the meeting with Caroline Evans fresh in her mind.

"What are you going to do with it?"

"Try a 'Sophie'."

Sophie would bring home punnets of overgrown seedlings and plants which, left unbought for too long, had yellowed or grown straggly. She had a special place in the garden for her invalids. The annuals seldom gained full vigour despite her devoted coddling, but the perennials, with a longer lifespan, allowed themselves to be coaxed back into bloom. "And I am crafty with cuttings," she would say.

She wasn't a good gardener, Nin thought fondly; good gardeners know how to be ruthless. They require their plants to stand up and do their duty — or else. Sophie only required hers to stay alive. Her garden never looked groomed but, boy! there was everything in it.

Nin sniffed as she touched the soft, ruffled petals. Why should it be doomed? That bloody woman —

The memory of Caroline Evans stalking away and leaving her to cope with the wreckage and the ill-humour of the café proprietor brought her ready temper to the boil.

Dan reached over her shoulder and lifted the pot from the sink. Water dripped.

"Look," he said. The stem was badly crushed and almost broken through.

"Stake it?" Nin asked, hope receding. She felt him shake his head. "Perhaps we could —"

"No, we couldn't."

"Why does everything have to die?"

He dropped a kiss on the back of her neck. "I'll deal with it, sweetie. You go and pour us a drink." He turned her round, pointed her towards the sitting room and gave her a gentle push.

Tears fell as she trudged through to the quiet room striped with sunlight and shadow. She left behind the brisk action in the kitchen and the opening and closing of the door into the garden. Incinerator or compost bin? she wondered, and wept afresh as she slopped out the gin.

God, what a mess I am! she thought, huddling in one of the huge, soft chairs. How long will Dan stay patient if I keep on confronting him with these helter-skelter emotions? How long before he begins to hint at the menopause?

If only I could talk to him about this, as I can about almost everything else; but his mind would snap closed. Sophie, instead, was with me every step of the way. "If you think it might do any good," she said. I can't bear to think about that now.

"If only Nell were here," she said once, to my great surprise. From what I had heard, Nell was a stirrer, not a soother.

The garden door opened and there was the sound of running water and Dan humming. He came into the room, rolling down his sleeves, and made straight for the drinks table.

"Forgot to tell you," he said, "there was a telephone call last night while you were out. From Nell Martin."

Nin came upright in the chair. "I don't believe it! I was just thinking about her!"

"She is casting her shadow," Dan said, busy screwing on bottle tops and mopping up. "She told me she is coming up here and is particularly anxious to meet you."

"Why? I don't know her! And where did she get our telephone number?"

"Don't ask me, sweetie."

"That's the second time you've called me 'sweetie'," Nin said, becoming prickly. "Whatever next? Poppet?"

Smiling with relief, Dan spread himself over the couch and settled to enjoy his drink. "That's my girl," he said.

Nin looked at him with love. Sorry, my darling, she thought.

Aloud, she said, "Did she know the boys were here?"

"Didn't seem to, and didn't show any interest. She wanted to speak to David and was cross because he wasn't at home."

"When did she say she was coming?"

"Next week."

Nin took a deep, enjoyable drink of her gin. If she wants to see me, she will want to see Caroline Evans too. She remembered Sophie saying once, "Nell will be here! Please God, don't let Caro turn up!" and then being pale and fed-up because Caroline had. "Nell can be a devil," was all she said afterwards. Now Nin thought, in anticipation, she can be as much of a devil as she likes!

"Nin," Dan said, and there was a different note in his voice. "What do you make of Sophie's boys?"

"How do you mean?"

"Do they strike you as being typical?"

"Of what?"

"Well ... children who have lost their mother under traumatic circumstances."

"I don't know what is typical." Her voice rose. "This is the first time ..."

"Watch it!"

She watched it.

"What I mean is," he said carefully, "they are being surprisingly normal. One would have expected —"

Behaviour more like mine, she thought. Wild grief, incoherent questioning, inability to eat and sleep. They were sometimes quiet, often boisterous, always hungry and fell into sleep as though into a chasm. They spoke of Sophie without any visible distress. Thinking about it, she could see that most people would say they were not "typical".

"Do you think it could have anything to do with their being twins?"

Having each other, were they born with an inbuilt security? she wondered. Most of us seek security in another person all our lives, and some of us never find it. Was it natural to them?

"Watch them, will you?" Dan said. "I don't want their stutter to come back."

He looked serious and, as she watched his face, she was aware of thoughts rumbling between them like the quiet threat of thunder. Quickly she pushed them away.

She nodded and smiled at him and, for a moment, they both sat quiet. Then she roused herself. "They certainly eat well. We're out of bread, Vegemite and ice-cream."

"And I need a haircut."

He was up on his feet and obviously glad of the chance to get away.

"The *large* Vegemite," she said.

When he reached the door, he turned, "We don't hear much about Zak these days." Zak had moved in with the boys. Dan, like David, was impatient with the time and attention given to the imaginary playmate. His own boys rolled up their eyes and pulled faces whenever he was mentioned, but Nin felt it would be a kindness to go along with the fantasy — until the Martin boys had said who he was.

We are not opening that can of worms, she had thought, and stopped laying an extra place at the table.

"So, don't mention him."

"Do you think it likely? We can do without Zak!" But, she thought uneasily, and was exasperated with herself for such foolishness, is Zak willing to do without *us*?

CAROLINE

I know where Kate Hamilton lives. All I have to do is knock on her door. And yet I hold back. I have become apprehensive. Sophie did not tell me she knew her. Why not? Was she a friend in whom she confided? Did she tell this woman of her suspicions about me? When we meet, will she look at me with accusation in her eyes?

Fear is crippling me. It thins the lips, clenches the jaw, cords the neck and corrugates the brow. I see all the signs when I face myself in the mirror. I marshal all my expensive creams and lotions and devotedly follow the routines which have kept my complexion so clear and the lines of my face so clean and firm. If one is to keep one's looks, discipline is needed.

I cannot afford to relax it, for my looks are both defence and weapon.

I am told that I resemble my mother. I wouldn't know. She walked out on my father and me when I was little. All I remember of her is a cross voice saying to my father, "It's your fault she is such an unlovable little brat!" No child should grow up feeling it should never have been born. They lost no time in making me aware that I was the result of a casual coupling bitterly regretted by both parties. God knows why they married — surely there must have been abortionists around. Resentment and aggression were programmed into me. My father made money and drank himself to death. I have no idea what happened to my mother.

I knew little about either fun or love until, in my teens, I met Sophie and was gathered into her family.

"You must meet Hairy," she said, "You'll love him".

Hairy was her father, a smooth-faced man as bald as an egg. And I did love him.

I didn't know that parents could laugh and tease and not mind being teased back by their children. I didn't know about spontaneous displays of affection. The first time I saw Sophie's father suddenly throw his arms round Sophie's mother and without any obvious reason and in front of everybody, give her a great kiss, I was startled and embarrassed. When he said to Sophie, "Morning, sweetie, I love you," and nuzzled a kiss into her neck and ruffled her short curls, I was astonished. I gaped when he picked up Sophie's little brother, gave him a great hug, and said "How's my Tiger?"

I felt as awkward as though I were in another country and did not know the language.

Thinking of Tiger — he wasn't at Sophie's funeral. Funny I should not have realised it until now. Funnier still, when you think how fond they were of each other. Perhaps the poor lad had had enough. He was in England doing his medical training when Hairy died and, of course, came home to be with his mother and Sophie. He stayed with them for a few weeks before he went back. He could not have had time to unpack before he was in the air again, because his mother was dead. He did not stay long this time, he went back to England and has been there ever since. He didn't come back for Sophie's marriage to David either. Just sent a ribald telegram.

He was left most of the family money. The house, which has meant so much to me, was left to Sophie, and she and David made it *their* home.

"Caroline always seems to be underfoot," I once heard him say in exasperation, and did not forgive him for it.

"She always has been," was Sophie's soft reply. "We took her in."

I didn't much like that, either.

Well, David might be "in", but there was no way I was going to be "out".

Tiger and Sophie kept in touch. She used to read me his funny letters. She must have read them to David, too, so surely David must have let him know when ... Here I go, fruitlessly, foolishly, churning it all over. How long can an obsession last before one becomes deranged by it or, given my temperament, so chronically bored that the only thing to do is to say "Sod it!" and cast it away?

The day when I can do that glimmers on the horizon. I will get there. I have to. But before that is possible, there are a few things I must clear up.

Kate Hamilton.

Since I have no idea what she is like, it is hard to choose the persona I must put on to face her. Some of the people Sophie choose to befriend are anathema to me.

What reason do I give for knocking on this stranger's door?

Do I say, "Good morning. I believe you were a friend of my friend, Sophie Martin. I am giving cuttings of plants we bought to other friends of hers. I think it is a nice way to remember her, don't you?"

Surely that should do it. People seldom refuse freebies.

And if she is not the gardening type, I can say I am a close friend of the family and am contacting all Sophie's other friends, as I am sure they would like to have a memento of her, and is there anything in particular she would like?

The woman is bound to ask me in, and I can take it from there.

I will do it tomorrow. Now to choose the clothes I will wear. Naturally, I will start with the new lingerie I bought last week. It was impossible to resist. I believe money spent on glamorous undies is well spent. Knowledge that the concealed you is looking exquisite gives one a lovely confidence. Sophie was fascinated by my taste and extravagance and always eager to see what I had bought. The elegance of the cut and the sensuousness of the materials delighted her. David would *love* these, she said. "What a pity I am not that sort of girl!"

The tussore trouser suit and foulard scarf, with what Soph used to call "The Shoes", that should do it.
That unspeakable old mother of David's once said, "Caroline *Evans*. One would have thought she would have married if only to change her name. Evans! It makes her sound like the grocer's daughter."
She hasn't paid for that yet, but she will.
And what will Kate Hamilton have to pay for? One wonders.
Out on the balcony, the night air is warm; high summer will soon be here. And Christmas. What are we all going to do about *that*? The moon is high and shadows lie hard and striped. Car lights twinkle through the trees in the distance, as the slow flow of traffic creeps along the coast road away from the village, where the fairy lights cluster and a shop alarm is sounding. If there were a burglary every time the alarms sound, our village would be as crime-prone as Dodge City. Why do people go in for tacky technology? A shopkeeper here could leave his doors open all night and find nothing gone in the morning.
I have the urge to go down and set upon the bloody alarm with a hatchet. It will run for at least twenty minutes before dying of its own accord. In my mind the heavy metal falls with shattering, satisfying blows. Wonderful!

When I open my eyes, I realise the noise has stopped. Laughing, I go back inside. I feel so enormously better that I am reminded I haven't had a drink since the day of the funeral. To my joy I find a bottle of Glenfiddich, unopened, and still wearing around its neck a card wishing me a happy birthday.

It is signed "David".

DAVID

Nell and Henry are coming to see me. She has announced the impending arrival with the usual fanfare of trumpets and a degree of aggravation because I was not on hand to receive the news at the moment she had it to impart.

"I was very tired. I had gone to bed," I said, and brought down on my head a barrage of accusations. The inconsideration, the impoliteness. Never an enquiry as to why I had been exhausted enough to feel the need to retire so early.

She expects me to take time off from the office and be at her behest while she is here. "There is much to discuss and even more to settle," she said.

As far as I am concerned, there is nothing to discuss with her and even less to settle. I will not talk to her about Sophie. I am my own man in this. The days of being Nell Martin's son — period — are over.

I do, however, have to make practical arrangements for her accommodation. I have dumped the bags containing Sophie's clothes in the spare bedroom. There are other things too: her easel, her tapestry stand, word processor, funny little spinning wheel, a mountain of notebooks containing cuttings about cooking, gardening, beauty preparations, alternative lifestyles and medicines. They mean little to me, but I can't just throw them out.

My one effort with regard to her clothes was shot down by Nin Savage so I am nervous to try elsewhere. If only Caroline ... I would not dare approach her. Her grief has a cutting edge which adds to my own lacerations. But I have to make space for Nell and Henry.

Kate Hamilton has crossed my mind often recently. I am nervous about what she may disclose but, since she is not prepared to be my client, I have no control over what she might say. On the other hand, she appears to have been a good friend of Sophie's and, from all the indications, is a nice woman, only bent on doing what she feels is "good". Her perception of what that is is open to question, but one gets the feeling that her instincts are right, no matter how childish her notions of behaviour. It could be in my best interests to stay close to her.

I worry a little about how my disposing of Sophie's things will seem to other people. I feel that since they were hers, I will be expected to want to keep them; that to rid the house of them is to behave as though I am ridding myself of her, wiping away all the traces. When you love someone, they will say, everything about them is precious, and the things that belong to them have special significance. I loved Sophie, but I cannot wait for everything of hers to be taken away. I cannot bear to be reminded that she is not here and chose not to be here.

If she had died from an illness or accident, it would have been different. Grief would have been deep and I could have clung to many lovely memories. But she made the choice to die, and that changes everything.

I cannot forgive her for doing this to me. But there is no point in going over and over it all. I have to get that damn room ready, and Wednesday is not far away.

I did not like the idea of approaching the Hamilton woman,

but she made things surprisingly easy. She understood, she said. She had faced a similar dilemma when her husband died. I explained about Nell and Henry, the need for space and the shortage of time.

"There might be things your mother would like to have," she said. I had not thought of that.

"And other friends of Sophie's might like —" she added gently.

I took a chance. "Look," I said, "you know them better than I do, you would be a better judge. Could you ...?"

She was silent for a second. "What you could do," she said at last, sounding careful, "is bring them all round here. I have plenty of space and could store them for you until there is time to —"

I blessed her for her kindness and commonsense. "There's nothing very heavy," I said. "Can I bring it round on Sunday morning?"

As I put down the receiver, feeling eased and thankful, I was struck by a sudden thought. The man she used to work for and had stolen from, is an estate agent. If I asked, surely she could give me advice about selling this house. It is becoming more and more clear that continuing to live here is more than I can take. I have never bought or sold property before. This house belonged to Sophie's parents and came to us when they were dead. It is a big family house. Now the boys will be away at school most of the year, a two-bedroom flat in town would make a lot more sense.

The more I think about it, the more it seems that Kate Hamilton is going to be very useful.

I have just spent a very strange Sunday morning. After I had packed Sophie's things into her station wagon and was ready to take them round to Kate Hamilton's, I realised there was space left for more. On an impulse, I shoved in her little button-backed "nursing" chair, her sewing machine and the dressmaking model adjusted to her measurements, on which she fitted the clothes she made. There was room to fit her sewing table, too, the drawers spilling with patchwork squares cut out and ready to sew. Under the bed in the spare room, I found a big plastic bag containing smaller bags of dried flowers and leaves, a box of thick white powder and some little bottles of scented oil. That went with the rest. I went round the house in a kind of frenzy, bent on clearing decks.

The Hamilton house is further up the hill than ours. I had not known it was there, for it is on the low side of the road and down a steep, heavily treed drive. I drove down cautiously and found myself on a wide sweep of gravel in front of a huge semicircle of glass walling, open to the sky, and with a door in the centre. As I switched off the engine, I saw shutters beginning to close over it to make a roof and Kate Hamilton appear at the door.

She came across to the car. "Here we are, then," she said, "Come on in."

I have never seen a house like it.

It is built into the hillside on three descending levels. Each level is semicircular. The second level is wider and larger than the top level, the third level is proportionately larger than the second, so there are three roofs and all can be opened to the sky.

"My husband was an architect, and a very enthusiastic amateur astronomer," she said, obviously amused by my reactions as she led me around.

I had been totally unprepared for anything like this: the glass walls, the wide, tiled balconies, the plants, the sky.

"It's stunning," I said, "absolutely stunning".

"He was a stunning man," she said. "He won the House of the Year Award for it."

She cocked her eye at me mischievously. "At least you can see that I didn't do it for the money."

The casual way she referred to the calamity hanging over her was disconcerting. I took refuge in looking around. She had said she had plenty of space. She certainly had. There were archways and, beyond them, rooms. I glanced, but did not care to be seen looking too closely.

"I like a drink about this time," she said. "How about you? We can unload afterwards."

The stiff whisky she poured for me was just what I needed. The chair she indicated was deep and soft and had a footrest. She took her own drink and crossed the room to a companion chair and sank into it. The feet she lifted to the footrest were bare, the soles soiled, the nails like brilliant, polished shells. Silence settled round us.

I am grateful for the relief alcohol can bring. As I sat in that chair in that amazing room, with a woman I barely knew, I felt peace begin to settle on me. I had not been so free of tension in a long time. All I wanted was to stay where I was — no Sophie, no Caroline to confuse me. Just plain David Martin, no strings attached, no strings pulled.

I think I slept.

When I opened my eyes, the amused smile was waiting for me.

"Up you get," Kate Hamilton said. "We have work to do."

We off-loaded everything and stacked it just inside the entrance door.

"I can decide where to put it later," she said.

"I don't know what you'll make of this," I said, handing her a tatty string bag bulging with books. "A complete stranger came to the house the day after the funeral. Said these were Sophie's and she thought I would like to have them. She said her name was Mackenzie."

"That would be Maggie. Would you mind if I kept these?" she asked.

Of course I wouldn't, but who the hell was Maggie Mackenzie, and what had she to do with Sophie? I felt as though I were walking through fog. Alcohol-induced emotion was very near the surface.

"I don't understand," I said. "I don't understand a fucking thing."

All the pleasure ebbed from her face. "Oh dear," she said flatly. "She didn't tell you."

I gave a short laugh. "Does that surprise you?"

I could feel her weighing me up and trying to come to a decision.

"You know Nin? Nin Savage?" she asked at last. "She had that awful accident and a little girl was killed. Do you remember?"

I did, but very vaguely.

"I can only tell you what she has told me. The poor thing became obsessed about having taken a life. She went on and on about it. She nursed her guilt complex until everybody got fed up with her. But Soph didn't. She hung on in."

I felt a flash of impatience. Trust Sophie. Always the soft touch.

"Then Nin heard of Maggie. She is a 'sensitive' a clairvoyant. People go to her for advice about —"

"I know, I know," I said impatiently.

No wonder Sophie had never mentioned her to me; I had had a basinful of that sort of thing when Nell had had her "spiritual" phase. People arriving for "sittings" at inconvenient times. All the talk about "messages" and the afterlife; a person who looked perfectly ordinary suddenly going glassy-eyed and beginning to speak in "tongues". One woman had even told me she was worried about the colour of my aura. I had had more than enough of such nonsense, and Sophie knew it.

"Nin persuaded Sophie to go with her to see Maggie."

The flash of impatience came again.

"I am so worried about her now, though. The other day she told me about the accident, as though it were something I didn't know. It was eerie. She went on and on about how much she had depended on Sophie and Maggie."

Nin Savage and her problems were of no interest to me.

"Sorry," Kate said. She was extraordinarily quick at picking up nuances. "But Maggie is a very interesting woman. Sophie saw a lot of her."

Now I was getting irritated and let it show.

"She needed someone to depend on," she said defensively. "The problems with the boys were getting heavy."

"The problems? What problems? *Our* boys? Tom and Ben?"

"She should have told you," she said miserably.

There seemed no end to the things Sophie should have told me.

Kate Hamilton was obviously feeling very uncomfortable. "I can't explain it to you," she said. "You will have to talk to Maggie."

I certainly would NOT talk to Maggie.

"I can assure you," I said, with what I hoped was chilling finality, "there is nothing wrong with the boys. They are eating well and having the time of their lives with the Savages."

"If you say so."

We had obviously reached an impasse. It was time for me to go.

As we were saying goodbye at her door, she suddenly said, "Caroline Evans".

I was startled. "What about her?"

"She wants to meet me."

"So?"

"Sophie used to talk about her a lot. She admired her. 'Caroline always knows what she wants and sees that she gets it,' she said. But I don't know if I'm up to that sort of person. You must know her. What do you think?"

I looked at the steadfast eyes, the calm certainty of the mouth, and was amused.

"It could be a case of when Greek meets Greek," I said and found myself giving her a valedictory peck on each cheek.

Driving back down the hill, I was passed by a pale blue Mercedes sports car swooping upwards. The driver was bareheaded, hair and scarf flying. Caroline. We each faltered for a second as recognition flared, then drove on. I didn't know whether to smile or not when I reached home. When Greek meets Greek, there are usually tears before bedtime.

I cleared the room and made the beds ready for Nell and Henry. One problem was off my back but, going over the conversation with Kate Hamilton carefully and slowly, I was aware of others I did not know I had. The boys. What could possibly be wrong with the boys?

CAROLINE

There isn't much Glenfiddich left. Well, what can one expect after a day like yesterday? I needed a welcome home and, amazingly, feel fit and focused this morning. And what is one to learn from that one wonders.

I started yesterday early. Lying in the scented bath with the window wide open and the water making swaying patterns on the ceiling, I wished for an overhead mirror. One is familiar with one's standing-up appearance, but lying down — that could have some unwelcome surprises. One spreads. Something to remember when one is the underneath partner. Equally though, one can hang, or even swing, if taking the aggressive role. Thank God I stay reasonably firm. There is no-one around to express appreciation these days, but I am the one to please, not other people. And when I was bathed, made-up and dressed, I was very pleased with myself, indeed.

I know why old actresses, like Nell Martin, find it hard to give up the theatre. There is such a wonderful sense of Occasion as one smooths on the creams, shadows the eyes and takes down the costume hanging on the door. I felt like that yesterday morning. I looked wonderful and was more than ready to confront Kate Hamilton.

The window-cleaner had given me her address.

"Watch out for the drive," he said, "it's real steep."

I was driving up the road fairly quickly when I saw Sophie's station wagon coming down and my heart turned over. As it passed, the driver turned his head towards me and I saw it was David.

For a second our eyes met and held, then it was over and there was only the road ahead. The sudden, unexpected glimpse of his face shook me. He looked so blessedly, comfortingly *familiar*. At least he is still here, I thought thankfully, surprising myself.

"Look out for the big Illawarra Plum," the window-cleaner had instructed.

There were big trees everywhere. Which one was an Illawarra Plum? I inched along until I came to the end of the cul-de-sac and had to turn round and inch my way back again. I only found the damn place because I recognised his description of the murderously steep drive.

As I carefully negotiated the bends, I thought that if Kate Hamilton walked up and down this, she must have thighs like an Indian brave.

I had no idea of what she might be like, but surely Sophie could not have made a friend of another creature like Nin Savage!

When I came out onto the gravel and the house came in sight, I saw a tall slim woman, hands on hips, standing with her back to me. She was wearing well-cut, pale blue slacks. She turned when she heard the car. I saw to my rage, confusion and astonishment that she was the woman who had been with Nin Savage in that bloody café. She was the one I had thought so pleasant and good-mannered.

As I cut the engine, she came across to the car and bent to the window.

"Are you looking for me?" she asked.

"Kate Hamilton?"

"Yes."

"Caroline Evans."

"Yes, I know," she said, straightening up. "I've been half-expecting you."

I do not faze easily and am reluctant to admit that I found everything that happened next difficult to handle. Especially since she seemed to find no difficulty at all.

I was required to make swift mental adjustments. The discovery of her identity naturally set me aback. And then there was the house. I was wholly unprepared for that. I am used to being considered the last word in taste — people gasp with pleasure and astonishment when I show them around my home — but at least I can recognise superior talent. Kate Hamilton's place, for design and effect, left mine for dead.

"I'm glad you've come," she said. "I'm going to ask you to help me with this lot."

She led me through a huge glass door in a huge glass wall into the house.

"This lot" was a mountain of plastic bags and a jumble of miscellaneous furniture stacked in an untidy heap just inside the door.

With a lurch of the stomach, I recognised Sophie's pink, button-backed chair.

"David Martin has asked me to store these things for him," she said. "He needs the space."

She caught sight of my face and stopped. I poked the pile of bags with my foot and it collapsed softly, giving off clean, spicy whiffs of scent.

"They took her away in a plastic bag, too. Did you know that?" I asked.

"O-ho-o!" she said, and blew out her cheeks and clicked her tongue before turning directly to me. Her enunciation became clear and clipped. "Bit below the belt, wouldn't you say?"

I had intended it to be. As I stared at her and she stared back at me, I realised I was up against more than I had expected.

She was quick off the mark. Her voice became smooth and polite.

"I think we should start again," she said. "Nin Savage tells me you want to see me. So do come in and tell me why."

When I saw her at the café, I had been impressed by her pleasant looks and easy good manners. She was obviously what many people would describe as a "lovely woman". Now, although I had to grant that her looks *had* been good and her bones and eye-sockets would still see her through, I was glad to see that, at closer quarters, the lines on her face were as deep as though scored by a pastry cutter. I have no patience with the ravaged-but-interesting look. In my book it denotes either slackness or insolent self-confidence. I did not think her likely to be slack.

I followed her across thick white carpet to where a spiral staircase curved downward at the side of the room. The shaped wooden steps were polished and pristine. "Mind how you go," she said. Her bare feet made no sound as she went down. My jewelled sandals slapped.

The whole front wall of the room we reached was open to a huge, curved deck which looked out over the ocean. Her view of the cliffs and the waves breaking at their foot was better than mine.

"In or out?" she asked, indicating the chairs outside and the big couches in the room. There were no umbrellas on the deck.

"Inside," I said. I had not brought my dark glasses and did not propose to sit, screwing up my eyes against the sun.

She let me settle in the chair, made sure the cushions were comfortable against the back, and the small table for drinks within reach and then took up her own position facing me and side on to the light. I could see she was about to ask a question, so I pre-empted her.

"Why are Sophie's things here?"

"I told you. Her husband is expecting guests and needs the space." With the boys not at home and a guest bedroom and bathroom that was nonsense.

"Why *here*?"

She lifted her eyebrows. "Why not here? It's convenient. We live near each other."

My house is closer than hers.

Her eyes roamed over my face. I could feel her mind working as she searched for words. "What you are really saying," she said, slowly and carefully, is, 'Why her?' You probably think he should have come to you."

I felt the strangle of rage. That bloody Savage woman! What had she said? Surely she had not caught on about me and David!

"How long have you known Sophie?" the maddening woman was asking.

"All our lives," I snapped. It was a lie, but how much did childhood matter?

"I only knew her for the last two years," she said. "Is that it? Do you see me as an interloper?'

"She never even mentioned you," I said roughly.

"Well, she often spoke about *you*. She used to call you 'my Caro'."

Pain struck and tears were slipping down before I could get hold of myself. Deft as a conjurer, she produced a box of tissues and pushed them towards me. I hated her from the bottom of my heart.

"What else did she say?" I managed to croak.

She considered, taking her time. "Nothing much," she said, "of any consequence. That I remember. But then, we had other things on our minds."

"What things?"

"You don't know?"

Some people betray themselves by body language and facial expressions. Kate was not one of them, but she was not clever enough to conceal that here there was something she did not wish to talk about.

She stood up. "How remiss of me! I should have offered you a drink. I drink whisky," she said, as though defying me to choose anything else.

The glasses were squat and heavy; the bottle familiar. We sat and sipped. I could have wished she were not here and I could have prowled around the place, just looking. I would not give her the satisfaction of knowing how much I admired all I saw, so made sure I did not appear to be aware of it.

"I need your help," she said at last, putting down her glass. "I told David I was sure there were friends of Sophie's who would be pleased..." her voice trailed. "He said I would know what to do better than he did. So, if there is anything you want or if you know of anybody who would like anything special..."

I cut her short.

"I have all I need to remember her by."

This is something I will not forgive David. To expose me to the ignominy of an upstart stranger daring to offer me ... Something clicked in my mind. "How well do you know David?" I asked.

Implication and accusation were clear in every syllable. As soon as the words were out, I knew I had blown it.

I watched the soft features sag and then begin to harden as she took the question in and started to deal with it.

"I was going to ask you to lunch," she said at last, in a low voice.

"You haven't answered my question."

"I don't intend to," she said.

She got up and walked out on to the deck and leaned out over the balustrade.

"Go carefully up the staircase," she said over her shoulder. "See yourself out."

On an impulse, as I passed Sophie's belongings lying strewn around the entrance hall, I scooped up the little button-backed chair. There was just room for it on the back seat of the car.

When I got home, I threw up.

It had all been a waste of good whisky and was a morning which got me nowhere

I had barely found it safe to release my clutch on the lavatory bowl and get up and wash my face when the telephone rang.

It was Kate Hamilton.

"I'm sorry," she said. "I overreacted. And I hope it eases your mind to know that you are absolutely wrong in surmising —"

"All right, all right," I said impatiently.

"I know how it is," she went on, "we all look for scapegoats."

"What do you mean?"

"Oh, come on," she said wearily, "don't tell me you don't wake in the night and worry that it might have been because of you, that there was something she just couldn't take ..."

I could find nothing to say.

"Are you there?" she said.

I still did not answer.

"I'm glad you took the chair," she said. "I'm sure Soph would have wanted you to have it."

I put the receiver down.

It was only later I realised I had not asked her what it was that kept *her* awake in the night wondering ... It is unlikely she would have told me.

But I will find out. Don't think you have done with me, Kate Hamilton. We have unfinished business.

HENRY

There was drama before we got away.
The police had been notified of our impending departure and the Gas, Electricity and Water Boards informed, by letter, that their services were to be turned off until further notice. Nell insisted that copies of the letters be kept.

"Is it really necessary?" I asked.

"Of course," she said. "Proof. Just let them try and charge us for usage while we are away!"

Mrs Phillips, who comes in twice a week to keep us clean and tidy, was detailed to collect the mail each day, so that its accumulation could not alert intending burglars; to go round the house each day to make certain all was well, and to water the plants.

She pointed out that if the water was turned off, she couldn't do that, and did Madam expect her to bring water from home?

The Water Board was informed, by letter, of the change of plan.

Then, the day before we were due to leave, Mrs Phillips became ill.

"My plants!" Nell cried. Apart from the big pots of dramatic-leafed ones, there were twenty-four small ones of African violets.

She had read, she said, in some magazine, somewhere, that plants could be left on their own if a watering device were set up. She was sure she had not thrown the magazine away. Nell's searches are always frantic. The magazine was found, after nerves had been stretched to screaming point, under the cushion of her chair, among other jots and tittles she was keeping for reference.

The system was simple. Plants are positioned above a source of water with a wick leading from the water to the pot. They drink as needed.

I do not like to think of the hauling of the pots to the bathroom, the finding of things to stand them on to keep them just above the level of the water in the bath and the heaving of the pots into the bath. Nell helped. She cut old towels into strips to make the wicks. The African violets posed a different problem. Finally it was decided that I should take them to the nursery from which they came and board them there until our return. The woman was very nice. They could do with some looking after, she said.

By the time we reached the aircraft, I was so exhausted I could hardly keep awake.

"*Not* the window seat," Nell said sharply to the solicitous young flight attendant, "I do not need reminding of how far we have to fall."

I did not care to remind her that in the hoo-ha about the plants, burglars had been forgotten. No provision had been made for the emptying of the mailbox. Our personal correspondence is meagre, but the postman relentlessly delivers the junk mail which the notice informs him is not welcome. The box will be filled to overflowing in a week.

A week. I settled in my seat and let weariness take over.

"Don't dare go to sleep before we take off!" Nell said, reaching for my hand. "And why are you smiling?"

A week. God bless all bloody-minded postmen. At the end of the week I could alert her to the fact that the piled-up mail was announcing the house was empty and available for ransacking. The plane tickets were open-ended. The betting was strong that, in eight days time, we would be back at home. I could afford to smile.

David was waiting for us.

He and I exchanged a small wry grimace as Nell employed the kiss-and-you-look-awful routine she had subjected him to since he had reached adolescence and his clothes and haircut had not been of her choosing.

He looked surprisingly fit and well turned out to me. I wondered who was looking after him. Nobody, I discovered, after we reached the house.

"Mrs Thing does the cleaning," he said. "The boys are with the Savages. I manage quite well."

"You will, of course, bring the boys home," Nell said.

He looked surprised. "Do you think you can manage them?"

"Manage them?"

Not for nothing had Nell played Oscar Wilde. Lady Bracknell and the handbag immediately leapt to mind.

"I'll be at the office most of the time," David said. "I can only take short breaks —"

"Short breaks?" Lady Bracknell was in evidence again.

"I have a practice to run, Nell," he said, "a living to make."

Her basilisk glare did not seem to affect him. "I'm glad to see you, of course," he said, "but you must realise —"

What she had to realise we did not discover for she made an explosive sound, picked up her bag and swept towards the staircase.

"Better go with her, Henry," he said. "It's the far door on the right."

"This is what I call getting off to a good start," I said, preparing to follow her and found, to my surprise, that we were both laughing.

I think it was the first time I actually liked him.

David brought up the bags. Nell never travels light. "I hope you haven't been carrying these," he said. I had, but there was no point in admitting it.

Nell was standing looking out of the window. David planted the bags down. "Plenty of room," he said, indicating the wardrobe and Georgian tallboy. "And why not have a lie-down to get over the journey?"

Nell turned away from the window and towards us. Her face wrecked and messy with tears.

"Who killed her, David?" she said brokenly. "Who killed her?"

As bad moments go, that had to be one of the worst.

I doubt if two men ever handled a tricky situation better. My years of experience with Nell and David's outraged anger made us a formidable team. He silenced her with an authority I did not know he had, and she was too astonished to resist taking the sedatives I knew she needed. We dealt with her in a very summary fashion. Within an hour, she was in bed and asleep, and we had left her, and stolen downstairs.

"It's the strain," I said. "When she's strained, she becomes irrational."

"It doesn't take strain to make Nell irrational." He was still very angry. "I can do without this, Henry," he said. "I have enough to cope with without Nell's histrionics."

"She is suffering," I said, trying to placate him.

"And we all know *how* she suffers! There has never been suffering like it in the history of the world! I didn't want her to come! I knew there would be scenes. And accusations."

"I think she might be in need of your help," I said, knowing I was taking a chance, but deeming it worth it. "She hasn't said so directly, but I get the feeling that she thinks Sophie might not have forgiven her for something."

"What?"

"I don't know."

"And are we about to find out? Are we to have the beating of the bosom and the high Cs of agonised remorse?"

"I don't know that either," I said, upset that I could not calm him. "All I do know is that she is very unhappy and not at all well."

"And how about you? Are you well?"

I didn't much like the way he was scrutinising me. "I'm all right," I said. "You know me."

"No," he said, "actually I don't. I've never bothered enough. Stupid of me." As we looked at each other, streaming between us were thoughts that could never be expressed. Nor did they have to be. We were each aware of the extent, if not the detail, of Nell's effect on our lives. Comrades-in-arms, I thought, and reached out and patted his shoulder.

"Thank you for loving her," he said, as though I had relieved him of a crippling burden. "No-one else could."

"I'll not argue with that," I said, and there we were, laughing again and Sophie lay dead and Nell was drugged and lost to the world.

We sobered quickly as though the same thought had struck us both.

"Enough of this," he said, "there is dinner to cook — and I know you are good in the kitchen." We went through to the comfortable place which I remembered as the heart of the house. It was much tidier than usual. There were vegetables, ready-chopped in little bowls, chicken drumsticks marinating in larger bowls, and wok, oil and spatula standing at the ready.

"I've opened a bottle of red," he said. "Shall we leave it in the bottle or decant it? And do you mind if we eat in here?"

We busied ourselves peacefully.

"Henry," he said, as he unwrapped small cheeses. "She has come to flay me alive I know, but however it goes — and it could go very badly indeed — I want you to believe that I loved Sophie — and nobody else."

"I've never doubted it," I said.

I was taken aback by the blazing gratitude of his thanks. It was then I became aware of the danger of the ground beneath our feet and began to feel that even a week in this place would be too long.

Nell did not wake for dinner and slept on till morning.

The birds are noisier here than at home. I was awakened by the raucous shouting of kookaburras. Sophie and the boys used to feed them and, apparently, they are still expectant. I wonder how long it will take them to realise that, with only David here, they will shout in vain.

I went out onto the balcony and looked down at the sea. Although the house is high above it, one hears it breathing. The first time I came here, urban man that I am, I thought someone had left a car engine running.

I was glad to have time to myself to adjust to this house-without-Sophie. From the moment we entered the door, I had been aware of emptiness. God knows how David stands it. He should get away from here.

I loved Sophie. How could one not? But now I feel critical of her. Her health was good. No problem there. She may have had other problems. Don't we all? We have to face them.

Death is the easy way out, the soft option. Whatever troubled her was surely transitory. All she needed was the capacity to endure. I would have sworn she had it.

Nell is rabid for answers. I am afraid of the questions.

David appeared, dressed for the city, with a tray of breakfast coffee and fruit. "I have to go to the office," he said. "I'll bring something back for lunch."

"Don't bother," I said. "She raided the delicatessen before we came." I had had the presence of mind to shove the plastic bag of goodies into his refrigerator.

"Oh God," he said, "and I was hoping for *food*."

We were getting into the habit of exchanging meaningful glances. I would have to watch it.

The coffee had become cool before she woke. "Can't that boy do *anything* right?" she said.

When she was fed and dressed, she began to prowl around the house. "It is stripped!" she keened. "Stripped!"

I was thankful that David did not come home for lunch. He rang to say that there were clients whose demands on him could not be ignored; that he was sure we would find plenty to eat, and that he would be home in time to take us out to dinner.

"Does he think I am going to waste a whole day?" she cried. "What is the telephone number of that Savage woman?"

A startled female voice said, "Oh, did you arrive already?" She said that the boys were out, but would be home to lunch. Perhaps we would like to come down and join them? She gave instructions as to where to find the house.

"We are without transport," Nell said.

"Then I'll give you the number to call for a taxi," the voice said.

It was not the reaction required. "Can't the woman drive?" Nell asked in high dudgeon.

Travel and trauma had played havoc with her hair. This was obviously a Haroun-al-Raschid day. I had never asked where she had learned the art of turban-winding. She never let me see her effect it. Nell likes to be mysterious. "How do I look?" she asked when she was dressed and ready. She looked like Nell at her flamboyant best to me; what she might look like to strangers was another matter.

The taxi arrived on time, drew up at the gate and the driver hooted. She had trained our local taxi-men to come and ring politely at our front door. They were not supposed to leave their vehicles unattended, they had said, but they did it for her.

The driver had to hoot twice more, before she was ready to emerge from the house. "You are not calling the cattle home," she said to him icily, waiting for me to open the car door for her.

"No?" he said. He was young and had all the cheeky imperviousness which goes with ignorance and adolescence. "Where to?" He rolled up his eyes when I told him. The house is only at the bottom of the hill.

"David may not like our doing this," I said, as the short journey came to an end.

"Then he should have stayed home and kept an eye on me."

She was herself again, the exhausted hysteria of yesterday forgotten. She was Nell, firing on all cylinders and ready to go forward full throttle; the Nell from whom the boys retreat in sullen bewilderment.

"Take it easy," I said.

I knew it would come. She turned on me with a scorching glare of scorn. "Bloody Henry," she said.

Nin Savage was all I expected her not to be, and many of the things I most like. I saw Nell drop her suspicions the minute she set eyes on her. *David would not go for this* was written all over her face, and her manner became amused and patronising.

"You are *so* kind and I am *so* grateful," she said.

I pressed the small, warm hand offered to me. "And so am I." I don't do it on purpose, but it happens. I do not exactly distance myself from Nell, but a twitch of the lip and a glance under the eyebrow establishes my separate identity and, regrettably often, complicity with the new acquaintance. It happened now.

"The boys are expecting you," we were told, and invited into the house.

The expectation had obviously alarmed them into an uncharacteristic spruceness. Hair was slicked, shirts and ties were being worn.

"These are our blazers for the new school," one of them said, offering himself up for inspection and blocking Nell's path towards a large, comfortable-looking armchair.

"Your father has obviously been busy," Nell said wryly.

"Mrs Savage took us to be measured. Do you want to see our hats?"

"No, thank you," Nell said, and used her handbag to push him aside so that she could reach the chair.

"I'm sorry my husband isn't available yet," Mrs Savage said. "He is with a patient."

"A patient?"

"He has rooms here. He is a speech therapist."

The mention of the word "speech" sharpened Nell's interest.

"You remember, Grandma. He's the one who st-st-stopped us st-st-stuttering. He taught us to say —"

"I remember." Nell cut him short and sank down heavily into the chair.

"Would you like some coffee?" Mrs Savage asked.

"She'd rather have a gin, wouldn't you, Grandma? She always has one in the mornings."

"Tom ...! Ben ...!" Tom was the livelier of the two and the most upfront, but one could never be certain. She got round it by addressing both of them as "Tomben".

"*I'd* love a gin," Mrs Savage said, quick as a flash. "How about you, Mr —"

"Call me Henry," I said.

The boys snorted. "You'll never guess what his name is," one of them said. "Henry Knickerbocker."

One of the conditions of my marriage to Nell was that she would never be required to answer to Nell Knickerbocker.

"Tonic or Martini?" The voice squeaked a bit as our hostess turned to leave the room.

"Martini," said Nell. I hoped Mrs Savage realised that both gin and Martini are alcoholic. She came back with a drinks tray and, indicating bottles and glasses, invited us to pour our own. "You know how you like it," she said.

"Grandma likes it..." one of the boys began and stopped, open-mouthed, as Nell snapped at him. "Don't keep calling me that!"

He could have been doing it for devilment, for it had been well established, when the boys were staying with us, that she did not like being labelled a grandparent.

"Well, what shall I call you? I can't call you ... Nell." He said the word in a hushed, shocked tone, which did not deceive me.

"I know," the other one said brightly. "When somebody doesn't have a name, they are called 'X'. We could call you 'X-ma'."

"Sorry," said Dan Savage breezily, suddenly appearing in the room. "Oh good, I see my wife is looking after you."

He is a strikingly handsome man and has a confident, easy manner. I was grateful for it. I hate to think how Nell might have behaved if he had been otherwise.

"Good Lord!" he said to the boys, "aren't you hot in that rig-out?"

He smiled at Nell. "They were so keen to show off to their grandparents! Off you go now. Get it all off, and hang things up! And there's coke in the fridge if you want one."

The boys took off like sprinters from the block.

"How's your drink?" he asked Nell. "And are you comfortable in that chair? Is it too low?"

Nell often reminds me of a cat. Now she reacted to the soothing voice and the concern for her welfare with half-closed eyes and a graceful movement of the head. "You are very kind," she said, and no-one would have dreamed that, only a few moments before, there had been a wildness in the eyes and an unsheathing of claws.

"David was damn lucky to get the boys in," he said. "It's my old school. I would have liked ours to go there, but it costs an arm and a leg, and Nin wanted to keep them under her wing." He stopped short. "Oh," he said, and leaned down and put his hand on Nell's shoulder. "Sorry again."

For a second we all sat and thought about the wings that could no longer shelter Tom and Ben. Nell brought us out of it.

"For once my son has shown good sense."

She swept her lighthouse smile around the three of us. "We have much to talk about," she said.

"After lunch," Dan said indulgently. "First we must show you around and then feed you."

His wife looked a good deal less at ease than he did.

"I'm afraid you'll find the cuisine filling rather than haute," she said. "I tend to cook for the boys. If I had known ... Fortunately, we do have some really good wine."

I hoped it would not turn out to be unfortunate.

"Red?" Nell asked with interest.

"If you like."

My heart sank. With Nell and vino, one often got far too much veritas.

KATE

The small mountain of Sophie's things still lies, untouched, inside my door. After the fracas with Caroline Evans, I felt drained and sat about, wasting the rest of the day, staring at nothing. I should never have become involved.

To be honest, I walked right into it. All David Martin was asking for was space. I was the one who jumped in with the suggestion that there were people who would like mementos of her and, quite naturally, he said that, knowing her friends, I would have a better idea than he had ... Oh God.

I could feel the Evans woman's hatred like a blowtorch. I don't know what to do. One always wants to do the right thing. But what the hell is it? Sophie's belongings cannot be left lying there. I will stack everything in Geoff's old studio and close the door.

David had used ordinary green plastic bags, not the heavy-duty kind. They were tightly packed and splitting. Gathering up one containing her clothes was like taking Sophie in my arms. I never want to experience another moment like that one. The closeness, then the emptiness, the finality. The wolf-howl of loss.

She had become indispensable. Her warmth, her wholeheartedness, her naughtiness and sense of fun. And, most of all, the way she cared. When I told her about the scam and the way innocent people were suffering, her outrage was as great as mine.

Her conviction that something must be done fuelled my determination that it would be. When I told David Martin that she did not know how I did it, I lied. There is no need for him to know how we schemed and how joyfully we celebrated each turn of the screw! We were so caught up in the exhilaration of seeing a wrong redressed that we didn't think about being found out. It was mentioned, of course, but somehow we felt that the good we believed rules the universe just had to be on our side and would see us through. We weren't doing it for ourselves, we said, there is nothing to be punished for.

When I was arrested, she was terribly shocked. "It should be me, too!" she kept saying.

I thought she must surely have told David when she stood bail for such a large amount of money.

I don't know whether it is a case of God tempering the wind to the shorn lamb but, although the length of time these things take to come to resolution wears one down, I have never felt panic or desperation. I survived the worst thing that could possibly happen, Geoff's death, so … if it has to be prison, then at least I have the comfort of knowing that other people are happier than they were, and that I have it in me to be a good prisoner and make the most of my seclusion from the world.

Thinking about it, though, I have become increasingly convinced that the case will never reach court. Anger made that man react too quickly. There are others involved, "names". They surely will not want unwelcome publicity. I have the feeling that, before long, there will be pressure on him to let it drop.

I was building up to telling Sophie what I thought when … Commonsense tells me that her distress and worry cannot have been enough to make her feel that life was no longer worth living. She cannot have been that afraid of David's reaction when he found out — as find out he must. But ... Do any of us really know the ones we think we know best? I fight off the feeling of guilt like a bat from the hair.

It has been a very strange two days. The thought of anyone else arriving and finding Sophie behind my front door galvanised me into moving the great heap of her things. They are all now safely down in the studio. It is as though she is keeping company with Geoff. All his things are there, too.

Now that I am over the worst of it, I quite like to think of the pair of them sitting together gossiping and making wry comments about the way we are all behaving. They never met. He was dead before I got to know Soph, but they would have got on. I hung some of her slacks and shirts with his slacks and shirts in his cupboard. The smell of him is still there. I suppose it is a measure of how much she had come to mean to me that I am pleased to feel they have each other's company.

David has obviously just swept drawers, cupboards and wardrobes clean and stuffed everything into bags. In a strange way, I enjoyed sorting through it all, making tidy piles. It was as though I were reconstructing her.

I was surprised by the clothes, the bags and bags of them, and many I had not seen before. These last were the real surprise. They were so elegant. And elegant our Soph was not. Her charm was in her lack of sophistication, her bloom of health and freshness and total lack of self-awareness and guile.

Together with the simple cotton bras were underclothes of the type one drools at in the shop windows but would not presume to buy. Sophie had bought them. A lot of them. They made me uneasy. I piled them together, shoved them to one side and turned to the Sophie I knew.

The tapestry she was working on is not here, but the bag which held the wool and hung on the back of the stand, is. I will have to take that up with David.

I enjoyed sorting out her sewing gear, disentangling the reels of cotton from the lengths of elastic and zips of assorted sizes and colours, and lining them up so that they could be coordinated and placed neatly on the spindles in the sewing box. I came across cushion covers she had embroidered, the designs bold and free. I could remember her working on one in particular.

For some reason, she had decided to smoke because she had been to a restaurant and had been seduced by the scent of French cigarettes and coffee. She bought a packet of Gitanes. And she inhaled. She sat with her legs tucked under her and looking twelve years old, squinting and coughing and plying her needle, dropping ash and grumbling, until neither of us could stand it anymore and I took the cigarette away from her and made her some chamomile tea. As I now held the cushion over to my face, I hoped it would still hold the smell of smoke, but it did not. The design is Chinese peonies and a ginger jar. I will ask David if I may have it.

And, dear heaven, I find I am lusting after the patchwork pieces. She had made the design and cut all the dozens and dozens and dozens of pieces needed to make the bedspread, but had only just begun to put it together.

I sat for hours with the notebooks and scrapbooks. I recognised so much in them that we had shared: the recipes, the controversial articles in the daily paper, lovely illustrations pinched from art magazines, medical hints.

"Did you know pee is good for burns and scalds?" she once asked, searching for the scissors. "But it has to be your own pee." She loved bits of information, the odder the better. When I put the books aside, I found I was smiling. It was as though we had spent a comfortable afternoon together.

What was not comfortable was coming across a wig on a polystyrene head.

I took away the soft, pretty material in which it was wrapped and set it up. It was a lovely wig, and I could see it had been worn. The smooth black wing of hair fell across the forehead and curved across the cheek. The style was unmistakable. I knew at once who owned it, but I was damned if I could have any further dealings with that woman. David could give it back to her. She had obviously left it with Sophie to keep secret. She was not the sort of woman to admit needing help with her looks.

I will enjoy giving it to him and saying, "Caroline Evans, I presume!"

NIN

Nell Martin is all I thought she would be. I well understand the amused affection with which Sophie said, "She can be such a horror!"

When I told the twins she was coming for lunch, one of them smacked himself on the forehead and fell backwards onto the carpet; the other muttered a sepulchral "Ho-ly cow!"

I am getting very fond of those boys. They make me laugh. They fit into the family as unobtrusively as a joey into its mother's pouch. Although they are only nine and our own boys are so much older, Ian and Peter don't mind them tagging along. And tag they do. The four of them move like a pod of dolphins.

I do like Henry. His quiet, old-fashioned dignity and good manners charm me. And I love the way he puts the brakes on Nell when brakes are needed, and needed they were during our first, memorable meeting.

Lunch was a solid meal of lamb stew and apple pie. I do not believe that heavy meals late in the evening are good for adults, and certainly are not for youngsters. I have behind me the English tradition of dinner at midday, tea in the afternoon and supper in the early evening. I have seen no reason to change. I just call *dinner* "lunch" as lip-service.

If I had had more notice I would have adjusted, as I often do, to the current mores. But things were sprung upon me. The crockpot was on, the pie baked. People who invite themselves must take potluck.

Nell made it obvious that potluck was not something she relished. She picked at her food. Henry tucked in. The boys ate devotedly, without raising their eyes from the plate.

Her attempts to be winsome and engage them in conversation failed. They grunted. They nodded. And that was as far as they would go.

Fortunately, the wine was good and she appreciated it.

The turban she wore was multi-coloured. Her face became flushed. The boys exchanged glances under their eyebrows.

As she reached out to replenish her glass yet again, Henry laid a hand on her arm. "No," he said pleasantly and removed not only the bottle but her half-filled glass.

"My watchdog," she said, with smiling malevolence.

The boys escaped as soon as the meal was over; Dan led our guests into the sitting room (I would die rather than call it the "lounge room").

I took my time in the kitchen preparing coffee. I knew that interrogation lay ahead ...

I had barely entered the room and set the tray down before she weighed in. "Why?" she said. "Why did she do it? I have a right to know."

It was the claiming of a right which did me. I, too, had enjoyed the wine. I busied myself with the coffee. As I handed her her cup, I said, light as a thistle and as provocative as a slap in the face, "If she had thought that, she would have left you a note".

I felt Dan and Henry stiffen. But I was up and running.

And then she floored me completely. "Love has its rights," she said, "and I loved her very much. I need to know if anything I said, or anything I did, could have —"

"S-sh-h!" Henry, his face creased with concern, was up with his arms across her shoulders. He shook his head at me. "We are all in distress. Why not try and help each other?"

I felt like a dog.

"Don't tell me you don't worry, too," Nell said, without venom, unhinging me completely. "Everybody who was close to her must surely wonder if . . ."

Dan took charge of us all then. "I doubt if any of us here has anything to worry about," he said heartily.

In no time at all he had Henry re-seated, with a coffee cup in his hand, and me, with my eyes wiped, seated with one in mine.

"An after-dinner mint?" he asked Nell.

Nell shook her head and took a sip of her coffee. "Actually," she said, "I do have reason to worry." And the cup rattled as she put it back into the saucer.

I was so struck by how old her heavily-ringed hands looked, the skin wrinkled and soiled-looking against the bone-white china, that I almost missed what she said.

Dan was still being hearty. "Oh come on, my dear —"

She raised her chin, and though she looked at him, I felt her words were directed at me. "I told her to beware of her friends," she said.

I bristled anew. "ALL of them?" I asked.

"Naturally, I had a particular one in mind. I thought she could work it out for herself."

"How cruel!"

"It was kind. She was too naive. It is dangerous to think you live in a world which holds no deception."

"So you decided to destroy her faith in everybody?"

"I wanted her to learn to discriminate."

She sat there, her face as implacable as a dreadful old mandarin, calcified in the certainty of her own wisdom.

Rage got the better of me. "What you mean is that you didn't have the guts to tell her what you knew."

"I didn't *know* anything," she said with maddening patience. "I felt it. Here." She pressed her clenched fist against the space between her eyes.

It was too much. I gave a great whoop of derision. "For God's sake!" I said. "What have we here? She-to-whom-all-is-revealed? Don't tell me! Sitting among us we have the poor man's Maggie Mackenzie!"

Both Dan and Henry made noises of alarm. I didn't care. I fronted up to her. To my astonishment, I saw a look of incredulous joy spreading over her face. "Did you say Maggie Mackenzie? Do you *know* her?" she asked.

"Of course I do."

She slowly settled back in the chair with a deep sigh of satisfaction. All her antagonism was gone. "Then you can take me to see her," she said, as though bestowing a privilege. I was about to make a sharp reply when Henry stood up and came between us. He raised admonishing eyebrows and gave me a quizzical, conspiratorial look. "Sorry, my dear, but I'm getting sleepy. That was a lovely lunch. Thank you so much. Now I'm afraid I have to ask you to let me call a taxi."

"The phone is out here," Dan said, darting me a murderous look as he led Henry away.

When they had gone, Nell and I measured each other in silence.

"I mean it," she said at last. "I want to see her."

I was not going to let her hector *me*! "She's a busy person."

"She won't be too busy to see me. Arrange it as soon as you can."

How dare she issue her bloody orders!

Dan and Henry came back into the room, and Nell held out an arm to be assisted to rise from her chair. Her face was blotched. As she swayed upright, she fixed me with a hard stare. "Ring me," she said.

I stared back at her blankly. Let her make what she could of *that*!

The taxi came.

Dan opened the door for her, and Henry took her arm to help her into the back seat, but she wrenched away from him testily and her foot missed the opening. She fell awkwardly, sprawled half in, half out of the cab. Hearing her cry of pain, Dan moved forward, but Henry held him back. "Thank you," he said. "I can manage."

Nell is a tall, heavy woman. As he struggled to help her up and ease her into the seat, I felt more concern for him than for her.

Feeling unhinged, we stood and watched the cab drive away up the hill, before turning back into the house.

"I didn't behave well," I said, before Dan had the chance to reprimand me.

"You certainly did not."

"I don't want to see her again — ever."

He was very stiff and cross. "I'm sure that can be arranged."

Oh no it can't, I thought. She will hover round me, relentless as a blowfly over putrid meat, until she has things her way.

He looked at me sharply. "I would rather you didn't," he said.

"Didn't what?"

"You know damn well."

He didn't mention Maggie Mackenzie. He didn't have to.

Now look what you've done, I said to Sophie.

DAVID

"I am very worried about Nell," Henry said.

Worried about *her*! I was worried about *him*! His face was the colour of paper, and he kept rubbing his chest with his knuckled hand. I was furious. Trust Nell! She had hardly been in the place twenty-four hours, and already there was drama.

I had come home from the office early, looking forward to having a rest before taking them out to dinner, and was confronted by a taxi in the drive, with Henry and the young driver attempting to haul Nell out of it. I brushed them aside and bent over her to pick her up. Her wine-laden breath made me turn my head sharply.

"Did you *have* to go out?" I asked Henry, after we had got her upstairs and into bed. "Couldn't you have waited? Had a rest after the journey? And why did you go to the Savages?"

"You know how impatient she is, David," he said. "And she is very distressed. She will know no peace until she gets to the bottom of what happened to Sophie."

My feelings towards Nell have always been ambivalent. Now they became very specific. I hated her. I hated her with an intensity which took away the breath. How dare she come here and interfere in my life and muddy the waters with people I knew! How did she bloody *dare*?

"I know how it will go," Henry was saying. "The bruising is obviously going to be very bad, and if there is a haematoma ... Once she starts to bleed, it is very hard to stop."

I couldn't listen to him. And tending to Nell had turned my stomach. The shock of the fall had made her wet herself. Henry had taken off her slacks and peeled off her shredded tights, but the warm sickly stench had reached me across the room. Her shin-bones were sharp, the calves slack and the skin loose and wrinkled. Higher up, I could see the blue rope of varicose veins. I could feel no compassion, only distaste.

"She needs a doctor," Henry said.

"I'll send for him tomorrow. I'd prefer him not to see her while she's half-cut."

"Then I will go and sit with her," he said. I was glad. I didn't want him sitting with me, I was too annoyed with them both. He went upstairs very slowly.

Dan Savage rang up during the evening. "We're feeling a bit worried," he said. So they should be. They should have had more sense than to let her drink so much.

"We didn't think Henry looked well," he said. "He was near to collapse after lifting your mother."

"He's all right now," I said brusquely.

"And your mother?"

"Sleeping it off."

"Sorry about that, but with guests, you know, you can hardly —"

"I know."

"Well," he said, "she's seen the boys now..." It sounded as though he hoped she would not wish to see them again.

"Thank your wife," I said, remembering my manners.

"Sure."

I was about to hang up when he suddenly said, "Do you know a Maggie Mackenzie?"

"I don't think so. Should I?"

"Your mother seems very interested in her."

I didn't care who or what Nell was interested in, so I just thanked him again and left it at that. It was only later when I was lying in bed, sleepless, that I remembered the strange woman who had appeared at the door with a string bag full of books which, she had said, were Sophie's.

Her name, Kate had reminded me, was Maggie Mackenzie.

I certainly was not going to get up and ring him to tell him that. It would probably have meant nothing to him, anyway.

Nell had not said how long she and Henry proposed to stay. The sooner I got things organised, the sooner the visit could be over. It was unlikely she would return home without crossing swords with Caroline. I had always felt they enjoyed their waspish exchanges; they are, after all, two of a kind, but this situation called for very careful handling.

Nell had her suspicions, that I well knew. Would it seem strange if I said that Caroline and I no longer saw each other, that she was Sophie's friend, not mine? Or would it seem more natural for us to have stayed in touch as ordinary friends would?

Should I ring Caroline and ask her what she thought?

I had just made up my mind that I would, when there came the sound of a heavy crash from upstairs. I was halfway up when Nell began to scream.

When I burst into the room, Henry was lying on the bed. He was a frightening colour and his breathing was ragged. I know he has Parkinson's. Was it a Parkinson's incident? Or a heart attack? Or a stroke? What the hell did one do?

Nell struggled up from between the beds where she had fallen. "Don't stand there like a fool," she hissed. "Call an ambulance!" The hospital is only a short way out of the village. I rushed downstairs and dialled the number Sophie had outlined in red on the list hanging up by the telephone.

"Ten minutes," the calm voice said.

Nell, half-dressed and still wearing that terrible turban, was kneeling by the bed holding Henry's limp hand. "Henry!" she was saying sharply. "Stop it! Henry!"

I got her up from the floor, found her dressing-gown and struggled to get it on over her embarrassing underclothes, then turned to Henry. I braced myself. God knows how one gives the kiss of life, but I had to try. I took hold of his poor pinched nose and forced his mouth open. His top teeth dropped quietly downward. I was seized with such a paroxysm of love for this dear, gentle man that I felt no squeamishness. I just took the teeth out and applied my mouth to his and blew. And kept on breathing and blowing until I heard the scream of the ambulance and the urgent ringing of the doorbell.

They asked if Nell was to go with him to the hospital. "No," I said firmly. I was determined Henry would get undivided attention.

As the ambulance drove away, she stood by the window, watching for each glimpse of it as it rounded the downhill curves. "What will I do if he dies?" she said.

Nell's first thoughts are always for Nell.

I rang the hospital just before midnight. He is sleeping peacefully and is in no danger, I was told. I tapped at Nell's door to give her the news, but she was already asleep.

Going to the office the next morning was obviously impossible. I got up, showered, had a leisurely breakfast by myself.

Once Nell rose, peace would be gone. I did not go up to call her until nearly ten o'clock. She was lying with her eyes closed. Without make-up she always looks very pale, but today even her lips were without colour. As I stood looking down at her, she opened her eyes.

"Sorry," she said. She looked so wretched I felt a twinge of pity.

"Nothing to be sorry for," I said.

"Oh yes, there is."

With an effort, she turned back the bedclothes. The mattress was soaked with blood and, as she moved, it squelched.

"Sorry," she said again. "When I fell last night, the vein ... I thought the bleeding would stop ..."

"Ten minutes," the hospital voice said again.

There was nothing I could do for her while we waited for the ambulance to arrive. I did not dare touch her. I stood by the window and watched the road.

"You coming?" the young ambulance attendant asked. "No. I can't leave my children alone in the house," I lied.

"Don't worry, sport," he said, "we'll look after her."

As I watched the white shape of the vehicle wind its way down the hill, I thought, what if she dies? I was thinking about Henry.

What if she *didn't* die? In that case, my thoughts were all for me. If she didn't, she could be here for weeks! What sort of a prospect was that?

KATE AND NIN

"I need your advice," Kate Hamilton said into the telephone. "I offered to help David Martin, and I think I've painted myself into a corner."

"And I need yours!" Nin Savage replied. "That dreadful old mother of his is here and has me in her sights."

"O-ho!"

Nell had gone to live in Adelaide before Kate and Sophie had become friends, so to Kate she was a name without a face.

"I can usually handle her," Sophie had said, but without certainty. The name was often mentioned, much in the way people who live below a fabled volcano speak of it, aware of past disasters and alert to the possibility of future devastation.

"We live in interesting times!" Kate said lightly. Nin moaned. "Tell you what," Kate said, "Let's go and sit and look at the sea. I'll bring a flask of coffee and some biscuits."

They sat on the beach, side by side like children, digging their toes into the sand and watching the waves hiss forward and breathe away, yet all the time creeping inexorably forward.

"Have you noticed," Nin asked, "that no matter how dry the sand may seem, you always get up with a damp bum?"

"You're still very English, aren't you?" Kate asked, amused. To her the damp bum was a natural phenomenon.

"Am I? Is that why people dislike me?"

"They don't!"

"Caroline Evans certainly does. My vowels enrage her."

"A lot of things seem to enrage Caroline Evans. I had a very stormy time with her."

"You did? She tracked you down?"

"Appeared on the doorstep, and I still don't know why she wanted to meet me. We got sidetracked. David had only just left and the entrance was piled high with the stuff he had brought round."

"What stuff?"

"Sophie's things."

"Why ever —?"

"He said he needed space to accommodate his guests."

"Bullshit!" Nin burst out. "What does he mean 'space'? It's a big house and the boys aren't at home. There are four bedrooms, two bathrooms and an outside shower room, that great sitting room and a kitchen you could bicycle round in."

"I can only tell you what he said. Perhaps there are rooms he doesn't care to use."

"Sophie did it in the upstairs bathroom, if that's what you mean," Nin said roughly, "and no, I don't imagine he does enjoy shaving there, but there's still the downstairs one —"

"Oi! Oi!" Kate broke in. "Why so angry?"

"Everything about all this makes me angry!" Nin was almost incoherent with temper. "He asked me if *I* would like Sophie's clothes, and I had to give him a flea in his ear about *that*! Now he's worrying you and trying to get rid of ... And there's that wicked old woman asking me if I don't think that perhaps *I* could have done or said something to make Sophie slit her bloody wrists!" She turned a piteous face upwards. "Oh, Kate, I have all the guilt I'm capable of carrying! I don't need more."

Kate put an arm around her shoulders, but she was not to be comforted.

"And you do know," she went on, her anger dying into a slick weariness, "I'm beginning to get exasperated with Sophie. Suicide is one hell of a self-centred thing."

The incoming tide had almost reached their feet. "Come on," Kate said, pulling Nin up. "Let's sit in the car and have our coffee." They turned their backs on the sea and ploughed through the soft sand, back through the clumps of marram grass to where the car waited under the trees.

Kate opened all the doors and windows and settled Nin in the passenger seat. As she unscrewed the flask, the good smell of coffee rose like a genie bringing promise of comfort. "And I made the Anzac biscuits this morning," she said.

But Nin was not to be diverted. "I have wondered," she said "perhaps I leaned on Sophie more than I should."

"I didn't know either of you then," Kate said. But she had often seen them together: two small women, talking absorbedly, one fair and fresh and joyous, the other dark, with a closed face and vehement hand gestures.

"But she was all I had. I couldn't ask Dan, he has no patience with that kind of thing."

"What kind of thing?"

"Talking to the dead."

"Nin!" Kate said warningly.

"No, listen. I was out of my mind. The wheels went over her *head*, Kate. Her little hand was stretched out ... there was a ring on it ..."

"Nin!" Kate said, on a higher note.

"To know you've done *that* is a lot to live with. It gets to be too much. I wanted to know if she was all right now, if she knew it wasn't my fault. And then one day I saw this woman walking down the street. You couldn't miss her. She strode. And she was wearing a hat nobody else could have got away with. 'That's Maggie Mackenzie,' the friend I was with said. 'Strange woman. They say she can talk to the dead.' And then, blow me down, the next day there was an article in the paper about the topiary in her garden and photographs. I recognised the fantastic shapes. You must have seen them."

Kate had. Too often, when driving along the narrow road, her eye had been caught by the unexpected sight of tall moons of green against the sky and the ungainly shape of what had seemed to be a leafy prancing horse.

"It seemed intended. I persuaded Sophie to come with me to see her."

"And did you? Talk to the child?"

"No. She didn't make things easy. She was forbidding, somehow. I could see she knew who I was — everybody bloody well does after the accident. But I couldn't talk. Sophie had to cover for me, said we had seen the article and were interested in her garden. She invited us in."

"And?"

"She and Sophie got talking. You know Soph. I just sat there."

Kate could imagine it. Nin, tight and glowering, Sophie smiling and at ease. "She was rattling on about the twins, about what a terrible stammer they had had and how good Dan had been with them, and then about Zak —"

"Zak?"

"This phantom friend they invented. How it was 'Zak this, Zak that, Zak won't like it, and where are Zak's bathers? And wait a minute, Zak isn't ready.' She was making light of it, but I could see she was worried. I knew David was no help. All he did was bring out the heavy hand. Much good that did!"

125

"I know children have imaginary playmates," Kate said. "That's considered quite normal. But it's usually an *only* child, isn't it? Lonely ones. I would have thought the twins —"

"That's what Sophie said. 'But they have each other' she kept on saying."

"And what did this Maggie woman say?"

"Not to worry. Zak had come in his own time, for his own reasons, and would go away again."

"Yuk! That's making something spooky out of children's imagination!"

"She told Sophie to make him welcome and treat him normally."

"How did that go down?"

"All right, I think. I don't know what else Maggie told her. Sophie went very quiet about it, but she was always wanting to know about karma and the afterlife. We used to go round to Maggie's on Wednesday evenings."

"Was it any help to *you*?"

"Sort of. Maggie was more interested in Sophie, though — seemed to feel she was the one with problems. I began to see there might be patterns. You know, the same people meeting in different lifetimes to work out problems of the soul together."

When people started to talk about "the soul" Kate felt immediate distrust. The past and future lives syndromes were particularly suspect. It might make sense if past lives were remembered and the lessons learned made plain, but they were not. And what had that child ever done to Nin in a past life to warrant such terrible reprisal?

She had had enough. "Don't tell me!" she said. "The thought of meeting Caroline Evans another time around is too much!"

The tension eased and they sat together, munching. "I'd like the recipe for these," Nin said, reaching for another biscuit.

"That shows you're still English. Every good Australian girl has it engraved on her heart."

Nin smiled, but was unable to shake off her mood entirely. "She was kind to me," she said, "but it was Sophie she was really concerned about."

And she was back again to her grievance about Nell. "The old bag! Asking me a question like that! What could I have possibly done to harm Sophie?"

Take her to see Maggie Mackenzie? Kate wondered, but did not dare say it out loud.

DAVID

"This is no way to treat your guests," the doctor said and I knew from his jocularity that all was well. Henry was suffering from exhaustion, malnutrition and acute dyspepsia. "His heart?" I asked. "I have often seen him rubbing his chest."

"Heartburn," the doctor replied. "Give him good simple food and make him rest. You can take him home this afternoon."

Nell had lost a great deal of blood and was very weak. She might need a transfusion. "And we'll give her a good going-over while she's here," the doctor said.

"How long will that take?" I asked.

He shrugged. "Depends on what we find."

She was pale and petulant, and in the public ward. And wearing a hospital gown.

"You must bring me my own things," she said before I could greet her.

"Henry is suffering from exhaustion and malnutrition," I said. "He needs care and rest. I will have to get somebody in to give me a hand with him. I'm taking him home this afternoon."

"Good," she said, "he can show you what I need."

I don't know if Henry was expecting me to take him to see her before we left, but I wheeled him straight down to the car, and he was too tired to argue.

As we entered the house, the telephone was ringing. "Bit of commotion up at your place," Dan Savage said. "We've been ringing all day to see if you needed any help."

The ambulance sirens must have alerted the neighbourhood. "Things aren't too bad," I said. "They've let Henry out, but are keeping Nell in."

"I'll just tell Nin," he said, and I heard him call out "It's OK, sweetie. Panic's over."

Nin sounded amazingly gentle. "Poor old Henry," she said. And then on a brighter note: "I bet you've had nothing to eat all day."

It was only then I realised that in the hassle I had indeed forgotten food.

"I've just made two steak-and-kidney pies for tomorrow," she said. "If you pop some potatoes into the microwave now, they'll be ready by the time Dan brings one up."

Henry did not eat much, but his enjoyment was a pleasure to see. It was a damn good pie. No wonder the boys like staying with the Savages.

I got him to bed early. I had dragged out the blood-soaked mattress and put it in the garden shed. Should I set fire to it or ask the Council to take it away?

I had piled some blankets on the bed base and covered it with a duvet, so that the absence of the mattress was not obvious. I didn't want him looking at the bed and being too forcibly reminded of what had happened.

I was knackered, but the least I could do before going to bed myself was to ring and thank Nin Savage.

"I've been thinking," she said. "You'll have to go to the office. Won't Henry be lonely in the house all by himself?"

"Well, the cleaning lady comes in," I said. "I'd thought of asking her if she could help out."

"I've heard about her from the boys," she said, and I could feel her grinning. "Better than that," she went on, "why not ask Kate Hamilton? Her days must be pretty empty now. I can ask her for you if you like."

"Thanks," I said quickly, "but if she is asked, I must do it myself. I am already in her debt."

"Yes, you are, aren't you?" she said. "Dumping all that stuff on her!"

"Has she complained?"

"No, but I have. The responsibility for dealing with it is yours, not hers. You shouldn't think you can just shuffle it off."

It had been a long and troublesome day. I didn't want more trouble at the end of it. "The problem is," I said wearily, "I just don't know what to do."

Her sigh was as gusty as though she were blowing in my ear. "Sorr-ee," she said. "I speak before I think, but my heart's in the right place, honestly."

"And you can cook," I said and, for the first time, we laughed together.

"I mean it about Kate," she said. "Do it for Henry. He'll love her."

She was right. "I'll ring her in the morning," I said.

As I was falling off to sleep, I realised the Savages had not asked about Nell, nor had I offered to tell them.

HENRY

Nell has dangerously high blood pressure and there are serious questions about her heart; consequently, she must remain in hospital. This does not please her. Although our medical insurance is for top hospital cover, the local hospital does not have private rooms.

This enrages her. Top-rank medicos and surgeons visit the hospital, so I have no worries. The doctors who have seen her are specialists in their field and, if surgical intervention is necessary, I am sure she would be attended by surgeons of similar stature. This does not console her.

David said that, if we insisted, she could be moved to a hospital in the City where she could have a private room. Then move me, she said. If you wish, he replied. I had to point out to him that the City was an hour's drive away, and Nell required to be visited twice a day. Up to her, he said, and shrugged.

He has become surprisingly hard.

She is still in the hospital down the road.

Meanwhile, I am the pampered guest. I had forgotten life could hold such ease. "How do you feel about parsnips?" asked the tall smiling woman, Kate, who often pops in to make certain I do not feel lonely.

"Friendly," I said.

"Then I will make you parsnip and orange soup, with chicken stock."

My digestion is much easier, although I still burp. But the burps are contented rather than painful. Nell has a sophisticated palate. Ham, chicken, oysters, fish must all be smoked, cheeses studded with fruit or full of holes, and fruit is only acceptable if soaked in liqueur. I have often longed for the luxury of fresh baked bread, a chunk of cheese and an apple.

I take note of everything I am given to eat. I wait, watching for discomfort to begin. I am a connoisseur of abdominal distress. Sometimes, as I wait, I fall asleep. Such sleeps are sweet.

David, of course, is at the office all day. He takes me to see Nell in the evenings. The girls, Nin and Kate, take me on the morning run. They are very good. They sit outside and wait for me. Nell never asks how I manage to get to the hospital. She complains endlessly about the food, the surliness of the nurses, the racket other patients make in the night and the offhanded way the doctors treat her.

"Don't they know who I am?" she demanded, and there was no way to tell her that indeed they did not and, even if they had, they would not have cared. Poor Nell. She has never realised that fame in the acting profession can be like the day of the mayfly.

She is sick and ill at ease, while I know a rare content.

"Now stop that!" the girl Nin said, when I expressed feelings of guilt. "Make the most of it; you deserve it."

And indeed I do. It is not admirable to think of oneself as an admirable fellow, I know, but there is no law against being objective and, as I stand back, all emotion put aside, and take stock, my judgement can tell me nothing less. And then the other voice speaks: Is Nell what she is because you allowed her to be?

I think about that. It is a tricky one.

Here, in Sophie's home, I am very aware of the girl's absence. David is a tidy man: once used, a thing is put away, surfaces are kept clear, cushions plumped up at bedtime. I see him cast an eye around before he puts out the lamps and helps me upstairs. The house has lost its bright disorder, the careless, comfortable evidence of life in progress.

I thought, before we came, that we would feel Sophie around the place, but she is not here. It is not just that David has obviously tidied away most of her things — it is more than that. Which is not to say I feel ill at ease. One can be grateful for the lack of pressure from the personality of even those one loves most. And I can use the silence.

And I appreciate the number and accessibility of the lavatories. There is one outside each bedroom. I remember remarking on it to Sophie's father, a genial chap.

"I had 'em put in," he said. "The house is always full of people, you never know whom you might meet prowling round in the night, and I was never a chap for the po."

He died from prostate cancer.

It is odd. In my mind's eye I see him clear as a bell, eyes twinkling, bald head shining, but when I try to bring Sophie's face to mind, all I get is a pain between the eyebrows and blankness.

Nell is really unwell. When David took me down to visit her tonight, there were screens round her bed and a doctor was with her. A young nurse, all bust and belt, came up to us as she saw us hovering. "She's had quite a day," she said. "Tests for everything and there was a hassle with Records."

"Hassle?"

"It says 'Knickerbocker' on her Medicare card, but she won't have it. Says her name is Martin."

I had been this way before. Nell's battles with bureaucracy amused me. She knew she would lose in the end — bureaucracy being what it is — but she had to make it known that she had been called upon to bear a cross she was unwilling to carry.

"You are Mr Knickerbocker, aren't you?" the nurse asked.

"Yes."

"And she is your wife?"

"Yes."

"Well then —"

"My wife has a musical ear," I said, speaking quietly and confidingly. "She was 'Nell Martin'. Can't you hear the softness, the flow, in that?"

I waited, and encouraged her with my eyes to listen as I said it again. "When she became my wife, she became —"

"I get it!" the nurse burst out and grinned.

"So, dear girl, tell Records to put 'Martin' in brackets after her name in their books, will you? Then we can all be happy."

"Lovely chap, isn't he?" she said to David and gave my shoulder an affectionate squeeze. It is ludicrous how my success with women grows in inverse proportion to my ability or inclination to take advantage of it.

A young doctor, looking harassed, came out from behind the screen and beckoned to the nurse. She nodded her head towards David and me. "Family," she said. "Ah!" He came towards us, rubbing the knuckles of his hand against his chest in a way very familiar to me.

"Bad for her to get disturbed," he said. "Her blood pressure . . ."

"I know about her blood pressure," I said. "What is disturbing her?"

"Everything, according to the nurses, and frankly, we haven't the staff . . . She's calmer now and will soon sleep."

"You've given her an injection?"

"Yes." He sounded defensive. "She does herself harm, and we have to think of the other patients."

"What are the results of her tests?"

"I don't know. Not back yet. Anyway, that's not my line of country. I'll call Sister."

David and I watched him make off down the passage, leaning forward, shoelaces flying. We exchanged looks. "Poor young bastard," David said.

He just beat me to it.

The nurse began to remove the screens from around the bed and motioned to us to take the seats beside it. Nell's eyes were closed, her hands lying slack beside her. I took one of them. "Nell," I said, "it's me."

Her lips tightened and she turned her head aside. I held on to her hand or she would have withdrawn it.

"Nell," David said from the side to which she had turned.

She let out a great sigh of exasperation. "Is there no bloody peace in this place? Go home. You can come and see me in the morning."

"I trust you will not," David said, as we walked back to the car. "Nothing excuses behaviour like that."

I did not argue with him. Nin or Kate would take me.

NIN

Talk about drama being high, thought Nin, tossing whites into the washing machine and coloureds into a pile on the laundry floor. Her feelings towards David Martin, usually of impatience, had turned into active sympathy. Heaven had been loosing thunderbolts on him very unkindly, Like that fellow in the Bible who was visited by a plague of boils, she thought. Her scripture was hazy.

Her sympathy did not extend, however, to easing pressure on him by making hospital visits to his mother.

"And don't think you can pressure me about Maggie Mackenzie, you old bat," Nin mentally told Nell, being vehement with the soap powder and slamming shut the washing-machine door. She did not wish ill on anyone but could not think of Nell's accident as other than God-sent.

"No!" she cried when Dan suggested taking the boys to the hospital to see their grandmother. "David must take them. Keep away!"

"You make it sound as though she has the plague," he said.

"She ought to carry a card round her neck," she said vengefully and earned his look of baffled disapproval.

"Sometimes, Nin..." he said, shaking his head.

"Just keep her off me, that's all I ask. Now can we leave it?"

They left it. They were good at leaving things which threatened, at turning the blind eye. They protected their relationship against the world and against themselves.

Now with the machine whirring satisfactorily, she tramped through the house to the big sunny room where five male bodies were sprawled, looped or draped over chairs and couches. Dan, with the pages of the daily paper spilling round him, was lying on one of the couches, engaged in his daily battle with the cryptic crossword puzzle. The four boys, all arms, legs, elbows and feet, and looking as ungainly as stick insects, infested the other chairs. All were reading devotedly.

"Oi!" Nin said. "Feet off the furniture!"

Five pairs of heels swung downward and thumped the carpet.

"Things to be done," Nin said. "Ian, the furniture; Peter, the windows, Ben and Tom can share the vacuuming. You all know where everything is, and Dan, I'd like a word."

"And I love you, too," he said, grinning and lazily capturing the pieces of newsprint to make the newspaper respectable again. He got up and stretched. "Come on, you lot. Get a move on."

The twins moved over to Nin slowly and stood in front of her, staring upwards in amazement.

"Vacuuming?" one of them said.

"The thing you shove backwards and forwards over the carpet and it picks up the dust. You know."

They looked at each other. "We're supposed to put our chairs under the table when we've finished eating, and roll the bedclothes back and leave them while we have a shower. Then we have to make the beds..."

"Oh, and to say, 'Is there anything you want us to do?' and not rush off before you can tell us —"

"But *vacuuming*!" Alarm and distaste were writ large on their young faces.

"Don't you have a vacuum cleaner at your house?"

"Yes, but the lady who comes in uses it. Mum never asks us!"

"Well, *I'm* asking you!" Nin snapped, irritation rising like sudden steam. "And after all, your Mum isn't here, is she?"

The twins moved closer together and their shoulders touched. "Yes she is," one of them said truculently, and narrowed his eyes.

Dan smote his forehead and headed for the door. "Come on, you two," he said to his sons. With eyebrows lifted high they began to follow him.

"We'll do it," the other twin said, Nin's expression obviously making him anxious. "We will, won't we, Tom? And we'll try not to bang the furniture. Mum hates the furniture getting banged."

Peter, halfway through the door, gave a strangled guffaw.

"Out!" Nin said. He shot out, and the twins, galvanised into life, followed him.

"I didn't mean *you!*" Nin cried, but it was too late. They were thundering along the corridor in the wake of the others, and she was alone in the room, feeling ruffled, contrite and completely at a loss.

Dan appeared in front of her. "You wanted a word."

"I did, but I've completely forgotten what it was. Oh God, I blew that, didn't I? They made me cross."

"Why change the habit of a lifetime?" he said. "After all, they are only two young kids who lost their mother in appalling circumstances."

She knew she would have to tread carefully. "What did our boys say?"

"Something on the lines of what's-up-with-the-little-blokes-are-they-nuts? I said, 'Give them a break, How would you like it if it had been your mother instead of Sophie?' That sorted that out. They are now giving instructions in the art of using the vacuum cleaner."

"I don't deserve you," she said miserably.

"No, you don't. It's a good job you married a masochist, You wouldn't last five minutes with anybody else."

"No," she agreed, and the tears slipped down.

He stood and looked at her, his annoyance turning to worry. "I think I must ask David to take the boys home," he said.

"No" she burst out, "you mustn't! That's unthinkable!"

"I questioned you about them, if you remember. I found it hard to know what to make of them. So, all things considered . . ."

She did remember. She remembered, too, the questions which had risen in her own mind, but had been brushed aside as too complex to answer.

"David had more than enough on his plate when we took them," she said. "Imagine what it must be like for him now that there is this hoo-ha with Henry and Nell."

"Ah yes. I'd forgotten."

Anybody capable of forgetting Nell deserved recognition with trumpet and drums. She threw her arms round him and dug her head into his chest. *Dan, Dan, my very own man.* The words in her head brought alive the old, rude jingle: "Dan, Dan, the lavatory man," and she choked on the sudden uprush of laughter. "Now what?" asked Dan in bewilderment, holding her off to inspect her face.

"I'm being silly. Sorry."

He planted a hand on each shoulder and anchored her to the spot. "Now listen," he said, bending his head and speaking directly into her face. "There is obviously some sort of problem with the boys. It is not our problem. We tell David about it. David will deal with it. Got it? It is no concern of ours, and we do *not* interfere."

"But . . ."

"No! I can't have you exposed to that sort of thing again. It does no good."

"What sort of thing?"

"You know perfectly well, and you know how much I distrust it. It don't want you running to Maggie Mackenzie again."

"Again? How do you . . . ?"

"Nin," he said lovingly, "you are no good at hiding things. Wednesday nights. Eight O'clock. Yes? If you were only going to Sophie's, as you said you were, why did you look so guilty?"

"I *was* going to Sophie's!"

"And then you both went to see Maggie Mackenzie."

"Yes," she said miserably, "I didn't want us to quarrel. I'm sorry, but I just had to try."

"Going to see her didn't do much good though, did it?"

"How do you know?"

"Sophie told me."

She felt as though she had been struck across the face. "She swore she wouldn't tell!"

"I asked her — point-blank. She would have to have lied."

"Then she should have!" she said savagely. Sophie knew that when she had told Dan she was thinking of consulting a woman who might be able to get in touch with the spirit of the little girl she had killed, disagreement had been fierce. "*Charlatans!*" Dan had said. "They take money from gullible people. I thought you had more intelligence." He had raised his finger to her. "Nin, I absolutely forbid . . ."

Her glare had been outraged and incredulous.

"I earnestly exhort you," he had said, altering his tone, "forget this nonsense, please. It offends me."

Sophie knew all this and still she had told him, Nin thought bitterly. She didn't give me the chance to tell him myself — in my own good time — when it seemed safe.

"I suppose she told you all that went on, gave you chapter and verse!"

"More or less."

"E-eeagh!"

"Don't be hard on her, darling. I practically had her at pistol point. She could see how upset I was. All she wanted was to do the best for you and me."

"All Sophie ever wanted was the best for everybody," Nin said bitterly, "and look where that got her!"

"Enough!" Dan said quickly. "We've had enough drama for one day. You'd better go and see how those boys are getting on."

The thought of Peter and his inability to clean a window without leaving streaks broke through her sick mood. And now there was the sound of too much merriment and an ominous thump.

"They're not supposed to be having fun," she said. "It's *training* — serious stuff. I do it for their wives. Someday two girls are going to rise up and call their mother-in-law blessed."

Dan's face smoothed and he looked at her with love. "What am I going to do with you?"

"Give us a kiss for a start," she said, "and I've remembered what I wanted to say. Next time David comes to dinner, I plan to ask Kate Hamilton, too. OK? People living on their own never eat properly. She's looking under the weather."

"Oh yes," he said grinning, thinking he saw an ulterior motive.

"No!" she said vehemently. "I'm only planning to feed them. I don't presume to know what's best for them."

"Attagirl!" he said, and gave her the kiss she had asked for. They went, arms around each other and smiling, to deal with the husbands of the future.

HENRY

Nell needs an operation. I will have to ask David to explain it to me, for my knowledge of bodily functions is minimal and, as soon as the doctor mentioned the word, all I could think of was the hideous inconvenience it would cause.

As far as I can make out, she needs a heart bypass operation, something I have, of course, heard of and which seems to be thought routine by the medical profession. But her general physical condition is not good. It was stressed that surgeons, as well as relatives, become upset when patients die on the operating table. It was suggested that the greatest care must be taken and Nell nursed into better general health before a decision can be made. Flying back to Adelaide is, at this stage, out of the question.

"Has she been told?" I managed to ask.

"Her state of mind made that inadvisable."

I was asked for the name of her doctor at home, so that her previous health records could be studied. I gathered there was worry about her veins, not only in her legs, but in other parts of the body.

When I went to the ward to see her, I was thankful to find she was asleep. "Don't wake her, *please*," the harassed-looking little nurse said. I was sad to see that whoever had done her hair for her had just parted it and combed it straight down on each side of her face. There is not much of it. And her nail varnish was badly chipped. It is a measure of how ill she must be that such things were permitted. But at least she was wearing her own beautiful nightdress and, when I bent to kiss her head, the scent of the sandalwood soap she always keeps in her lingerie drawer was warm and fresh.

The girls were waiting for me down in the car park. They seem to like to make an occasion of these daily visits. They had a newspaper spread out over the boot of the car and were bent over, studying it devotedly.

"She's wicked," Kate said, looking up with a smile. "She nicked her husband's paper and intended to enrage him by doing the cryptic crossword before he could get his hands on it."

"Only we're not getting very far," Nin said. "I'll have to buy another one, so the depth of my ignorance is not revealed. We've only got six answers, and two of those are dodgy."

Although I have known them less than a week, our relationship is very easy and I think of them, with pleasure, as "my girls". They believe I need looking after. And looked after I am. They do not treat me as though I were old and infirm — which, of course, I know I have become — but as though I had encountered a temporary misfortune and just need a "leg-up". They are nice creatures.

"How is she?" they asked. I told them. They listened with grave faces, and then Kate put her arm around my shoulders. "Well, the good news is that we won't be losing you yet awhile."

They are *very* nice creatures.

Each morning, when my visit to Nell is over, we take lunch together, usually at Nin's, where I renew my acquaintance with the boys who, I must say, seem extremely cheerful. Once we went to Kate's extraordinary house. Nell would love the drama of it. Sitting up there and looking down on the world and up at the sky, one feels a sort of detachment, not the loneliness of isolation, but a sense of freedom. I wonder what Kate thinks during the long hours she spends alone there.

She told me about the death of her husband, how she faced the unimaginable end of her world, and I told her about how Frances and the baby died — something I have never told Nell. People might find it hard to believe, but Nell does not know I was a widower when we met, and that my wife and little boy were burned to death. I was twenty-five at the time, Fran was only twenty-two. It was many years before I met Nell, my strident peacock, and I let her believe I had not been the marrying kind until then. I was willing to give her the rest of my life, but all that went before was mine alone. I was aware of a need to shield my memories from her scrutiny.

When I first met her, I was amused and intrigued. Her glittering world was a far cry from my own unostentatious one of "old" money. Money has to be mentioned, for it figured so largely in what attracted Nell to me. I doubt if she would have had any time for me at all had she not been aware that my forebears had ensured future generations would never have to toil as they had done. I watched her fizz and light up like a Catherine-wheel, her beauty, her charm, her presence lighting the gloom of others' everyday lives. I saw her when the adorers who fed her vanity went home to their wives.

I saw the child she claimed to be the crowning achievement of her life and realised that, as a mother, she was a famous actress. I felt profoundly sorry for both of them. As far as I was concerned, my own life was ended. It had been encompassed in the few years of joy and certainty that I had known, but time stretched ahead. Nell was a puzzle, a challenge and so very good in bed. During the years of our marriage, I have grown to admire her capricious mind, her lively spirit, the single-mindedness of her selfishness, which she has distilled into an art, and to love, in my own way, the fallible, vulnerable side of her that she would die rather than show to the world. Bloody Henry, she says, knowing that I know.

Lunch at Nin's is both a meal and a sermon. She tells me that I have to be intelligent about what I eat; that my very life depends on realising that I must ask, "What will this do for me?" before putting anything into my mouth. My malnutrition enrages her.

"No need for it," she says, "no need at all."

Nell requires bought food to be tasty and look good on the plate.

"Bugger the taste," Nin says, "And bugger bought food because, half the time, food it ain't. All it is is just stomach packing."

She is a vehement girl.

I love her soups. She says she has a spare slow-cooker I can take home with me. "Chuck a whole heap of chopped vegies, two or three lamb shanks and a handful of barley into it, put it on 'low', leave it overnight, and you've got food for several days," she says. "You can put chopped basil in one lot you heat up, or sage, rosemary and thyme … Suit yourself. And don't forget chillies. They're good for the gut."

She makes a lovely sweet I thought was chocolate mousse. "Good God, no!" she said. "I wouldn't give you *chocolate*. It's avocado beaten up in soya milk, with honey and carob." I didn't know what carob was. I have a jar of powder to take home with me. I am assured that I could survive on banana, egg, honey and milk beaten up together. The savoury meats of continental countries are denied me. The delicatessen is a forbidden place. And the cow is a dangerous animal. I am told I must befriend the goat or drink milk made from rice or the soya bean.

145

I can only say that I enjoy everything she gives me to eat and that my digestion is quieter than I have known it for a very long time.

David brings food home when he leaves the office, and we either eat before we go to see Nell or go to see her and eat at a restaurant afterwards. I find that I have no trouble with Chinese, Indian or Thai food, if I have just one course, with neither sweet nor cheese to follow, and that red wine does not give me the heartburn I get after the white wine Nell always insists upon. I am learning many useful things.

I did not ring David at the office to tell him the latest news about Nell. No point in presenting him with fresh dilemmas during working hours. I told him as we were sitting down to a dinner of curried prawns and fried rice, I could see his mind working furiously as he manoeuvred his chopsticks.

"How long do they think it will take to get her fit?" he asked.

"They didn't say. I would imagine at least a fortnight, wouldn't you?"

Two weeks! I could feel him thinking; *then* the operation, *then* the convalescence! It was all turning out worse than he had expected, and I felt sorry for him.

"There are air ambulances," I said. "Perhaps she could be flown home and have the operation there."

"And how would you cope afterwards, all alone in that great mausoleum?"

"I would employ nurses."

"And how long do you think they'd stay? The ones at the hospital can't wait to be rid of her — hadn't you noticed?"

I had. Nell is a fractious and ungracious patient.

"And what about you? Nell isn't the only one to be considered."

I told him that the new routine was suiting me very well. I felt rested. The girls were spoiling me, and I could feel strength coming back day by day. I told him how I enjoyed our quiet evenings together after the visit to the hospital and that I slept very well.

"Then let's keep it that way," he said.

"They are not operating on *me*!" Nell said, as soon as we arrived at her bedside. She was flushed with fever. "Get me out of here, Henry!"

I saw David's face tighten. "Stop that," he said curtly, and then gently but firmly moved me aside. "For once in your life, Nell. *Listen*. It isn't a matter of what you want, it's what you need. Your body has let you down. Without the help of an operation, you could die."

"So?"

Nell has a fine sense of the dramatic. I knew she would be seeing herself as the wounded matador facing the plunging bull. "So what?" she said, chin up and crackling with challenge. "Are you telling me I should be afraid of death?"

I was surprised to see that David was not intimidated. "Don't make a circus of it," he said unsympathetically. "We've had enough of that already."

I had not realised the depth of the bitterness he felt over Sophie's suicide, and my heart went out to him. I know what it is to lose someone dearly loved to an unkind fate, but to have the beloved say so clearly, "I prefer to die than to stay alive with you", is something more.

Nell was oblivious to the forces at work behind his words. "You can tell them to put their knives away," she said. "I'm going home."

"Very well," he said, rising from his chair, "we'll leave you to organise it."

They measured each other eye to eye.

"Henry!" she said.

"Henry is sick and needs looking after. You can't count on him."

"Henry!"

She had always been able to count on me. My function was to be counted on.

I felt the first lift of obedient response, and then an extraordinary thing happened. It was as though the power which drives the machine had suddenly died. I looked at her and, if she had been lying in the path of an oncoming train, I could not have moved to save her. I was spent. All I could do had been done; all I could give had been given.

I had not realised how peaceful helplessness can be. I felt the force of her self-will, formidable as an army with banners, moving down on me, yet was untroubled. There was nothing left for her to take.

"Sorry, Nell," I said.

She stared at me, her face incredulous and malevolent. Then she turned her full attention to David. "I want my clothes!" she demanded.

He was already moving away from her bed and, as he moved, took my shoulder and propelled me with him. "Talk to your doctor about it," he said over his shoulder and kept me walking towards the open door of the ward. I could not bring myself to look back; I knew I should, but doing what I should did not seem to matter anymore. I knew I was walking away when I was needed, but the shame I felt had no strength against the imperative to be free of stress.

"Sit here," David said, finding me a chair in the corridor. "I'll get a nurse to come out and look at you, and I'll get the doctor to sort Nell out."

I had not known he could be so brisk and authoritative. I must have slipped into a half-doze because, though I could hear sounds of commotion from the ward, it felt as though I were dreaming, and I let them drift away.

I found out later that Nell had got out of bed in temper, had fallen and the vein in her leg had begun to bleed again.

When David got me home, I was groggy but beginning to feel the benefit of the injection I had been given. He was wonderfully kind.

I attempted to apologise for the trouble we were causing him, but he cut me short. "Rest while you can. There'll be no more talk of her coming home for a while. The doctor is none too pleased. He said he could do without self-inflicted wounds, but she has to stay where she is now."

"And the operation?"

"God knows. Who's to say where things go from here?"

Who indeed?

Kate rang to ask about Nell and to say not to cook dinner, as she would bring a meal down for us. I excused myself after the soup and went to bed. It was good to lie and listen to the clink of plates and the low murmur of conversation.

The telephone rang several times, but David did not call me, and I did not have the energy to get up and enquire whether the hospital was ringing about Nell. The third time it rang, he did not answer it. When I slept, I dreamed that Nell, in her nightdress and with hospital tubes trailing from her nose and wrists, was furiously punishing the front doorbell.

CAROLINE

Tick poisoning! I am like a sick cat — off my legs, off my food, off life in general, and this country in particular. It is heinous that a day spent happily working in the garden should reduce me to this.

When I realised something was wrong, I summoned the acupuncturist. An acupuncturist does not ask you what is wrong as idiots of doctors do. He tells you.

"Oh dear," he said, taking my pulse, alarmed by my soaring blood pressure, stressed kidneys and labouring liver. I screamed when he touched my neck and shoulders. Yes, I had spent time in the garden. Yes, I had been bitten. No, there had been no engorged ticks — how the hell would I have missed them? Yes, the signs of scratching on the back of my neck came from my fingernails. On it went. He gave me a lecture about how important it is to protect oneself when out in the garden; detailed the long-sleeved, long-legged, high-necked clothing I must wear, as well as the wide-brimmed hat; the repellent I must rub into any skin left visible, the need to spray it on clothes and hat, too. I must also remove all clothing before entering the house, and leave it outside while taking a hot bath containing a large cupful of bicarbonate of soda.

"You are joking, of course," I said.

He wasn't. Had I done all that, he said, I would have been spared this mass infestation of ticks in the larval stage, which had left so much poison in my body. He left me, spiked like a hedgehog, to lie quiet while the needles did their work and he wrote up his notes. After a time he went out of the bedroom and sat on a chair on the landing and had inaudible conversations on his mobile telephone. It irritated me not to be able to hear what he was saying, but I must have relaxed and dozed because, when I felt him taking the needles out, an hour had gone by.

He produced a packet of vitamin C powder and told me I must take half a teaspoonful in fruit juice every two hours. Did I have comfrey in the garden? No. Then here was a packet of linseed meal. I must use it to make a poultice and apply it to the back of my head and neck to eliminate the tick poison locally. Simple, he said, before I could say it was not. Keep it in place with an elastic bandage and put on a beanie.

Did I look the sort of person to have a beanie? I asked.

Whatever, he said.

Before going to bed I must take a hot bath containing two cups of Epsom salts to stimulate the general elimination of the tick poison. The water must cover the kidneys, but not reach the heart.

And I must drink a great deal of water.

I hate water.

Heat it and drink it with your eyes closed, you'll think it's tea.

I hate tea.

Whatever, he said, and asked for a urine sample. He had to help me out of bed and squire me out of the bedroom and along to the loo.

Well? I said, as he stood, preparing to wait outside the door. Did the oaf think I would allow him to stand there and listen to me pee?

Ah, he said, and went back to the bedroom.

I left the sample carton on the washbasin. It was a long way back to my bed.

"You must take this seriously," he said. "I don't like the look of you at all."

He had always liked it before.

He stood staring down at me. "Do you have anybody who could come and stay with you?"

"My cleaning girl will do all the fetching and carrying I need," I said. "Send your bill."

"I have it here."

"Then leave it."

Like any civilised person, I confront my debts once a month.

"Whatever," he said.

When he left, I lay and drifted in and out of sleep. Every now and again, when I woke, I thought incredulously: I am ill! I am accustomed to my body behaving with the smooth precision of a Mercedes engine lovingly and intelligently maintained. I felt anger and outrage that anything so mysterious and microscopic could have the impertinence to interfere with such perfection. I felt terrifyingly vulnerable.

Did I have anyone who could come and stay with me? Of course I had. I had Sophie.

I drifted away again, smiling.

But when I woke, I knew I did not have Sophie. For her own selfish reasons, she had abandoned me and there was no-one else I could call upon. What a fool I had been to make her the centre of my world! What insanity had made me see her as a source of all joy and safety? My love for her was an obsession. But, but, and but yet again, there was nothing Sapphic in it.

The moistness of women repels me, the whiff of femaleness, the indignity of the messy lunar reaction. Oh no! A brief hug or quick kiss on the cheek is the only physical intimacy possible. Men, by comparison, are so clean.

The thing about Sophie was that she loved me. Unconditionally.

Nobody else ever had. By the time I met her, I had put on my glittering carapace as defence against the world, and that was all most people saw. Soph knew about the soft underbelly I tried to deny. She never spoke of it. There was no need. There never was a need of words between us — we knew. "My Caro," she said.

Who would say that again in such accepting love? Sophie was adept at giving out love. And concern. I wonder she had any blood left in her the way she spilt it for people.

"She has problems," she said when I complained about the amount of time she wasted on that creature, Nin Savage. Who hasn't? Why did she feel she was called on to be the universal Mopper-up of Tears and Binder-up of Wounds? And couldn't she see that all those ties of love and gratitude she was so busy spinning would turn into ropes around her? No, she couldn't. Let's face it, our Soph was not as bright as she should have been.

And what a way to spend a day this is!

Did I have anyone who could come and stay with me? That acupuncturist had asked.

No, I haven't. I know everybody; I am a Well-known Figure, but there is sod-all among people who know me whom I could ask to change my sheets and find me a clean nightgown. Think about that, Caroline.

I suppose I should marry. Then there would always be someone under the same roof to call on. I must start to think of marriage as an insurance.

David. Housebroken. With enough money not to be marrying me for mine. Well-trained in the techniques every man should have, but too few do. With children old enough not to intrude. Anyway, I quite like the boys — they have a quirky, adult sense of humour, but . . . No, David was not suitable. For obvious reasons.

My cleaning girl would do all the fetching and carrying

necessary. And she would do it well. She knew better than to give less than good service. In fact, I was sure my illness would delight her — she would see the extra money in it. But I wanted more than bought help. I needed to be cossetted.

My thoughts went round and round all afternoon. In the evening, weak and sweaty, I called David.

"I am ill," I said.

He cleared his throat. "Sorry to hear it."

I might have been telling him my car would not start. "I have been poisoned by ticks."

"Nasty."

"It isn't just 'nasty'! It's bloody awful!" I burst out. "And I am all alone ..."

He made noises he obviously thought conveyed sympathy. They did not.

"Well?" I said.

"Well what?"

"Can't you DO something?"

"Not at the moment," he said. "I have a guest. And Henry is here. He is ill. And Nell is in hospital and could be dying."

And bugger you, Caroline, his tone said. I told him I was sorry to hear it, and I was. He was clearly not going to be of any help.

I remembered my manners sufficiently to ask what was wrong with Nell.

"She needs heart bypass surgery and is resisting having the operation. She is being very tiresome."

I didn't blame her! I did not consider resisting the idea of having the saw put through one's thorax merely tiresome — and told him so.

He had the grace to apologise. "But, you know Nell," he said.

There was a silence.

"Hope you'll soon be better," he said at last. "Sorry I can't help. You've chosen a bad time."

Chosen! Did he think I had *elected* to be the prey of microscopic malevolence?!

"You should have taken care," he said. "Sophie was always in the garden, but she never got bitten."

No, she didn't. She went into the garden looking like something strayed from a Van Gogh painting: booted, trousered, wearing a hat which made her look like a peripatetic mushroom. My time in Europe had made me aware of how civilised a pastime gardening could be, in comparison with the ludicrous performance demanded of the Australian gardener before the perils of outdoors could be faced.

"Nell said she wanted to see you," he said tentatively. "Better not. Don't you think?"

"The only person I am seeing is my doctor. I am in pain, disabled, can barely see across the room. I drop things and, if pregnant, would be in danger of a miscarriage."

"You've been reading the tick pamphlet," he said, obviously amused. "Come on, Caroline. You don't sound all that ill . . ."

I slammed the receiver down. I knew how ill I was. How dare he!

Temper would not let me rest. I rang him again later. There was the sound of music in the background. So! His mother was dying, Henry and I were ill, and he was lying back listening to Mahler — with a guest.

"What would be my position if I decided to live abroad?" I asked, without preamble.

"What?"

"I can't put up with this country any longer. To go outdoors is to take one's life in one's hands."

"For heaven's sake! You've only been bitten by ticks!"

"Which have incapacitated me! And could ruin my health! My acupuncturist is very worried about me."

He gave what could only be described as a snort. Very unattractive. "You'll soon feel better," he said, in a falsely hearty voice. "And as for living abroad, why consult me?"

"You are my solicitor."

"Then make an appointment to see me in business hours. Or, better still, talk to your accountant."

"Are you telling me to piss off?"

He sighed heavily. "I'm just saying, not now, please."

And what was so special about "now"? I didn't ask him, I didn't have to. I just knew that bloody Kate Hamilton was the "guest". He was not a Mahler man, he was just trying to be impressive. I was not prepared to let him off the hook.

"What have you done with the tapestry Soph was working on?" I asked roughly. "I didn't see it among the stuff you dumped..."

"For heaven's sake!" he said again. "Leave it, can't you? I have enough on my plate with Nell, Henry, the boys — it's a matter of first things first."

How dare he not consider me a "first thing"? Before I could slam the receiver down, he said urgently, "Remember, if Nell tries to see you, better not."

"The tapestry," I said, and cut him off.

If I wished to see Nell, see her I would, for better or for worse. What had I to lose? Anyway, one had to admire the old bat, she was no cringer. If she was still alive when I became myself again, *I* would decide whether we met or not.

I slept surprisingly well and felt much better when I woke in the morning.

The vitamin C had proved so effective I took stronger and more frequent doses throughout the day. I would have words with that fool of an acupuncturist. He should have warned me of its alarming propensity for loosening the bowel.

NIN

"Is Grandma going to die?"

Nin, clutching an unwieldy bundle of soiled clothing, was stopped in her headlong rush to the laundry by Tom, planted like a small bush in her path.

The earnestness of his enquiry merited a considered reply.

"Well, she is very ill, and very old. It has to be expected."

"Oh bugger!"

She was too surprised by his vehemence to reprove him for his language. "I didn't realise you were so fond of her," she said.

"It isn't that," Ben said, materialising behind his twin. "It's just that when she's alive, at least we know where she is."

Nin swept them both aside without ceremony. "Talk to your father," she said, and made her escape. Oh God! Here it came again! Dealing with their physical needs presented no problem; she enjoyed having them in the house, which was big and came into its own when thronged with people, but getting involved with their oddness was something she would not do. I am not equipped for that sort of thing, she thought belligerently, though what sort of thing it was she could not put into words.

"Mrs Savage!"

Tom had caught up with her and, with a smile of great sweetness, was presenting her with a sock as though it were a gift. As indeed it was. The single sock could be the cause of much aggravation.

"You don't have to worry about us, you know," he said. "We don't *have* to have clean underpants every day."

"In my house you do," she grated, snatching the sock, all too aware that he was grinning wickedly. Oh God, what a mess! If Nell refused the operation, she would surely die. And when and where would she elect to do it? And how would it affect Henry? David? And me? And *me*, she thought in anger. How dare she!

Her self-regard had always been a source of amusement to Sophie, who had smilingly pandered to it. But it isn't bloody funny. Soph, she admonished the lost presence. It isn't funny at all.

She brooded as she cast garments into the maw of the machine. But you can't deny Nell the right, she acknowledged reluctantly, and you can understand her refusal to struggle to hang on. She was, after all, in her late seventies and might feel that the quality and length of life she might gain was not worth the price. What's the betting that Sophie would have agreed with her, stood by her and sent her off thinking that Sophie was the only one in the world to understand? That was Soph's forte. We all believed nobody understood us like she did. She pandered to us, each and every one.

Nin corrected herself hastily. "Pandered" was not the right word. Or was it? The uncomfortable question lodged in her mind. Oh, Soph! She saw the concerned face, the soft, charitable mouth, felt the arms open wide as heaven . . .

What is wrong with me? She thought, in a blast of astonishment. How can I question her?

But the questions came, on an uprush as acid as bile. When she had discovered how seminal a part Sophie had played in Kate's undertakings, her original reaction had been astonishment; then incredulous amusement. Now it was different. Her main desire was to pin Sophie down and ask her how the hell she could have sloped off and left Kate to face the consequences on her own.

You must have known how serious they could be by the amount of bail demanded, she accused. And did you not wonder what would happen to Kate when your bail was no longer available to her? You didn't know that others would come forward when you turned your back on her, did you?

And what about me? You had encouraged me to be dependent on you, but you didn't give a tuppenny damn about me. And you betrayed me to Dan. That was one hell of a farewell present, Soph!

It was a relief to hear the telephone ring.

"Are you ready for it?" Kate asked.

There was no merit in suffering alone. She rounded up the twins. "Your grandmother is coming out of hospital," she told them.

"Is she better?" one of them asked, his voice squeaking.

"No."

"Then ...?"

"She will probably die." They are always handing it out to me, she thought. Let them cope with that one. She was now used to the way they consulted each other with a look from under the brows. Their eyelids were smooth as slivers of almonds.

"She won't be coming here though, will she?" the livelier one asked winsomely.

"We're enough for you to cope with, aren't we?"

She looked at their young faces, open and disarming and quite unknowable. "You are more than enough to cope with," she said heavily. "Your father will have to deal with her."

"Then that's all right then!" Their smiles were serene; their attention already drawn away by the sight of the surf rising, creaming and pounding towards the beach that stretched wide beyond the great windows. They looked at her inquiringly.

"Yes," she said. "Go."

She stood and watched them running towards the water, arms waving, their shouts of joy trailing behind them like bunting.

Grown-ups and the grown-up world don't register with children, she thought, and why should we expect they should? Children have never been grown-up. They have no yardsticks. We will only become real to them when they look back later in their lives.

Now we are just presences on the edge, faces they see and hear, but with sight vague and sound muffled as though coming from elsewhere. She remembered how cardboard the grown-ups in her own childhood had seemed, engrossed as she was in her own small realities.

Ah well, she had done what she must and that was over. Now she had to face what could not be dismissed so easily.

"The hospital is not pleased," Kate said. "They say they will keep her there until she is stable enough to be sent home. After that . . ."

"Home" was not Adelaide. It was David's house, which already contained one sick man.

"David says he will get nurses in."

"Can't he insist?"

"He says that if she has decided to kill herself, she must get on with it, but he is very concerned about Henry. He asked if you and I could help out there."

"Of course! Anything!"

"We can only take it a day at a time. You are doing enough already, with the boys. I have plenty of free time. Up to now!" she added, sounding almost merry, and then collected herself and became practical. "David says she is nagging him about Maggie Mackenzie. She insists that since she can't go to see her, he must get you to bring her to the hospital."

"She would! She bloody would!"

The last thing I want is to displease Dan again and here that dreadful old woman is pushing me into it. But what choice is there? How do you become tough enough to refuse the dying?

"Nin?" Kate asked anxiously.

"Yeah," she said. "OK, I'll do it. But I don't guarantee anything. Nell can't just snap her fingers and, hey presto!"

And if she can't do it with me, she thought, how much less can she do it with Maggie!

"Nin!" the well remembered voice said. "I have been wondering about you."

"Yes, well . . ." Nin said, her throat suddenly thick with tears.

"What is it? You sound upset."

"No! Yes! Oh, I don't know . . ."

"Time for the deep breath, wouldn't you say?"

The force of Maggie Mackenzie's personality travelled down the wire as straight as an arrow in flight, and Nin felt the flooding relief of a weary traveller sighting home. She saw the rich pink of the unmistakable straw hat, the fly-away flowery scarf tied around it, the patrician nose and steady eyes beneath the severe brim.

"Oh Maggie!" she said, and wept afresh.

She wept into silence. There was no sign that anyone was listening. When, at last, she gained control of her breathing and her sobs quietened, she became anxious. "Maggie?"

"Nin!" The voice leapt at her. There was no consolation in it, only challenge. "What's wrong now?"

The "now" stung. As though I am always calling her, she thought, her ready anger awakened. "Nothing is wrong with me," she said stiffly. "I am calling on behalf of Nell Martin, whom you may or may not remember."

"Oh, I remember Nell!"

The implication that Nell was impossible to forget did not please her either.

"Well, she's dying," she said roughly. "And she wants to see you."

For a moment there was silence. "Why?"

"How should I know? I'm only the messenger."

"And not making a very good job of it. Come on, my dear, you can do better than that. She lives in Adelaide now, doesn't she? Is she expecting me to make the journey there?"

The implication was that Nell was quite capable of making that demand. It was good to know that her measure had been taken.

"She's here — in the local hospital," Nin said, softening. "I could take you there, but I'd rather not."

"Why? Is it me, the hospital, or Nell?"

She had forgotten that Maggie could be as forthright as she was herself.

"Do you have a car?" she said, ignoring the question.

"Yes."

"Then go pretty soon. They might not let you see her . . ."

"They'll let me see her."

Such silken confidence was irritating. "I wouldn't bet on it!" Nin said. "Nell isn't their flavour of the month."

"I'd be surprised if she were. But don't worry, they'll let me see her."

God, this woman could be maddening!

"No need to hiss like that," the amused voice said. "You're not local, so you wouldn't know, but I used to be Matron there."

So that accounted for the imperiousness, the lack of compromise.

"Blow me down!" Nin said.

Maggie Mackenzie had had enough. "Start from the beginning," she said, "and don't waste my time."

HENRY

Life can take some curious turns. When I woke this morning and lay and listened to the muffled sound of the surf and watched the patterned dance of leaves across the ceiling, I felt cushioned in content and with no concern that Nell, lying in her narrow bed, listening to the hospital clatter and staring up at the pallid plaster of the ward ceiling, would be feeling quite different. There was no knowing what the day would bring but, since there was nothing I could do to shape events, why should I worry?

"Leave things to me," David had said, and I had left them. Gratefully and without demur. Thinking about that easy relinquishment, I slipped back into delicious sleep. It was only later, as I took my bath, that I remembered the plants and Nell's testy instructions.

Nell had thrust the long strips of towelling she had cut into my hand.

"Can I trust you to do this properly? Push one end into soil — well down! Well down! Never mind about getting your fingers dirty! Now, trail the strip down into the water. That's it! Now do the next one."

The magazine article had said that this was the way to look after plants which would be left to fend for themselves for a while. But we had already been away longer than anticipated. How thirsty would they be?

Had I run enough water into the bath? And the mail! By now the letterbox would be spilling over and garishly coloured catalogues advertising unwanted goods would be blowing about the drive — clear evidence that no-one was at home. This was the invitation to burglars we had been warned against and which I had intended to use to persuade Nell to return home early. No hope of that now. But something had to be done.

"I have to ring the local police," I told David as we sat together over breakfast, "I need them to keep an eye on the house."

"I'll do it from the office," he said.

The plants, I had decided, must be left to their fate. I had never liked them anyway. They loomed, and made over-dramatic claim to notice. Since it seemed unlikely that Nell would see them again, I could be ruthless.

I realised in surprise that I was finding no difficulty in the thought of life without her. My strongest feeling was hope that she would take her leave of the world without too much suffering on her part and without inflicting too much on others. And what did that say about me? I asked myself, but had no desire to find an answer.

"Are you going to see her this morning?"

"Kate is taking me."

"Then would you give her a message from Nin? The woman she wants to see will be visiting her. Somebody named Maggie Mackenzie."

"Maggie!"

"You know her?" David looked surprised.

"She used to come to the house. She and Nell used to lock themselves away. She is a medium."

He made an impatient grunt. "More to the point she's a nurse, too. She was a matron no less. Nin is hoping she will help us out."

"If only she will!" I felt a real gleam of hope. Our conversations had been few and brief, but I had really liked that woman. It had irked me that Nell had kept her so much to herself. He looked at me curiously, but there was nothing I felt I could say to him.

"I don't want any medium nonsense —" he began.

"You won't get any. She is a no-nonsense woman."

"We'll see. I suppose I'll have to talk to her . . ."

"No, I will."

"Nursing Nell at home is going to cost a great deal of money, Henry."

"You don't have to worry about that. I'm just sorry for causing you so much trouble."

"You are not the one to be sorry."

David is changing. It is sad to watch an easy man becoming hard. I put my arm across his shoulder. "We'll get by."

"No thanks to them."

He did not mention her name. He never did these days, but Sophie was as potent at our side as though she were in the room.

Kate arrived carrying a covered dish and a plastic bag. "Steak and kidney pie," she said, "and vegetables, all washed and prepared. They will cook while the pie is heating up in the oven."

I looked at her with love. Looking at Kate is always a pleasure. Her dark hair is drawn back, but little tendrils escape. She uses soft colours on her eyes and mouth. She has lost her young beauty, but evidence of it remains and tantalises. She wears trousers better than most women can. I like her long legs and neat waist and the turned-up collars of her shirts. The young Henry stirs when I look at Kate.

She seemed troubled. "There is something you don't know and I think you should," she said. "I am afraid you are consorting with a criminal."

"WHAT?" I exclaimed, and laughed. My consort is Nell, who is many things, but hardly criminal.

"I mean being friendly with," she said quickly, "and I mean me".

Now I really laughed, and so she told me all about it. "If you don't want to know me now..." she ended.

I took her soft hand, kissed it and held it between mine. "Some people it is a privilege to know," I said, and saw her eyes fill with tears.

It was a long, delicious moment.

Later she took me to the hospital. As I entered the ward, I saw a doctor and a woman come out from behind the screens around Nell's bed and stand, some distance away, talking earnestly. The woman was Maggie Mackenzie. Once seen, never forgotten. Where does style turn into eccentricity? I wondered, intrigued as before by the raffish elegance.

"Ah Mister — er — er, Mister —" the doctor began as I approached.

"Mr Knickerbocker and I have met," Maggie Mackenzie said, holding out her hand, "How are you, Henry?" And you don't have to tell me, her eyes said.

"We have been discussing..." the doctor began.

"And can surely do it somewhere more comfortable," she broke in.

"Ah, yes, well..." The doctor was clearly flustered.

"The patient's sitting room?" she asked, eyebrows raised. "And I hope you have got rid of those plastic chairs."

They were ranged in a semicircle around an old television set. Pieces of a jigsaw were scattered over a table too low for comfort.

"Yes, I know," the doctor said, "but it's —"

"Money. I know it always is. But surely somebody —"

"Don't start Matron," he said, and grinned. They exchanged the warm glance of old and comfortable protagonists.

"She's a dreadful woman," he said, "she can persuade anybody to do anything."

"You mean my wife has agreed to have the operation?" I asked incredulously.

"Good heavens, no. I just made sure she understood what her refusal means, but she seems determined to do without our help and make it a personal fight."

My heart sank. I know what it is like when Nell conducts her personal fight with ill health.

She is not embarrassed by the bedpan or humiliated by soiled sheets. As our own doctor once said wryly, "Well, old chap, she's going to fight to the last gasp of your breath".

"You will need both day and night nurses," Maggie Mackenzie was saying.

"Would you engage them for me?" I asked. The face of the young nurse finding Nell very hard to handle was sharp in my mind.

"Certainly," she said, and there was a glint in her eye. "They will be hand-picked."

There was a moment's silence as the three of us exchanged looks and then, one by one, broke into slow smiles.

I must watch it. I find that, even more than before, I am sliding into unspoken complicities against Nell — and enjoying it.

"Why don't you sit down?" the doctor asked, lowering me into the grip of one of the frightful chairs. "I believe you spent a night with us recently."

"I was only tired," I said.

"Deal with him, will you?" he said to Maggie Mackenzie, patted me on the shoulder and left us.

She stood looking down at me. She has fine eyes, clear and quizzical. "Which would you like?" she asked. "The iron hand or the velvet glove?"

The impulse to flirt dies hard. "Be gentle with me," I said, and there we were, both laughing and exchanging a pleased look of recognition.

"She's going to die, isn't she?" I said, suddenly sobered.

"Who isn't?" she flashed back, daring me to go soft on her. I could have done, very easily. Tiredness overtakes me without warning and robs me of the will to think and move.

I could feel the warmth of her body as she bent over me. "How long have you had Parkinson's?" she asked. "Five years?"

It was longer.

"I take it your doctor is in Adelaide. I think you should see someone here."

"When we have..." I said, gesturing. She knew what I meant. "We needn't wait that long. It will be some days before they allow your wife home. I'd like to arrange an appointment for you."

I was in no state to argue.

"Come along now," she said, struggling to heave me out of the chair. "I'll drive you home."

I shook my head. "I have someone waiting."

"Is it Nin Savage?" She took me companionably by the arm and steered me towards the lifts. I realised with annoyance that my shoes were making a dragging sound.

"Not today. Nin will be my chauffeuse tomorrow."

"My word, you *are* being looked after."

"I am very lucky. Everything just seems to happen."

"Nothing just happens. Haven't you found that out yet? Nothing just *happens*."

We were out in the car park now and Kate was, as usual, sitting reading the newspaper while waiting for me. As she heard us approach, she looked up and smiled.

"My word!" Maggie Mackenzie said. "Some of the things that just happen are quite something!"

"She's going to make an appointment with a chap she knows, then let me know when it is and I'm going to take you to see him,"

Kate said, when she joined me in the car. After they had settled me in, the two women had walked a little distance away and stood talking earnestly. I watched them, half-dozing. Maggie was doing most of the talking, and Kate was nodding her head, sometimes emphatically.

It was cool in the car. Outside the sun was as yellow as egg-yolk, the sky a hard, enamelled blue. Kate was not wearing a hat. She should have been. I wanted to call out to her, but the words would not come.

"How was Nell?" she asked as she got into the car. I moaned in disbelief. I had left the place without seeing her! "Can we go back?" I asked miserably.

"No, we can't. I have my orders. You are to be kept free of all stress. It's lunch and a lie-down for you, my dear."

The idea was wonderfully enticing. As I began to drift off again, I remembered walking through the garden before Kate had called for me. Sophie's flowers had been looking sick and limp. There was a watering system, I knew, but it must have failed. Under this pitiless sun, the poor things would surely die.

"Tell David I think the timer needs a new battery," I said.

"What?"

"The garden. The flowers. Tell David . . ."

"Now, now. What did I say? No stress. I'll have a look at the garden."

I knew she would. Sophie's flowers would not die today, but did she understand about the timer? "Tell David . . ."

"Henry," she said. "Shut up."

I am surrounded by masterful women. I am used to showing a wry obedience, tongue in cheek, which leaves the essential me untouched. This is different. "Yes," I said, in gratitude. And dozed again. By the time we reached David's house, I was beginning to feel better.

"The pie?" I said. "And I think I know where to find a bottle of red."

"You're on!" Never has a woman looked at me more indulgently.

After lunch she gave the garden a long, careful soaking while I lay on the chair under the trees and watched her. There are many places where one can lie about in Sophie's garden. She loved her hammock. It still hangs there. Kate hesitated when she saw it, then made a movement as though about to take it down, but let her hands fall. "Not up to me," she said.

I could have done without the pervading presence: the trowel left in the flowerbed, the cotton glove, crinkled by rain, lying beside the secateurs propped against a tree? Did Sophie *ever* put anything away? I wondered.

"Hello," Kate said. "Who's this?" We heard the slam of a car door and running feet on the gravel. It was Nin. She was grinning. Something I had not seen before. She flopped down on the grass beside my chair and spread herself. As she flung her arms above her head and settled her limbs, her shirt burst open and disclosed the purity of a perfect navel.

"Boy, oh boy!" she said. "Can I a tale unfold!"

It was obvious that life was going to take one of its curious turns.

CAROLINE

I recovered from the tick poisoning remarkably well, or so my acupuncturist congratulated me.

I should hope so, I told him. At the prices he charged, I could legitimately expect to be raised from the dead. He liked that, he said. Had anybody ever told me I was a Trick? — and went off laughing. "Alternative" practitioners can be so *brash*.

However, there I was, feeling magnificently alive again and nothing, but absolutely nothing, was happening, or seemed likely to happen. So many people spend their days closeted away, tied up in their dreary preoccupation with making their way in the world. Sorry, Caroline, I haven't time, they say when I ring up and suggest doing something exciting and worthwhile.

Sophie was always available. When the boys were babies, we used to put them in their carry-cots in the back of her station wagon, and off we'd go. As long as the car was moving, the babies slept. How we talked on those drives out into the bush! The boys were more trouble as they started to sit up and stagger about, of course, but they were funny and good-tempered and they grew on me. They called me "Liney". Sophie was a light-hearted, light-handed mother. Some women make such a chore of it that it puts you off their child. You look at the little brat and think, "How can the centre of the world be *that*!"

I liked them even better as they grew older. They were such physical little creatures. They ran, they climbed, they swam with fierce enthusiasm. How often do you see a mother climbing a tree with her children? Sophie did. We all ran and swam together. She let them beat her. I never did. I think they liked me for it. And they admired my cartwheels. Wow! they said and flung themselves at the sand in comic imitation, and then laughed until they hiccupped.

We had such good times! David is not an outdoor person. I stood *in loco parentis*. I played cricket with them, hurled balls about, swam farther and dived deeper, outlasted them at every turn. They looked up to me.

Sophie loved it. "But for you I would have to nag him," she said, meaning David, of course. As far as I was concerned, a damn good nag was what he merited. David is not effete, just lazy. I told her so.

"I don't think it's that," Sophie said. "Nell made him feel that if he couldn't be Olympic standard, he should leave games alone."

Ah, yes, Nell! I had temporarily forgotten about her. She wanted to see me, did she? And David thought we should not meet. Well, here was one way of livening up a boring day. She might have David brainwashed, but she did not intimidate me. And anyway, what did it matter now?

The only person the truth could hurt was gone. If Nell was hotfoot in search of it, why not let her find it? It would only be what she thought was truth anyway.

David and I never *betrayed* Sophie. She was always the most important person to both of us. And how do you explain that? To anybody? But particularly to someone like Nell?

The obvious answer is that one does not try. One just hands out the facts and lets people find their own truth. And you can bet there will be as many truths as there are people!

I made sure I was looking particularly well-groomed and

healthy before I set out for the hospital. One-upmanship. She would not be looking well-groomed nor feeling healthy. Even I recognised that, with anyone like Nell Martin, one needed the support of every gun at one's disposal.

Why, at this particular point, Sophie's brother should leap into mind I cannot imagine. Tiger is two years younger than Sophie and three years younger than me. He had gone off to England to study medicine while Soph and I were at Nell's dramatic school. He had been barely registered by me then, and it was not until he came home for the funerals that I actually "saw" him — a taller, better-looking, more laidback version of Sophie.

When Soph had cried, "Remember Caro? Isn't she gorgeous?" there had been the stiffening of the nipple as his warm, slow smile of agreement washed over me. But it was a solemn time, and I do know my manners, so I had to let the electricity between us run to waste.

He didn't come home for Sophie's funeral.

Why not? And why had it taken me so long to realise there were questions to be asked?

Nell, like Heaven, must wait, I thought, and grinned at the unlikely association. The boring day was beginning to show signs of promise. Here was something I could get my teeth into.

David had not telephoned to find out whether I had survived the tick poisoning. He deserved to be punished. Sophie's brother was coming in handy. When I rang his office, the triumphant voice said that Mr Martin was in court and inaccessible.

Always to you dear, but only temporarily to me, I thought gleefully.

I thanked her nicely, said I hoped she was well, and wasn't it a lovely day?

"Is it?" she asked rudely, and put the phone down on me. Oh dear, oh dear, how prickly some people can be!

It's wonderful how cooperative Fate is when you have hit a winning run. As I parked the car in the village, I saw the baggy-trousered backside of Nin Savage disappearing into the little supermarket. I nailed her as she came out.

"Just the person I want to see!" I said.

She is another who doesn't know how to respond to charm. "I can't think why," she said.

"Then I'll tell you," I said agreeably. "Come and have a coffee."

"I don't have time. People at home are waiting for this milk." And the packets of Magnum Almond ice-cream I could see in her horrible plastic bags.

Why didn't she equip herself with a decent hessian hold-all and protect the environment?

But this was not the time to bring that up.

"Just tell me," I said. "You are, at the moment, very *au fait* with the Martin household. What news of Sophie's brother?"

"I didn't know she had one."

You don't hammer a telling point home, you allow time for it to sink in. I waited. "I've just realised Tiger was not at the funeral." I said.

"Tiger?"

"That's what they call him. I don't know his real name." I could afford to let her have that one.

I pressed on. "Do you know if David contacted him? It was all such a trauma, he may have forgotten. But I think he ought to have been told, don't you?"

"It's nothing to do with me."

"Sophie might feel badly about it," I said, hitting below the belt.

"Then Sophie shouldn't have done what she did," she answered roughly and attempted to brush past me. I put my hand on her arm.

"But she did. And we're all suffering." For a second our eyes locked. The flash of recognition was short, but we both registered it.

"Please," I said, "you can do what I can't. I was Sophie's friend, not David's. He will listen to you, but not to me. Please ask him."

She obviously had no suspicions about David and me, for she showed no disbelief.

"Why are you pushing this?" she asked, and, for once, there was no hostility in her voice.

"I don't know," I said, as honestly as I was capable of being with her. "But don't you ever get an *instinct*? A feeling that something is the right thing to do?"

She is an unnecessarily plain woman. The bright day shone into her eyes. The whites were clean, blue-tinged as scalded milk; her lashes were aggravatingly thick, tangled and upward curling. I could see just where colour was needed for dramatic effect. If I can tell what is needed to make her look striking and unusual, why in hell can't she?

"You're weird," she was saying. "Do you know that?" But though she didn't smile, she didn't scowl.

"Not as weird as some," I said. "I'm on my way to the hospital to see Nell Martin ..."

Then she did smile. It was only a small one but it escaped before she could contain it.

"Wish me luck?" I asked wickedly, cocking an eyebrow at her. Now the smile was open and full of an amusement she was willing to share.

As I walked back to my car, I knew she was watching me go. I would have taken bets she was shaking her head in disbelief.

Oh Caroline, I thought, you are indeed a Trick! Sophie had always laughed when I went into my Irresistible Routine. Now I had to learn to laugh alone.

And don't think you can't! I told myself. Don't be stupid enough to think you can't.

"We have no patient of that name in the hospital," the nurse at the desk told me.

"Of course you have."

"Don't you think we might *know*?" she asked archly, trying to bring humour into the situation.

"Do I have to answer that?" I asked aggressively.

"Well! Is this patient medical or surgical?" The winsomeness was fading.

"I've no idea."

"Then I'm afraid I can't help you."

"Oh yes you can. You can take me to the wards. I will point her out to you."

"Are you family?"

"No."

"Then," she said triumphantly, "I couldn't possibly do that."

"So what do you suggest?"

Her scanty eyebrows disappeared into her fringe, she made a parson's nose of her mouth, lifted her thin shoulders and spread her used-looking hands. It was an eyeball to eyeball encounter.

The telephone rang. I waited till she was answering it, then gave her a big smile. "Then I must see Matron, mustn't I?" I said, gave her a little wave and was off down the corridor, leaving her trapped and fuming.

I had never been in the place before. It was like a sanitised rabbit warren — with sound effects. There was a subdued hum of activity, overlaid by the rattle of crockery, clanging of unoiled wheels and the pounding of inconsiderate feet.

I attempted to stop a nurse hurtling down the corridor. "Matron —?" I said, but she just waved the bottle she was carrying at me and rushed on. If this was a hospital, Central Station was a hospice! And whoever had been told that green was a restful colour soothing to the sick, had serious eye problems. The walls were bilious. I was reminded of the mushy pea soup inflicted on us at school.

A large arrow and the lettering "WOMEN'S WARD, MEDICAL" had me on track.

"Yes?" a nurse said, confronting me and barring my passage.

"I am looking for a patient, Nell Martin."

"Are you a relative?"

"No."

"Then . . . ."

"I've been through all that," I said. "The woman is here and wants to see me. That should be enough."

"But there is no-one named Martin on this ward."

"Then where is she? She must be somewhere. Somebody must know her, she was a famous actress . . ."

"Ah!" she said, her face lighting up. "We do have an old theatrical. But her name is Knickerbocker."

It was a moment of pure joy. I had had it in for Nell for years. I had longed and failed to cut her down to size. Now this busty, starched little person had done it for me.

"Take me to her," I said.

"Only for a few minutes. Doctor will be doing his rounds."

Nell was lying high in the bed, her eyes closed. I barely recognised her. Her features seemed to have both sharpened and sunk, and the skin beneath her eyes was a livid colour. Worst of all, her hair — thin, wispy and piebald — straggled limply on either side of her face.

"A visitor for you, Mrs Knickerbocker," the nurse said, tinkling brightly.

Nell opened a malevolent eye, looked at me and closed it again.

"I believe you wanted to see me," I said, quietly and formally.

"The only thing I want is to get out of this place." Her voice was as nasally imperious as ever.

To my surprise, I was swept with an instant pity. My own recent battle with betrayal by the body was still vividly in mind, and I recognised the angry outrage she was clearly feeling. "I can imagine!" I said warmly, and shooed the nurse away.

There was some unlovely impedimenta on her bedside table: plastic jugs, a plastic beaker, a spilling box of very ordinary-looking paper tissues and two sad mangoes on a plate. I opened the drawer.

"What are you doing?"

"Looking for a hairbrush and a mirror, for God's sake. And where is your make-up bag?"

She snorted. "Where indeed! Henry and David brought me in. Men!"

There was at least a hairbrush. "Come on," I said. "We can't have you looking like this." She was too astonished or too sick to wave me away. I had that hair smoothed and drawn up and away from her face before she could argue. I always carry mousse and hair spray. I carry a great deal else too. I leave nothing to chance. "I bet if I asked you for a hammer and chisel, you would dig one out," Sophie once said. A small handbag may be smarter, but my bags, handmade for me of soft leather, are things of both beauty and usefulness.

I put away the mousse and spray and took out my lipstick. "Stretch your lips," I said, and leaned over her with it poised. She would not meet my eyes, but did as she was told. Her lips were so bloodless I had trouble finding their contour. In spite of her effort, they remained slack. But at least I made her look halfway human.

"Keep this," I said, putting the lipstick on her bedside table.

Since it had touched her lips, there was no way I could allow it to touch mine.

Now she did look at me, and I saw that the old knowing, cynical Nell was still alive. And I was strangely glad of it.

"What do I smell like?" she said. Somewhere behind the scent of talcum was the whiff of pee. The staleness of her breath made me lean backwards each time she spoke.

"You need a mouthwash and a shower," I said.

She nodded as though satisfied. "Ring the bloody bell," she said. When she lifted her hand to indicate where it was, I saw the state of her nails. "Good God!" I said.

Chipping one's polish is a daily hazard. Only women of questionable class or virtue would allow themselves to be seen with nails in such squalid condition. I always carry protection against emergency.

I whipped out the suede envelope containing my polish remover pads, cotton wool and an assortment of coloured polishes. "Why did you use such a dark colour?" I asked. Her nails were well-shaped, but the skin of her hands was liver-spotted. I really enjoyed taking off the vulgar-coloured polish.

"Now this is the colour you need," I said and was busy applying the polish when the screens were moved aside. A young man in a white coat appeared with acolytes and the nurse.

I held up my free hand. "Hold it!" I said. I made the last careful, sweeping strokes on her little finger and laid her hand down carefully beside the other I had placed on her chest.

"There," I said. "Just remember, polish takes time to dry." I made them wait as I gathered up my things and then smiled round at the circle of young faces. "All yours," I said.

I left Nell to it and went in search of a cooling drink. This is a woeful place. The bowling lady, who had obviously just taken time off from a chukka, or whatever they call it, to man the hospital shop, could not offer me a Perrier, but only some Johnny-come-lately-jump-on-the-bandwagon local mineral water in a plastic bottle. I refused it, of course. The only drink they had in a glass bottle was milk. I took the bottle to the car and laced it with brandy. One needs to carry a restorative in case of emergency, but I did not need restoring now, only refreshing. There was nothing refreshing about the way my teeth became furred and my tongue gluey. Now I had to find a washroom where I could cleanse my palate. I always carry a small bottle of Listerine with my toothbrush and toothpaste.

I took as much time as I saw fit — after all I do have myself to consider — and then went back to the ward. The screens had been taken away from around Nell's bed, and she was in full view of the other three patients in her little bay. She was now looking almost fit to be seen.

"You again," she said, but not unpleasantly.

"Just checking. What did he say?"

"Why wasn't I showered this morning? And that, providing David can supply suitable care, the ambulance will take me home at the weekend."

"What is suitable care?"

She flapped her hand. She was obviously very tired. Her eyes slid closed.

"Probably dying," David had said. She looked it. I have never seen a dead person, not my parents and certainly not Sophie. Did she look like this? Would I look like this?

"Wanted to see you," she was muttering. I drew the uncomfortable visitor's chair closer to the bed. "Well, I'm here."

"Wanted to ask you..." She frowned and began to scratch at the sheet, making little puffing noises of distress. This was not my sort of thing. I began to get up and go in search of the nurse, but her eyes flew open and she seized me quite violently by the arm. "Do you think I killed her?" she rasped.

"What?"

"I told her about you and David —"

She stared up at me, and there was so much guilt and confusion in the face I loved to hate that, before I could stop myself, I had taken her trembling hands in mine and was patting them, saying "Ssh! Ssh!" like a mother comforting a child.

She wrenched away and turned her face into the pillow, muttering and sobbing. It was dreadful to see the breakdown of such a dominant personality, and I knew how much she must hate me for seeing it.

I surprise myself sometimes. "Nell," I said, capturing her hands again, "of course you didn't kill her. No need to worry about that! You didn't tell her anything she didn't know. She'd known for years."

I thought she had stopped breathing she had become so still. "It was nothing to do with you," I said, beginning to pat her hands again. "So come on, my dear, cheer up. We want to see you getting better."

I had never spoken to her so nicely in my life, nor felt the concern which had sparked the inspired lies. "Nell," I said and bent down close, attempting to turn her towards me.

Her face was screwed up and her eyes tightly closed. She gave me one almighty shove. "Clear off!" she said, between clenched teeth. "Clear off!"

I let her fall back on the bed. I was stunned and outraged. I had meant so well.

I snatched up my bag, pushed the chair out of the way, glared at the interested patients in the other beds and stormed out. I felt punch-drunk as I raced along the corridor, my heels clip-clapping. This was what came of trying to be kind to people! And I had given her my lipstick. One of my favourites. I grew angrier by the minute. The worst of it was I had nobody to complain to, nobody I could *tell*.

Oh yes there was! David couldn't be hidden away in court all day.

It was hot in the car. I wound the window down. I needed fresh air, not the pseudo-substitute of airconditioning. I wondered about running the roof back, but there wasn't time. I had to get home to the telephone as quickly as possible. I blasted out of the hospital car park with satisfying speed.

Out on the road, the geriatrics were abroad. I could see the flat cap of the driver in front of me. I put my finger on the horn. It did no good. I pressed it again. The fool put on his brake and, before I could swerve to avoid him, I was ploughing into his boot, the bonnet of my car and the boot of his crumpling and rising in front of me.

I felt the impact in every bone in my body and, as I slammed forward into the rising airbag, I was jarred by a great thump from behind. My lovely car! I thought. My face!

The mind works in such curious ways. I was there and I was not there. I heard the noise, then the silence, then the sudden babble of hysterical voices.

The car door was being wrenched open. Hands were on me.

"Don't touch her!"

I watched it all. I was calm and clear-headed. I opened my eyes, and there was a face hanging above me.

"Tiger!" I cried.

Then I knew I was in trouble. I had lost the plot. I was out there, beyond reality. The face came closer, became the whole world.

It couldn't be Tiger. It must be Sophie. And Sophie was dead.

Somebody was screaming.

DAVID

"Why didn't you let me know you were coming?" Sophie's brother was lounging in her chair, looking so much like her it wrenched the heart.

"No time," he said. "When you're offered a break in our game, you snatch it and run."

I did not feel particularly warm towards him. He was only a doctor, for heaven's sake.

He had not snatched time to come to the funeral. "Why come now?"

"An odd compulsion."

"To run Caroline down, you mean?" I could not resist it.

He laughed. "Wasn't it the damnedest thing? When I saw who it was, I nearly freaked out. She certainly did. One look at me and she went off like a steam-train whistle. Fortunately, she's not too badly hurt. Just shock, bruises and a touch of whiplash."

"You don't realise what that 'touch' is going to mean," I said, with foreboding and in accusation.

"Don't blame me," he said. "I was the fifth car in the pile-up. They say she stopped dead. Some brakes that car has — or had. I gather it's a write-off."

"Just hope you're not around when she finds that out."

"But I will be," he said. "I've got three months."

"Look," I said, taking the bull by the horns, "I've got Henry

183

here, and he is a sick man, as you must have realised. Nell is on the point of coming out of hospital, two nurses arrive tomorrow..."

He was like Sophie, all ease and agreeableness. "Don't worry about me. I can go to a motel."

I was seized with irritation. The fellow had come halfway round the world, this house had been his home for longer than it had been mine, I was cluttering it up with my relatives, and here he was showing no sign of resentment.

"For God's sake," I snapped, "What do you take me for? I didn't mean that. I was about to warn you that it's going to be a bumpy ride."

"One is no stranger to the bumpy ride," he said, sounding excessively British, and grinned.

I don't know how I am going to cope with him. He peels the scabs from my wounds. The face that was beginning to fade is before my eyes again, and I need no reminder of how fatally easy it is to take mean advantage of cheerful selflessness.

The telephone rang. It was Kate. Hearing her voice was the one good thing that had happened all day. "You weren't home when I dropped Henry off," she said, "so I couldn't ask you. We've heard about Caroline Evans, and Nin and I wondered if we should offer to give her a hand. Or would she bite it off?"

"She's not badly hurt. It's mostly shock."

"That can be nasty. Has she anybody at home who could..."

"Why ask me? I don't know?"

"Well then," she said, and hesitated. "Actually, I wanted to tell you some news. Would you like to hear it?"

"Only if it's good."

"Well, it is, and it isn't."

My heart sank. "Can it keep?"

"Of course," she said, rather too pleasantly, and I knew I had said the wrong thing.

"No! Tell me," I said, before she could ring off. "You can tell me."

"Well," she said, "It's just that the charges have been dropped. I've just heard."

As far as I was concerned, that was very good news indeed. "You must be relieved," I said, warmly.

"I am, I'm ashamed to say. But I feel as though I've failed. I ought to have gone through with it."

"Kate!" I said in exasperation. "Do stop thinking you are obliged to put the world to rights. It's a waste of time."

"Oh," she said, and I waited for her to go on. "Oh. Yes. Well. Thank you. I will remember that." And she rang off.

"Anything wrong?" Tiger asked.

"No . . ."

But I was not sure. Women are such strange creatures, even the nicest of them.

Tiger was a great help. We lugged Henry's bed into my room and replaced it with an armchair for the night nurse. Henry had said he would stay with Nell in their room, but I wasn't having that. He needs all the sleep he can get. And what is he paying the nurse for, anyway? We took one of the boy's mattresses and put it on Nell's bed in place of the one she had soiled so badly. I must remember to buy a new one before they come home.

We turned the boys' room into a sitting room for the nurses. Tiger said he would be quite happy in the little room in the roof. He had liked to sleep up there when he was little. It was full of junk, some of which he greeted with pleased recognition. "What's happened to me hammock?" he said, rooting around. "And look at the view from this skylight." We soon got him fixed up.

"Don't use the top bathroom," I said. "We'll leave that for the nurses." I did not say that was where Sophie had been found.

"A woman, Maggie Mackenzie, has produced the nurses for us," I told him. "I gather she trained them. They're retired now, but she says they're good."

He whooped with surprise. "Matron! Oh fabulous joy! Will she be around?"

"You know her?"

"You bet I do! She talked Hairy into letting me take medicine."

I was past being surprised by anything.

Having him around is playing hell with my nerves. Sophie had a soft, tuneful whistle, but a limited repertoire. She whistled the same things over and over. It could be irritating. "Don't you know anything else?" I once asked her shortly. "No," she had said.

Now I could hear the plaintive keen of "She walks through the fair," coming from the kitchen.

He was boiling a saucepan of milk on the stove. He turned and ran his fingers through his hair in a gesture I knew too well.

"Hot drink before bed?" he asked. Sophie's nightly question.

I don't know what he saw in my face. "She used to whistle that," I said.

"I know. I taught her. We used to drive Hairy mad." He was altogether too cheerful and laidback.

"You didn't come to the funeral," I said suddenly, tightly. "You asked no questions."

He lifted the saucepan from the heat. "I didn't fancy the answers."

"What do you mean?"

He poured the milk into the beaker. "I'd been that way before."

What the hell did he mean? He looked at me indulgently over the brim of the beaker. "Ma," he said, as though explaining something to a dim child.

I felt my jaw drop. I remembered his mother well. A happy woman, uncritical, amused, at home in a world which pleased her — someone totally unlike my own mother.

"She was subtle about it," he said. "She had a heart condition and took liberty with her pills and her motor car. The doctor knew, but he was a good chap ..."

"But why?"

"She had lost Hairy."

"Well, Sophie hadn't lost me!" It flared out, the bitterness, hurt and resentment.

"Then one must ask oneself what she did lose," he said levelly.

It was the sort of conversation I could not endure. I turned away from him. "I'm going to bed."

"Just a minute."

He did not pursue the matter as I feared he might. "About Henry," he said.

"What about him?"

"You must know he has Parkinson's. What is being done about it?"

"Kate tells me that Maggie Mackenzie has made arrangements for him to see a specialist."

His face cleared. "Wouldn't you know! And do me a favour. Don't call her that. She's 'Matron'."

I didn't care what she was called. "Bed," I said again. "It's going to be hell on wheels tomorrow."

"Tell me what you want me to do."

I didn't want him to do anything, I just wanted clear space when Nell arrived so that I could establish my own terms.

"I suppose I ought to go to see Caroline," he said, showing apprehension. "What's she like these days? It's a dicey situation — any advice will be gratefully received."

I stopped myself saying that everything to do with Caroline was dicey. "Just tell her she's beautiful," I said. The cynicism came easy.

"Well, she is, isn't she? Sophie certainly thought so."

"Goodnight," I said firmly.

He followed me upstairs. "I'll just have a squint at Henry," he said. "I didn't like his colour."

I felt sudden gratitude that he was here. He was, after all, a doctor.

"Did you ever meet my mother?" I asked.

"Only at your wedding. Wonderful voice — more royal than royalty. She frightened me to death."

"Well, don't let her frighten you now," I said.

I went with him into Henry's room. The reading light was on, but he was asleep and his book had slipped to the floor. Tiger picked it up and showed it to me. "Lady Chatterley's Lover — according to Spike Milligan." We grinned at each other and stood looking down at him with indulgent affection.

"He could have an operation on his brain," Tiger said. "That's probably what Matron has in mind."

"For God's sake!" I burst out. "He's old!"

He snapped out the light and manoeuvred me towards the door. "Just a thought," he said. "He might prefer to take the chance rather than wait for the last stages."

I had had enough. "Don't you ever get tired of thinking about sickness and death?"

"Can't afford to," he said equably. "Where would I be if I did?"

When he climbed the ladder up to the little room in the roof, he was whistling softly again. I did a thing I very seldom do. I took two sleeping tablets.

KATE

My house and Nin's are so different: up here, it is all silence and sky; down there, all voices and water. Our days are different, too. Hers are overflowing; I have difficulty in filling mine. Yet it was not entirely the emptiness of the day which gave me the idea of going to see Caroline Evans. I felt under an odd sort of compulsion.

Nin thought I was mad.

"Come on!" I said, to amuse her. "I do owe her a house call! And you did say she was pleasant when you met her in the village."

"The smile on the face of the tiger."

She had toughened up again. When she had told me of their encounter, she seemed to have softened towards Caroline. "Another sufferer," she had said. "I hope Soph knows how many people she is putting through it."

"Henry says she reminds him of Nell. 'Sad girls,' he said."

Nin gave a great whoop of derision. "I can think of a lot of words that apply to those two, but 'sad' isn't one of them."

I have not met Nell and I have never before met anyone who behaves in the least like Caroline. It will be interesting to find my own words for them.

"You're not going to see her, are you?" Nin said, then quickly answered her own question: "No, of course you're not!"

Caroline's house is far too big for one person. It must cost a fortune to keep the lawns mown and the drives swept. I fight a losing battle with falling leaves; her place is intimidatingly tidy. But then, she can easily afford to have people keep it so.

As I brought the car to rest by the gleaming white paint and shining brass of the front entrance, the door flew open and a young, good-looking and highly agitated girl rushed out to greet me. "Thank heaven you're here!" she said, bending down to the window. "She's *waiting* for you!"

"I'm sorry?" I said, bewildered.

She looked at me sharply. "You're not the acupuncturist?"

"No. I'm just a ... I came to see if Miss Evans needs any help."

"You bet she does! Bloody hospitals! If you're breathing they say you're making good progress. You should see the state of her face!"

"Perhaps she won't want ..."

"Well I do!" she said, opening the car door. "Please. I'm worried. You know what she's like — well she isn't being like it."

Her young face was lively and full of concern; she obviously wasn't going to let me get away.

"I want to go down to the village," she said urgently. "Get her some yoghurt that will slip down easily. And jellies. I could get her some jellies. Please. Oh pretty please! Do stay until the acupuncturist comes!"

She didn't wait for me to agree or refuse, but pressed my arm in warm thanks, flashed me a brilliant smile and was off round the corner of the house at top speed. She reappeared astride a bicycle and, to my alarm, jetted off down the drive, scattering the gravel.

"The hill!" I called after her.

Traffic comes down it at full pelt with scant regard for emerging drivers and, sure enough there was a screech of brakes as she turned out into the open road. Once someone you know has been involved in an accident, you become nervously alert to the perils we face. I listened, but there was no sound of drama unfolding. There was nothing for it. Caroline Evans here I come.

The girl had left the door wide open. I was immediately charmed by the uncluttered space into which I stepped, though the whiteness of the walls was too stark. A touch of carmine in the paint would have given subtlety.

I see houses as paintings made from the owner's personal palette. I often find that if I didn't care for the house, I have nothing in common with the owner. I liked this house very much. Which was a worry.

"Who's that?" Caroline's voice sounded husky and muffled. I found her in a big sitting room, which opened off the entrance hall. She was sitting bolt upright in a deep chair, propped about with cushions. Her arms stretched out along the chair arms, her feet, in their jewelled sandals, set neatly on the footrest. She was wearing a neck brace.

"I heard" I said. "I'm sorry. How are you feeling?"

"The way I look. Weird."

I would not have recognised her. Her top lip was swollen, split and crusted with blood; her eyes were slits in puffed and discoloured flesh. Her whole face seemed to have slopped sideways. "I'm so sorry," I said. And I was.

"They tell me my nose is not broken, but it feels like it. They tell me I am lucky. It doesn't feel like it."

"You were damned unlucky!" I said warmly. From what I had heard, the accident had not been her fault. A car had stopped in front of her. The elderly man driving it was shaken, but unhurt, the drivers of the cars behind had got away with it, although their cars had not. She had been the unlucky one.

"Thanks," she said drily. "Now where is that wretched acupuncturist?"

"Do you want me to ring and find out?"

"We've done that already. Twice. Petronella has everything under control. You must have met her. Don't laugh. She can't help her name."

I felt very far from laughing.

"I never expected to see you," she said. "What made you come?"

I could hardly tell her that the day had stretched ahead empty, leaving me with too much time to brood. "I thought it was what Sophie would have liked me to do," I found myself saying. It might not be the truth, but it was not wholly a lie.

She was silent. "You get to think the damnedest things," she said at last. "I have even wondered if she wanted me to have this accident."

"That's ridiculous!"

"Not really," she said sadly, "not really."

I was out of my depth and mightily glad to hear the doorbell ring.

"Let him in will you?" she said. "He'll only take an hour. Do you feel like putting your feet up for a while? There are drinks on the tray."

"No, really, I only came to see if you needed help."

"Well, I do," she said. "I can't bend and I can't turn my head because of this wretched collar, so how can I water my pot plants?"

The acupuncturist, a very ordinary-looking young man, took her away to her bedroom for treatment. He offered to carry her, but was refused, and when he tried to support her, she fended him off.

She made it clear that only his needles would be allowed to touch her person. I wondered how she would have behaved if he had been handsome.

I was about to make a start with the watering when he

suddenly reappeared. "She says, do you know that herbariums need very little water?"

"Ask her what makes her think I don't" I said. He beamed at me with approval and I was left to myself to find watering-cans and the nearest source of water. Being left alone in someone else's house is like being given temporary use of the keys of the kingdom. I knew immediately what it was like to live here. I knew what had moved her to place the Bristol blue glasses beneath the aggressively modern painting. How rarely painters can catch that particular shade of blue! I knew why the floors were bare and why so few rugs — and such colourful ones — were on them. I saw with her eyes as she chose the spot for each one. The chairs and couches were exactly what I would have bought, if I could have afforded them. In each of the rooms I prowled through, the windows were low and wide. She kept out the sun but let in the sky and the glint of sea. She had chosen beautiful pots for her plants, but not always the right plant for the pot.

Petronella, arriving back triumphantly with yoghurt, jellies and a plain sponge cake, found me hoisting plants around. "Oooh!" she said, "What are you up to?"

"Taking liberties."

"Rather you than me," she said, and laughed. She was very pleased with herself. "I'm going to make her a trifle. There's plenty of sweet sherry and I got this, but don't tell her." *This* was a carton of ready-made custard.

"Do you do all her cooking?" I asked.

"Good heavens, no! I do the cleaning. She does her own cooking."

I had never thought of Caroline in a kitchen.

"She makes her own bread." That was a definite shock.

"She's got one of those new contraptions." Now that figured.

"Don't smirk. It makes very good bread."

193

"I'm sure it does," I said, keeping my face straight.

"How long has that acupuncturist chap been here?"

I looked at my watch. An hour had fled by. No wonder I was tired.

He appeared as suddenly and silently as if he had been conjured up.

"Oh, here he is!" she said, greeting him as though he were the leading player in our little drama. "Cup of tea, Mr Howard?" She turned to me. "I'm sure you'd like one before tackling the garden room." I hadn't known there was a garden room to tackle.

"You look pooped," he said. "Sure you wouldn't like a treatment, too? I've got time." I declined rather more hastily than was polite.

The garden room stood a little apart from the house, at the back. It looked to be part conservatory, part sunroom. When I opened the door, I reeled back from the blast of sweltering heat. Rushing forward to open some windows, I stumbled against Sophie's little button-back chair. I couldn't believe it.

This was the last place it should be! The velvet would fade, the rosewood crack. That wretched woman!

I was hauling it out into the open when, suddenly, there she was. "Oh dear," she said. "Oh dear..."

"Yes," I said tightly. "You had to have it, but you can't take the trouble to look after it."

She was unsteady on her feet and holding on to the doorjamb for support. She said something I could not catch and began to slide slowly down to the floor.

"Petronella!"

It took time and effort to get her back to her chair, prop her up with cushions and set her feet in place. I stood in front of her, hands on hips. I was angry. I expected her to react angrily, too, but she did not. There were tears in her slits of eyes as she lifted her hand towards me.

"Don't go, Kate," she said.

Petronella and I took our lunch — a rather leathery omelette — out into the garden. "Told you I am the cleaner!" she said gaily. She also told me she is a student taking a year off from her dress-designing course to make some money.

Caroline insisted on being left alone to deal with her yoghurt. "I am bound to slurp," she said.

Petronella was still in a state about the accident. "Her *face*," she said, "anything but her *face*!"

"You like her, don't you?" I asked, a touch too curiously.

"You just have to know her," she said. "She can behave like a spoilt kid, and you long to shake her, but she's up-front. What you see is what you get. Yes, I do like her. Don't you?"

"I barely know her."

"Then it's very nice of you to help. Anyway, she obviously likes you." I had the uncomfortable feeling that if Petronella knew me better, she might not like me at all.

After lunch I sat with Caroline while the girl worked joyfully around the house, spreading the sweet scent of wax polish, burnishing mirrors and gilt picture frames into brilliance.

The chair was on Caroline's mind. "I tried it all over the house," she said fretfully. "In every room. No matter where I put it, it just wouldn't look right. It was as though I couldn't bear to let her go, and she was insisting she didn't want to stay."

"Now, now," I said, very aware of the acupuncturist's admonition to see she was kept calm. "You mustn't get worked up."

She gave a weak laugh. "I was born that way."

195

"And don't talk."

"I know. I say too much."

"I had noticed." It was out before I could think, and now she was laughing, a small, difficult and painful contraction.

"I'm sorry," I said, "I didn't mean..."

"Oh yes you did."

Now I was laughing, too. "You bet I did!" To my surprise, a strange sort of ease was beginning to flow between us. I found myself thinking, "She must have *something*. Otherwise Soph wouldn't have been so fond of her."

"When I first met you with that Savage woman, I thought you had such good manners. I admired your looks," she said.

"And when we met again?"

"I still admired your looks." There was pleasure in the light cut and thrust.

"Neither of us behaved well that time," I said.

"We could be forgiven. The shock Sophie gave us would have unhinged anybody."

I knew I was being drawn on to dangerous ground, but could offer no resistance. I was shocked by that poor battered face and the evidence that there was inward damage to match. "She was very fond of you," I said. "She often told me so."

"She never mentioned you."

"She wouldn't. There was too much to hide."

"I don't know what you mean."

I told her. Once the tongue becomes loosened, there is no holding it. As I heard myself talk, I was back in the heady days when outrage gave birth to plans for retribution, and Sophie and I lent each other fire. "She understood so well," I said. "She made me feel how right I was, how admirable."

"And then she just pissed off and left you to it," Caroline broke in.

It was a thought I had tried very hard not to have.

We sat there in our separate pools of dejection. At last she spoke. "Now I'll tell *you* something. See what you make of this. I actually tried to be kind to Nell Martin. Can you believe it? I went to see her in hospital, and she was in a dreadful state. Smelly, unkempt. Well, I soon fixed that up. Then it all came out. The old bat was torturing herself because she thought it was *her* fault Sophie killed herself. She had told her that David and I were having an affair. It's hard to believe, but she was pitiable. I don't know what came over me. I told her she had nothing to worry about. Nothing at all. She hadn't told Sophie anything Sophie didn't already know. Had known for years."

"You didn't have to lie as much as that!" I said, shocked.

"Lie?"

It was one of those moments when you know that the next one is going to be catastrophic.

"You can't mean that you and David really were lovers," I managed to say at last.

"No!" Her denial leapt out like flame. "Of course we weren't *lovers*. We just liked to fuck."

HENRY

Maggie Mackenzie — "Matron" as I must now call her — is constantly in and out of the house, making sure the nurses she has engaged for us know what is what. They are large, capable-looking girls wearing wedding rings and uniforms too small for them.

"I can call you 'Maggie' when we're alone, can't I?" I said. "And would you ask those girls to let their belts out a notch?"

"I'm going to have to talk to you," she said darkly, but her eyes smiled. She had a great deal to say. Did I know that it has been discovered it is possible to have an operation to remove the symptoms of Parkinson's?

It was brief, expensive, carried some risk, but had mostly been found to be successful.

"What about the three-score-and-ten years allowed us?" I asked. "I've had mine."

"Don't go bibilical on me, Henry," she said. "I thought better of you."

"I'm quite enjoying being an invalid," I said. "I hadn't realised it could be so pleasant."

"You don't dribble yet, and you can still undo your own zip."

She didn't fight fair and, to prove it, added, "You still have time for yourself. Nell isn't going to last the year."

It can't be often that a man of my age is encouraged to look forward hopefully, but even if it were to be life without the strain of Nell and with good health, would I want it? What could be offered but a repetition of things I have already had. Been there, done that, as they say.

"I am doing you the most enormous favour by getting this chap to talk to you," Maggie said.

"Then I accept gratefully." No point in making a stand; let things unfold.

"Good. It isn't your time yet." *And which hat are you wearing, dear Maggie*, I thought, *medium or Matron?*

"But was it Sophie's 'time'?" I asked heavily. To me there could be few things less timely than her death.

She saw my face. "Leave it," she said.

I could not. "But what, in God's great name, had she ever done . . . ?" I burst out.

"It isn't always what we do, but what we are," she said gravely.

"And what was she?"

"Think about it, Henry."

She bent and pressed her cool lips to my forehead. I was too upset to register it at the time; it is only now, as I lie sleepless, that I wonder at it.

"Anything wrong?" Tiger said, emerging from the gloom as I tried to close the lavatory door quietly.

"Too much to drink before bed," I said. "Sorry to wake you."

"You didn't. Not enough to eat before bed. I was just going down to get something. Join me?" Why not? I wouldn't go back to sleep now.

"I know all the tricks," he said. "Don't tread on the bottom step. It creaks. And watch out for the grandfather clock. It sticks out further than you think."

I had already stubbed my toe to prove it.

"You shouldn't go barefoot at your age," he scolded, pressing the toe and making me wince. "You probably won't be able to get your shoe on tomorrow."

He helped me limp into the kitchen. "There's some exotic-looking pâté in the frig," he said. "Like some?"

"No!" I said, "and don't you have any! Nell brought it, and it must be off by now."

"Too late," he said. "And it tasted all right to me."

I began to laugh. "Then it will be your turn next. We're dropping like flies."

We threw away the pâté and made up some packet soup. "Nin Savage puts Guinness in hers," I said.

"We haven't any. Shall we try port?"

As midnight feasts go, it was one of the best. By morning, my toe was the size of a large radish. Tiger was bursting with health. "What price those falling flies?" he said.

David had stayed home from the office and had asked Maggie to be with him when the ambulance brought Nell home. "She must realise, right from the start," he said, "that she just cannot throw her weight about".

"Shall I go or stay?" Tiger asked.

"Stay."

We all waited as alert as a garrison expecting an attack. At noon the telephone rang. Would Mr Martin please go to the hospital: his mother was refusing to leave.

"Come with me," David said to Maggie, his face rigid with temper.

"We'll stay here," Tiger said, pressing me back into my chair.

"I'll make some tea," the nurse said.

The telephone rang.

"How are things going?" Nin asked me. I told her that Nell was refusing to leave the hospital, was being difficult.

"Wouldn't you know!" she said. "Have you rung Kate?"

"No."

"I will. Have you had lunch?"

"The nurse makes us cups of tea."

"Us?"

"Me and Tiger, Sophie's brother."

"He's turned up then, has he? Caroline Evans was rabbiting on about him. Can't he *cook*?"

"I haven't asked him."

"Then do," she said. "Now! It's well past lunchtime. He's a doctor, isn't he? Doesn't he know people need to keep their strength up?"

"I do a very good bacon sandwich," Tiger said, "with tomato sauce". I settled for water biscuits, cheddar and some oversoaked watercress and radishes. When I bit into the radish, it squelched.

"Sure it isn't off?" he asked.

It was four o'clock before we heard wheels in the drive. David came in first. His face was grey. He brushed past us, holding up a hand to fend off questions, and went straight upstairs and closed his bedroom door.

Maggie followed more slowly. She looked pale and exhausted.

"Nell's dead!" I burst out.

"No she isn't," she said tightly. "She worked herself into a hysterical rage, collapsed, was revived and then started all over again. She is now asleep. Under sedation. And I have to tell you I am very, very fed up."

I know Nell under sedation: she snores. The other people in her ward are going to be fed up, too.

I led Maggie to a chair. I was angry with Nell for making her look so wretched.

"Cup of tea?" the nurse asked.

I let a decent interval elapse while we all sipped the scalding brew. Tiger was obviously bursting with curiosity. "How ill is she?" I asked Maggie at last. "And why was she hysterical?"

"She could have had a little stroke, it's not clear yet, And I think David should tell you the rest."

"He doesn't seem in a telling mood."

"I can understand that," she said, and sighed. "Ah well, you won't like it, but you'll hear it anyway, so I might as well tell you. She accused David of having an affair with Caroline Evans and said that was why Sophie killed herself. She refuses to set foot in this house and demands you take her back to Adelaide at once."

"Oh Nell!" I said, exasperated beyond bearing. "How can you talk such nonsense!"

"Are you sure it is nonsense?"

"Of course."

"She says Caroline herself told her."

"Then it *is* nonsense! How could she have?"

"She could," she said gently. "A nurse and some patients say that a well-dressed woman visited Nell and, after a time, rushed away, leaving her very upset."

My stomach clenched. The unbelievable was becoming possible. Suddenly, as clearly as though he stood before me, I saw the desperate honesty in David's face when he said to me, the night we arrived, "However it goes — and it could go very badly indeed — I want you to believe I loved Sophie, and nobody else."

I had believed him then, and I believe him now. The male reacts willingly to temptation. Nature is cunning and uses all the tools at her disposal. And that is a Freudian slip, if ever there were one. It might be true that David had an affair with Caroline Evans, but I was cast-iron sure, as Sophie should have been, that it in no way meant the end of her world.

"Spell it out," I said to Maggie, "from the beginning."

I learned that as soon as David had arrived at her bedside, Nell had begun to scream accusations at him. "You know how she loves the theatrical gesture," Maggie said. "The other patients were upright in their beds."

I groaned. "What did David say?"

"Nothing. He walked away. That didn't stop her. She ranted on, used words she shouldn't, worked herself up into hysteria and, as I told you, collapsed. They've got her under sedation now. David apologised to everybody and has signed her out of the hospital, taking all responsibility for her discharge and guaranteeing to see she gets treatment elsewhere. She'll be arriving here tomorrow."

It was like looking into the pit. "Can you stay?"

"Have you enough beds?"

"Certainly," I said.

David might not have been in a talking mood, but there were practicalities to face. I sent Tiger up to bring him down to face them. He became surprisingly brisk and efficient. The boys' bedroom, which had become the nurses' sitting room, has now become Maggie's room. My bed, which had been dragged into David's room for me, was now dragged out again and put in Maggie's room for her. Tiger found his hammock among the junk in the little room and slung it up; I have taken over his bed up there.

"Watch out for your toe when you climb the stepladder," he warned me. I had forgotten my toe. Now I realised it was hurting, but this was no time to worry about that.

There was much stripping of beds and linen replacement. "How do nurses *stand* it?" Tiger moaned.

The day nurse was sent home, the night nurse was telephoned and put off for the moment.

"Aren't you hungry, Henry?" Tiger asked, when our labours were over. "I'm starving,"

"I know the best takeaways," David said. "Chinese or Indian?"

"Indian," we said in chorus.

When he was gone, Tiger sat looking unusually thoughtful. "Do you believe Nell?" I asked him. He made a seesaw movement with his hands. "About Caroline, probably yes, but about blaming David, no." He looked at me, his eyes clear and candid, "That is down to Sophie".

I looked at Maggie and raised my eyebrows. "That's enough," she said. Maggie has authority. Tiger and I bowed to it as one man. We sat in silence and waited for the arrival of the vindaloo.

KATE

"I have come to bring you news AND to escape the revolting sight of male bodies slumped in front of the television set and idiot faces grinning because England is losing the Test Match," Nin cried, bounding in.

I had to smile. Her loyalty to the country of her birth covers the sporting spectrum and leads to loud dissent in her household, summer and winter. "It's FIVE to one now," she complained. "Sophie's boys are worse than ours!"

"I'm glad to see you," I said. "I am incredibly glad to see you."

"Even though I bring tidings of woe and come evil-tempered?"

"Wait till you hear *my* tidings," I said. She laughed. "We're going to have to watch it. We're turning into 'double-double-toil-and-trouble' girls."

"Gin?" I asked, knowing her predilection and glad of it.

She kicked off her shoes and propelled me towards the spiral staircase. "Lead on!" she said, "but bags I be the first one to tell the news!"

She was in high and facetious good humour. Tears before bedtime, I thought, and decided to go easy on the gin.

"How could you?" she cried a short time later. "You let me go jabbering on about Sophie's brother when you *did* go to Caroline Evans and have been in *her house*!"

We were on the top balcony and her words went winging out like startled birds. I sat her down and gave her a drink. I would have to go carefully or the village down below would become alarmed by the cries from the top of the hill.

I began to tell what had happened, speaking slowly and carefully, leaving nothing out. She was the perfect audience, round-eyed, breathless and as reactive as litmus, but when I got to Caroline's amazing revelation, she seemed less surprised than offended. Her face screwed up in acute distaste. "Trust her to say 'fuck'!"

I thought Caroline had shown commendable honesty in using the word, but this was not the time to say so. "Ready for the rest?"

"You mean there's *more*?"

"Yes, and I need help with it, so keep the decibels down." Her glass was empty and must stay that way.

"I just sat there," I said. "You can imagine, I didn't know what to say. Then, fortunately, Petronella, the girl who's helping her, appeared bringing some exotic-looking iced drinks. So we sat and sipped. Everything was going round and round in my mind until, for no reason, I suddenly remembered Caroline's wig among the things David had brought round.

"Since Nell's hair was looking so awful, I wondered if the wig could help. I was glad to find something to say. "'Henry will be going to see Nell tonight,' I said. 'There is a wig of yours among Sophie's things. Do you want it, or do you think it would be a good idea if I gave him it to take —

"'Wig?' she broke in. 'What are you talking about? I don't own a wig.'

"'Not now, I know, but . . .'

"'I tell you,' she said, with a finality it was impossible to question, 'I have never, in the whole of my life, owned a wig'.

"'But it's your style, your hair colour. It's unmistakable.'

"'And it was with Sophie's things?'

"'Yes.'

"She was quiet for so long I began to get fidgety. 'And there's another thing,' I said at last, hoping to get her attention: 'When you feel better, I'd be grateful if you'd take a look at what there is of hers. I can't think what to do with the underwear.'

"'Underwear?'

"'Yes. Lots of it. Lovely stuff. Such a surprise. I wouldn't have thought it was Sophie's style at all.'

"'Would you say it was mine?' She positively shot the surprising question at me.

"'We-ell, yes, I suppose,' I said, remembering the sumptuous silk, the daring cut of nightgown and scraps of panty. Garments meant to please the senses rather than to cover the body.

"'Yes,' I said firmly, 'now I think about it. Definitely, I would. Just your sort of thing.'

"Then she frightened the life out of me. She threw back her head and gave this great baying howl of grief. I was so startled I began to shake. She pummelled the arms of her chair, crying, 'NO!, NO! Oh, please God, no!'

"Her split lip opened up and blood started to trickle down her chin. Oh Nin! It was *bad*. I was so sorry for her I put my arms round her and, all the while, part of me was thinking: what are you doing, woman? You are holding *Caroline Evans*!"

Nin was open-mouthed. "Then what?" she managed to say.

"She quietened down eventually and we just sat there without speaking. Then she gave a sick sort of half-laugh. 'So I wasn't lying to Nell after all. Sophie did know. She must have known for years.'

"I thought of poor Sophie, keeping silent, laying no blame, feeling inadequate and unattractive and wishing she looked like Caroline. And then it hit me. 'Caroline,' I said, 'if she *had* known for years, it can't be the reason why suddenly she should ... *now*.'

And there I was with my arms round her again and she was weeping and weeping and saying, 'Why are you being so good to me?'

"Oh, the relief when the doorbell rang. We unscrambled ourselves, smoothed ourselves down and tried to look as normal as possible. I expected Petronella to answer the door, but there was no sign of her. Caroline was looking so awful I expected her to refuse to see anybody, but she didn't. She motioned for me to go and answer it. There was a young man standing there holding a bunch of flowers. Oh, Nin! I heard myself making a funny noise. The shock! I could have been looking at Sophie."

"Tiger!" Nin said triumphantly. "Then what did you do?"

"I rushed him in, handed him over to her, and made off. I chickened out. I'd had more than enough for one day."

Nin cast her eyes upward. "And I'm sorry to tell you," she said, "there's still tomorrow. Nell is coming out of hospital." It was as though she were crying, "Doom! Doom!"

"Oh-o-oh! Poor David. Poor Henry," I said.

"Never mind about poor them!!" she replied robustly. "What about poor us? What did you do with that gin?"

It is fortunate we had been near the end of the bottle.

DAVID

There must be many degrees and varieties of wretchedness; at the moment I am experiencing a very strange one. Henry, bless the dear old chap, is doing his quiet best to make things seem as normal as possible. Tiger is out most of the time. The house is overrun by women I am at pains to avoid. Kate and Nin Savage treat me with the scrupulous politeness given to those suffering from a disease too indelicate to mention. Nell is a silent, uneasy presence. I have not been into her room to see her, not even when she slept. I have not been to see Caroline either, though I am truly, deeply sorry about what has happened to her. I asked Tiger to tell her so.

"Go and see her," he urges. He does not appear to bear me any ill will, and I find that strange. But everything is strange these days. I am an ordinary man. I am adrift when things become extraordinary.

A local doctor has been called in. Tiger's presence is regarded as useful, but not official. People have to die officially. The doctor is a raw-boned, short-fused young Scot, recently returned from the turmoils in Africa. It is clear that he finds it difficult to transfer his concern about the deaths of innocent, starving children to that of an indulged and difficult old woman. *Nature can be allowed to take its course, can't it?* he was asked, and was in entire agreement.

Matron likes him. She calls him "my lad". I am nobody's lad. Certainly not my own. Self-dislike is very hard to bear, and I do not bear it well and feel resentment against those who have forced it on me. Against Sophie, for being so damned amenable and not making her due demands; against Caroline, whose demands were undue, and inescapable; against Nell, for not being what I needed and everything I did not; against Nin Savage, for making me obliged to her when she was the last person in the world to whom I could give obligation easily; against Kate, for becoming so delicately but unmistakably distant the other day; against the boys, who obviously prefer to be with the Savages rather than at home with me.

"Could do with having a word about your two," Dan had said.

I immediately realised I should have offered to be responsible for the cost of their keep and I took care of that at once.

"Not only that," he had said carefully. But had not got round to saying what else.

I was not sorry. I have enough on my mind and don't want to confront more difficulties. But I have been asked for Sunday lunch. They are in wait for me.

"Christmas is coming. We have to make plans," he had said.

He might have to. *I* will not. I am in no mood for decorating the halls with bloody holly. The boys can tell me what they want and I will get it for them, but that is as far as I will go. Anyway, what are the odds against Nell dying on Christmas Day? She would relish causing the inconvenience.

I would like to talk to Kate. I want to know more about the dropping of the charges against her. Does she know why? What exactly did the letter say? From what she has told me, the man in question is a ruthless and unscrupulous fellow. "He is out to get me," she has said in that maddeningly unconcerned way of hers.

I don't doubt he is, and don't imagine the dropping of the case came from the kindness of his heart. Being a solicitor teaches one a great deal about the evil in human nature. I gather that she and Henry are also invited to lunch with the Savages. I will have to try to talk to her about it then. If she is willing to talk to me at all.

Tiger seems entranced with Caroline. "She's a hoot," he said, laughing. "Wind her up and off she goes!"

I had never found anything humorous in Caroline "going off".

"How is she?"

"Coming on well. She's as strong as an ox."

"And her face?"

"Colourful," he said, and laughed again.

"You're not winding her up about that, are you?" I asked, in sudden concern. I know how much Caroline's looks mean to her.

"Of course I am! She worked off nearly all her steam about stupid old men who drive when they're past it, and stupid young men who drive in the back seat of the car in front of them; now we're concentrating on compensation for grievous bodily harm. I keep telling her how grievous it is. Actually she'll be as good as new before too long."

"I'm surprised she lets you see her."

"She *likes* me to see her. I sit and stare at her and tell her I've never seen anything to compare —"

I had to laugh. "You're as devious as Hairy."

"He really liked her, you know. He said Caroline's trouble was that nobody had ever loved her enough, so she had to love herself to make up."

"Sophie loved her," I said morosely.

"Didn't she just! She thought she was marvellous: those long legs, that dramatic face! What wouldn't she have given to look like that! 'No hope for us,' I told her. 'We chose the wrong parents.'

Ours were short and round. I was always put in the front row when they took the school photographs."

"Did you mind?"

"Of course I did. Soph and I often used to bewail our fate. 'Think how much simpler it would be if people looked like they really are,' she said."

"I thought Sophie did."

"No way," he said.

Conversations with him always became disturbing.

"Caroline is very indignant because she says she was only trying to be kind to Nell," he said suddenly, switching back to his favourite topic. I snorted. The idea was ludicrous.

"She says that Nell was distraught because she had told Soph that you and Caroline were — you know — so she thought it was her fault that Soph — you know. She was weeping and carrying on, so Caro told her it couldn't have been her fault because Sophie had known about — you know — for years. Had she, by the way?"

"How do I know?" I snapped, and pushed past him and out of the room. I have had enough. All around me are people who know more about my private life than is comfortable. I have to meet their eyes knowing they are thinking, "How could he have done such a thing to Sophie?" But nobody accuses me. Except Nell. Why does she always have to be the one to hold the whip? I have forgotten what it is to sleep well.

Henry spends all his time sitting with Nell. He was a great deal brighter when she was in hospital and Kate or Nin Savage took him to see her each day. I have asked Tiger to keep a close eye on him, and he said not to worry, that no eye was closer than Matron's.

"I don't know what to make of that woman," I said, "or how to treat her. She's supposed to be a medium, isn't she?"

"Just treat her with deference," he said. "Bags of deference for Matron! And don't go asking her for a reading, or she'll have your whatsits off."

"Just look out for Henry," I said irritably. His schoolboy humour gets on my nerves.

HENRY

I am sorry for David. The revelation about Caroline hardly comes as a surprise to me.

Given Caroline's sensual appeal, it is hardly to be wondered that, when temptation was put in his way, as I am sure it was, he succumbed. I long ago recognised the younger Nell in Caroline. I saw the same need to be desired by every man who crossed her path and the same casualness in the granting of sexual favours. To them it was just like offering a drink to a guest.

After Nell and I married, she seemed content to relinquish the persona — or was clever or considerate enough to conceal it from me. I was not over-troubled. We were working out the structure of our marriage on a different level. The ties that really bind are seldom physical ones.

Tiger spends much of his time with Caroline. "She's amazing!" he says, his face alight. Tactful enquiry revealed that she looks like a boxer after an unsuccessful fight. Out of loyalty to Nell, I did not ask if Caroline had told him about her visit to the hospital. I am no gossip, and for us to discuss it all behind their backs seems tawdry in the extreme. But his rueful shake of the head when he said. "Some people have a genius for getting things wrong," certainly whetted my curiosity.

He shows no animosity towards David. I think David finds this baffling and wishes he would. It would be easier for him if he had something to defend himself against; since there is nothing, he is faced with his own accusations.

I sit with Nell for most of my days. It is hard to tell how sedated she is. She sleeps a great deal and when she wakes is not Nell. Sometimes she knows me, sometimes not. She is adrift on waters where I cannot reach her. I feel bad about this.

Maggie insists that I take time out, so Nin or Kate collect me, and we go to the beach, where the salt wind is fresh, or to Kate's eyrie. I am moved hither and yon by loving hands. I am aware that my feet are starting to drag as I walk, and that Nin is at pains to see I have a napkin tucked under my chin as I eat. I have to ask Kate if she will please do the same. I see tears in her eyes as she bends over me.

Nin wants Maggie to take Sunday lunch with us all. Surely the nurse can manage by herself for a couple of hours, she said. Maggie decided that she could.

Nin is remarkable. It is as though she has found the secret of the five loaves and two small fishes. She feeds the multitude without visible effort.

"I won't ask Tiger — this time," she said. "I'd rather wait until I know him better." I did not tell her that I was sure Tiger was already spoken for and would have found an invitation difficult to accept.

It was one of those warm, clear days when Nature seems to have got everything right. As we swooped down the hill to Nin's, the car engine hummed, clean and purposeful. It would have been very easy to fall asleep.

"Don't worry," I heard Maggie say, "I have him". I sagged, delightfully and comfortably.

"This barramundi had better be good," she was saying. "I had to fight to get it."

"Herbs," I said, my eyes closing. "It needs herbs."

"Shut up, Henry," she said.

"Let him sleep," Maggie said. I did not want to sleep. I could smell the hot oil of the barbecue and my tastebuds were alive. I could feel people hovering over me. When I forced my eyes open, I looked straight into those of one of the twins, "Don't worry, Grandpa Henry," Ben said. "We won't let them eat it all."

When we arrived I had caught sight of outside tables bright with umbrellas and flowers. After a short, sweet sleep, I heard Nin's voice calling, "Come on, you lot! Placemats! Get the tables set!" Then came the thunder of young feet. Her two boys are large and fair, ours small and dark, There was much clattering of cutlery.

"How many of us are there?"

"Nine."

"No, ten." One of the twins piped up.

"Knucklehead! Can't you count? There's only nine."

"What about Zak?"

The question silenced the clatter. "Knock it off," one of Nin's boys said. "What are you trying to do? Upset everybody?"

The twin — I don't know which one, I never do — looked mutinous, but remained silent.

The big boys gathered placemats and cutlery and, as they prepared to take them out into the garden, brandished them at the small ones. "*Nine*," they said in unison.

I was amused to see that, as they prepared to follow them, one of the twins, his small jaw set, was holding an extra placemat, knife, fork and spoon behind his back. "Who is this Zak?" I asked him.

"Our brother."

"I didn't know you had one," I said, smiling at what I thought was a childish game.

"Not many people do. Mum wouldn't let him get born," he said, and off he went.

"What's the matter?" Maggie asked, coming in to collect me for the meal.

"Nothing." I said, unable to find words.

"Henry!"

"Just something silly one of the boys said."

She would not allow me to dismiss it. "They claim to have a brother," I said unwillingly.

"Zak?"

"Yes. How did you know?"

"Never mind." She was staring beyond me. "Don't mention this to David," she said at last.

I was completely at sea.

"No sense in letting the food spoil," she said, becoming brisk and heaving me out of the chair.

"This is the barramundi to end all barramundis."

It was, too. Delicate, moist, exquisite in taste.

I will never eat it again as long as I live.

NIN

It was such a good idea; we could kill two birds with one stone; Dan could talk to David about his boys, and I could talk to Maggie about me. We were all in need of cheering up, so what better way than a Special Occasion? And what better occasion than the Feast of the Barramundi? I have a particular feeling for this fish. It is so strong, so beautiful, so princely. I can understand cannibals who eat their warrior-enemies so as to take into themselves their valour and strength. Dan says he still loves me and won't let them take me away, but don't tell me that other people haven't thought the same thing.

I had a dawn tryst with the fishmonger, who brought me the magnificent creature straight from the market, I prepared it lovingly. A light seasoning of salt, a heavy one of black pepper, butter and a careful wrapping in foil. Simplicity is all. Nothing must adulterate the taste.

I had made the pavlova the night before, I am not allowed to have a party without producing one. I have decided to wean my lot onto cheesecake, it's easier on the whipping arm. The salads were crisping in the refrigerator; my beautiful white china, elegant and as pure in line as in colour, stood waiting. How *can* people serve food on patterned plates? Fresh bread would arrive at eleven o'clock.

It was going to be a perfect day. There was not a cloud in the sky. The ocean whispered. As I took my ease in a moment which was mine alone, I felt the real joy of anticipation.

That was then. Now is now.

I should have known.

The meal was superb. At least I can say that. Maggie looked at me as though she were seeing me for the first time. All four boys ate devotedly, as usual and, as usual, were off like bullets as soon as I got up to make the coffee.

"Can Henry have a little brandy?" Dan asked Maggie.

"Certainly."

We all had a little brandy.

I remember what I have come to think of as those Last Moments with aching clarity. Henry was lying back, smiling, his eyes closed. I thought how decorative Kate and Maggie looked as they hovered around like butterflies before settling one on each side of him. Dan and David, long elegantly trousered legs outstretched, were the stuff of the fashionable magazine. I had even made one of my Efforts, and the startled appreciation had been welcome. I saw this golden creature reflected in the curved balloon of my brandy glass and was well content. The mindless pleasure cannot have lasted long.

"You said you wanted to talk to me about the boys," I heard David say and knew everything was beginning to slip away. "I'm sorry if they are being . . ."

"No, no. They're great kids," Dan said, and hesitated, "It's just that —"The change in his voice was obvious. I hurt for him.

"I don't know what you think," he went on, "but, childish imagination . . . You certainly don't want to stifle it, but it's hard to know how far it's wise to let it go."

"I don't get you."

"This business of Zak," Dan said — and nothing was ever the same again.

David sat up in his chair, exasperation showing all too plainly. "I thought I'd put a stop to all that!"

"I'm afraid he's still around," Dan said, trying to be whimsical about it.

David was not feeling in the least whimsical. "I told Sophie I wouldn't have it but she didn't seem to care ..."

"I don't think it was quite like that."

"Then what the hell was it like?" He had really lost his patience now. "Well," Dan said hesitantly, "they say Zak is their brother."

David snorted. "All part of the nonsense!"

"No. Their *real* brother."

David looked at him as though he had lost his mind.

Dan blew out his cheeks. "Sorry about this," he said, "but there's no way round it. They must mean the child Sophie aborted."

I doubt if any of us will ever forget that great cry of incredulity. David was on his feet, turning now this way, now that, in an agony of bewilderment. "Sophie?" he said. "*My wife*! You are telling me Sophie had an abortion?"

"Yes."

"How can you possibly know?"

"She told me."

"Sophie *told* you! She told *you*!" The cry hung in the air. It was dreadful to see suspicion beginning to twist the stricken face.

Now Dan was on his feet. "Hold it!" he said authoritatively. "Hold it! Things are bad enough without them being made worse. If you want to be stupid, I can't stop you, but if you've got any sense, you'll shut up and listen."

David hesitated and then slumped back into his chair. "Do you think I like doing this?" Dan said more quietly and put his hand on the hunched shoulder. "I'm more sorry than I can say."

"Get on."

I had to listen to it all again: how Dan had met Sophie on the beach when her boys were only a few months old and she was crying because she was pregnant again.

"You'd been married less than a year," he said to David now, "and you were already a family of four. She was feeding the twins and was tired all the time. The broken nights were getting you both down. Remember? 'It isn't fair on him,' she said. She was afraid she might have twins again. 'Imagine!' she said, 'a family of *six*! How could I expect David to put up with that?'"

"So you advised her to have an abortion."

"No! She had already decided."

"Without saying a word to me? Without asking me how I felt?"

"Don't be hard on her. She was only trying to do her best for you."

"Dammit man, she was my *wife*, not my nursemaid!" He was on his feet again, his good-looking face had lost all its bland smoothness. His eyes were hard, his lips thin. "What *she* thought was best! What about *my* best? Did she never think of that? But that was Sophie, always doing *her* bloody best for people!"

The lovely meal was forgotten; the day lay in ruins. And not only the day, I thought, worried by the hard, set face.

Dan had told me that Sophie had had the operation during three days David had been away visiting a client. Was he thinking back now to a time which had seemed so ordinary, but had not been ordinary at all?

He was looking round at each of us sombrely, at Henry, at Kate, at Maggie and at Dan and me. "There isn't much you don't know about me now, is there?" he said bitterly. We all looked away and stared at the ocean.

Dan cleared his throat. "There is one more thing. Sorry again."

"What more can there be?"

"The boys talk as though they are in touch with Sophie, as though, to them, she isn't dead."

"Well, she is to me," he said shortly, "so leave it." He kicked off his shoes and began to strip down to his bathers. He piled his clothes neatly on his chair, then turned and began to walk away out over the sand to the ocean.

We watched uneasily as he skirted spread-eagled bodies and sun-bemused children under canopies and splashed out through the small breakers, past the knots of lazy swimmers to the clear, blue emptiness beyond. He dived through the last wave and began to swim with long, clean strokes, out towards the horizon.

"I can't see him," Henry said anxiously.

"He's there," Dan said. "He'll be OK. He just needs some space." I hoped to God he'd got it right.

Henry was the first one to pull himself round, "Maggie," he said. "Can you help? I'm lost."

We all were.

"I'll tell you what I know," she said tensely. "Make of it what you can."

Her face was set and, as she spoke, her eyes, as did mine, followed the head moving further and further out into the water. "She tried to avoid trouble with David over what he said was stupid nonsense, she tried to keep the boys happy, but when they always had Zak tagging along, chattering their heads off to him, she got fed up and lost her temper. 'Shut up!' she said. 'Zak gets on my nerves!' That's when it all fell apart. Apparently, they ganged up on her. Tom asked her if that was why she didn't let him get born, and Ben said, 'You shouldn't talk like that about my brother.' She was devastated. She had only ever thought about the abortion as a sensible escape from problems, she had never felt that a Person was involved. *It was only ten weeks, for heaven's sake*, she said. But she started to feel guilty. And they didn't help. They still kept Zak around. The guilt grew and grew and, worst of all, she felt they were accusing her all the time. She got me worried. I could feel the darkness building up ..."

"Please!" Kate said in distress, but Henry quickly silenced her.

"What did you do?" he asked Maggie.

"You know those boys," she said, "normal as all get-out, except for this one thing, this capacity to see that bit more, be that bit more aware, than most people. To them it's quite ordinary, so you go carefully. I told them that Zak was very happy to be around for now; that Mum was sorry there had been a mix-up when he was ready to be born, but that there would soon be another chance for him and he would be off, and they mustn't be sad when he went but be happy for him."

"What did they say?"

"Tom said 'Goodo,' and Ben said he hoped it wouldn't be before his birthday."

"I'm sorry," Kate was on her feet and beginning to move away, holding up her hands in rejection. "I'm sorry, this isn't my line of country at all."

Maggie shrugged,

"Do you believe this?" Henry asked.

"They do. That's what matters."

"And do they talk to Sophie?"

"I don't know."

"Oh Maggie!" he said, shaking his head at her. She became Matron. She is very much a thus-far-and-no-farther woman. "Time to get you home, my lad" she said.

I could see Dan was glad to hear it. Within seconds he was up, collecting glasses, straightening chairs and flashing me get-on-with-it looks.

Henry refused to move. His eyes strained out over the sea. "I can't see him," he kept saying.

"He's there, he's there," we kept replying.

He would only agree to move when we could tell him that David had turned round and was now striking out for the shore.

It was a wretched end to what should have been a lovely party.

"Henry was limping rather badly," I said to Kate as we watched Maggie's car climbing the hill.

"He's a bad colour too," she said.

Neither of us mentioned Sophie.

We worked silently, clearing away all evidence of the beautiful meal, now sadly forgotten. My mind was in a ferment, going over and over all that had been said. I still could not let go of my resentment that Dan had kept so much from me. I hated the idea of him sharing something which excluded me with another woman, even though that woman was Sophie. I had accepted her reasons for the abortion as valid, as had Dan. They were logical and believable. But now my mind ranged wider, as his never could.

Pregnancy can be cruel to a woman's body; it leaves scars, stretch-marks, sagging flesh and small humiliations, The clean firmness taken for granted is gone. The bladder leaks, milk leaks; smells take over from scents. The wife becomes unrecognisable in the mother. It must have been when Sophie felt most vulnerable that she found out about David and Caroline.

I tried to *be* Sophie, to feel as she must have felt. She had no self-love; she laughingly deprecated her own looks and openly admired Caroline's splendid physicality. She loved both her and David; that was as clear as daylight. Did she think, "What could I expect?" and be humble about it or, did something stir and rebellion against being even more disadvantaged take hold?

The thoughts came up, flooding my mind. Maybe the abortion had not been for David's sake. Maybe Sophie had had it done just for Sophie. Maybe she was right to feel guilty.

"We didn't know Soph very well, did we?" I said

Kate put down the dishes she was carrying. "All those months," she said, "she was with me every step of the way. We were like one person. Totally committed. And she was carrying all that inside and never said a word to me."

"She was escaping," I said. "She was using you as an escape."

She put her hands to her ears. "Stop it!"

I put my arms round her and we stood and rocked together, Kate and I are very straightforward people. This was no more my line of country than it was hers.

Suddenly Dan was upon us, "Don't just stand there," he said. "Give me a hand with these!" He was holding out three huge cornets of ice-cream. "Hokey-pokey!" he said. "The ice-cream man cometh! And so does David, He's already back,"

Nothing had ever been more blessedly ordinary or more welcome. We stood about, licking the great mounding domes of wicked indulgence, smiling at each other and feeling the nerves settle.

We were down to the last crunchy bits when we saw David trudging up the beach towards us.

He looked tired and pale, as though there were no more emotion left in him.

"Could have done with one of those," he said with a wry smile.

Dan immediately leapt into action. "Right! I'll catch him!" he cried, and was off in pursuit of the disappearing chimes. The three of us stood around looking helplessly at each other. "Sorry, Nin," he said, "so sorry. I've spoiled your lovely day."

He looked so sad and his words were so unexpected that, before I could think, my arms were round him. "What about *your* day?" I said.

He was nice to hold. He has a giving body. He gave me a big squeeze. "Just a few things to get used to," he said.

225

There certainly are! I never thought the day would come when I would actually feel fond of David Martin.

The garden telephone was ringing.

"Is Mrs Kate Hamilton there?" a voice asked.

"Yes."

"I need to speak to her, Urgently."

Puzzled, I handed the phone to Kate. As she listened, her face paled and she closed her eyes.

"What is it? What is it?" She looked helplessly at David and handed him the receiver. "Ka-ate!" I almost screamed. "What *is* it?"

"Someone has tried to burn my house down," she said.

David was taut as a drum. "And we know who it was, don't we?" he said savagely, flinging down the phone and rushing to collect his clothing.

"Come on! Come on! Kate! We've got to get over there! The keys are in the car!"

Dan, returning triumphantly with a fourth ice-cream, was just in time to see David's car screaming up the hill. "Now what?" he said.

"You'll never believe me."

He did. Within minutes, our car was out and we were tearing round the bends in pursuit. I was still holding the ice-cream cornet he had pushed into my hand. "Don't let it drip all over the seat," he snapped. "Get rid of it!"

My wits had left me. "But it's for David," I said.

"Oh my God!" he said and, with one twitch of his hand, had it out of my grasp and through the window.

"Get a grip on yourself," he said. "Can't you see the smoke?"

CAROLINE

I am leading a very strange life. I feel not only like a bird in a cage, but a bird in a cage under a blanket, I cannot go out because I have no car. If I had a car, I could not drive, because the neck brace does not permit me to turn my head and, most compelling reason of all, I cannot go out because if I did, Tiger says I would frighten the horses.

Tiger comes every day. And stays. Petronella comes every day. And stays. I am visited by the acupuncturist, a masseuse he insisted I need, a physiotherapist who talks too much and a doctor who barely talks at all.

The first time he came, the doctor seemed to regard me as light relief and, after assuring me I would live to fight another day, took himself off with Tiger to bitch about governments and the hassles of practising medicine.

The first shock has worn off. I do not feel ill. Merely peculiar, I refuse to look in a mirror. When I did and saw what was now me, I literally felt the earth shift. Primal shock.

They tell me I will be relatively unscathed, but do not specify what "relatively" means.

Tiger said it means that people will be able to recognise me — just — but I saw him wink at Petronella. I could hit him. And frequently do. He makes me laugh, And it hurts. What is so weird is that I am having *fun*.

He has taken everything over. He has been on to the car wreckers, the insurance companies, mine and every one of the other drivers involved in the pile-up.

"Sign this!" he says, producing forms. He gives a running commentary on every interview he has, imitating voices, sending up officialdom.

He is fascinated by the state of my face. "Photographs!" he cried, "We must have photographs!" Over my dead body, I am afraid of dropping off to sleep when he is in the house, I wouldn't put it past him.

He has discovered my bread-making machine. And the old coffee-grinder his mother gave me when Hairy went all modern and bought ready-ground beans and filter papers. "This is how a house ought to smell," he says.

He has Petronella in a whirl. Between them they have baked enough bread to feed the village. "Look! Rolls! See how they crunch!" I cannot chew, so he tied a large napkin round my neck, broke off pieces of roll, dipped them into red wine and fed me with them. Petronella laughed so much she got hiccups.

I know everything that goes on in David's house. Once I would have given much to have had such inside information. Now, well...

Tiger knows everything that happened between me and Nell. I told him. "Didn't do her much good," he said.

He doesn't ask me to explain about David. I wouldn't know how to, but if I did, I think he is the one person in the world I could try to tell.

He likes David. He speaks easily of Sophie. He has fallen in love with Henry and Maggie Mackenzie. I remember Henry as a quiet, grey man. This Maggie I cannot wait to meet.

He makes everybody sound interesting and fills the days, which could have been so difficult and empty, with noise and good humour. We talk a lot about the old days. The riotous meals, the house spilling over with Hairy's friends, our friends and large, young men who followed his mother around; Sophie and I starting to find our social feet and making the little brother dance with us.

"You knew every word of every popular song," he said. They were good days for me, the best I had ever known.

"Did he used to be your boyfriend?" Petronella asked. Which made me think. So I asked him about his love life.

"Girls, yes," he said, "floor to ceiling. Girl, no."

"Why not?"

"There was nobody in England I could play 'do-you-remember?' with. And don't pick that scab."

Don't try telling me how clever Nature is. If it's so damn clever, it could surely have done a better job of healing than coming up with a scab. To be seen scabbed always seemed to me to be the last word in humiliation, and here I am being inspected with positive interest by a man who Petronella thought could have been ... Damn it, I was laughing again.

And then he said, "I've just realised I'll have to get used to you when you look normal again, I don't fancy that! What if I go off you?"

And I was crying and laughing and biffing out at him when Petronella rushed in.

"Didn't you hear the fire-engines?" she almost yelled, "There's two gone past already! It's that big house, the one with all the balconies."

"Kate!" Tiger and I said in unison.

For a second, he stood wavering, as though torn between staying with me and going. "Yes,! Yes!" I said. "Go!" He bent and kissed the top of my head and rushed out of the room. Kate's lovely house on fire. I could hardly believe it. I had admired it so much. It was a house I could have lived in myself. I *remembered* it, which is something one rarely does with other people's homes. Poor woman. The house was all she had. Like me, I thought. What do I have but my house? And turned cold.

"You're not going to be sick, are you?" Petronella said. "Shall I get you a cup of tea? What are you doing? What are you *doing*?"

I shoved her out of the way. I was trying to get to the telephone, of course. What the hell did she think! Emergency. Telephone. It was obvious. I had just got my hands on it when it began to ring.

"This is Dan Savage. Is Tiger there?" The line was crackling badly. It was obviously a mobile phone.

"No. He's just..."

"Never mind." And that was it. He was gone. I stood there thinking how much I did mind. I didn't want Tiger to be where flames were blazing and timber and bricks falling and the temptation to try and save whatever he could might override his commonsense.

At least Kate wouldn't be in the house. She would be at that party at the Savages. Tiger knew all about it and had told me of the barramundi he was missing just to have the pleasure of my company. Well, the party would be broken up now.

"There goes another fire-engine!" Petronella called. "Or is it an ambulance?"

The howling wail swept past the house and up the hill. I realised that David would probably be up there. *God*, I mentally admonished Him, *don't let anything happen to David but, please don't take your eye off Tiger.*

Petronella took the phone out of my hand. "Come on now, sit down. There's nothing we can do." If there's one thing I hate, it's not being able to do anything about anything.

Then I remembered. He had kissed the top of my head just before he rushed away. I have been unable to wash my hair since the accident, and brushing it is too painful. I put up my hand to where the kiss had been dropped. My hair felt greasy but, as I sniffed my fingers, I breathed in the lingering scent of Roger and Gallet. One small mercy granted.

I put in an immediate demand to the Almighty for more.

The day dragged into evening, and I was in a positive sweat when, at last, the phone rang. "It isn't as bad as it might have been," Tiger said, his voice sounding scratchy. "The fire-engine got here pretty smartish. She's lost a bedroom and the studio, but apart from the mess —"

"How is she?"

"Stunned. They've established the fire was deliberately lit. David reckons he knows who did it — or caused it to be done — but he's having to keep mum about it, naturally. He's fit to be tied. He's still here — and the Savages. We've been working our butts off. But we're bushed. We'll have to pack it in now. The fire's dead and we've saved what we could."

It was past imagining.

"Look," he went on, "will it be OK if I bring Kate down for a shower and a meal? David has his hands full with Henry and Nell, and the Savages are overrun with kids. I'll pick up some takeaway —"

"You'll do no such thing!" I said. "There's plenty of food here. I'll make omelettes and there's all your bread. And Kate must stay ..."

"Attagirl," he said, and made kissing noises. "See you in a few minutes."

"What do you think you're doing?" Petronella said, heading me off as I used the furniture to steer myself towards the kitchen.

"Just get me in there, and sit me at the bench," I said, "and get things out for me. And then put fresh towels in the bathrooms. Both of them. The bed linen is in the cupboard on the landing."

"Bed linen?"

"Sheets," I said, "pillowcases. And open the windows in the bedrooms."

"You're not up to having people stay."

"You don't know what I'm up to," I said.

One must always rise to the occasion. It is a matter of pride. And of excitement. I have very ready adrenalin.

"Pick me some herbs," I said, "and not just parsley!"

I require my *omelettes aux fines herbes* to be very "fine" indeed.

HENRY

When Maggie brought me home from the Savages, we found the nurse on the point of calling us to return, for Nell was awake and restless. She looked at me balefully, as though accusing me of deserting her, but could only mumble incoherently. When I took her hand in mine, it was flaccid.

Maggie became Matron at once and bundled me out of the room. "Only a minor incident," she said later. "It will probably resolve itself."

"I will sit with her," I said. I held her poor limp hand between my own, and we looked at each other with the here-we-go-again ruefulness to which we had become accustomed. And then her eyes flickered closed. When I am fit to go out and she is not, she demands to be told everything I have done and everybody I have seen. What did they say? she presses me and then berates me for being a poor observer and raconteur. She does not like to miss things. I was glad I would not have to tell her about the disastrous time we had all just spent. Her vitality was too low to either speak or listen. She had exhausted herself grieving about Sophie.

It sometimes seemed that Sophie was the only person she really cared about. Largely, I thought ungenerously now, because the girl gave her the open admiration which was meat and drink to her. Had it been real? Or was it Sophie doing her best again?

Ah well, little of it matters now. Sophie is gone and we each have to tread our own stony roads. I have just remembered Maggie's evasive reply when asked if she believed the boys did indeed talk to Sophie. I expect better of her than that. I must pin her down.

I have no difficulty in believing the boys could be "sensitives". Nell often used to tell the story of how her mother had insisted on sitting up all night because one of her sons who had been presumed killed in action was coming home. Her father had been furiously angry and there had been high words, but when Nell had come downstairs in the morning, she had found her mother and her brother quietly taking breakfast together.

When I first knew her, her interest in spiritualism had seemed part of her theatrical background: Madame This or That who read the Tarot cards and gave "readings" not only of the future but of past lives. I had no patience with it until I realised that she was testing herself, and being bitterly disappointed to find she had the five senses and no more.

I knew the frustration of finding that out for myself. When Frances and my child died, anguished love and the desperation of loss had made me reach out, frantic to burst through the veil which separates the living from the dead. It had done no good, of course. Then one day, at a crowded business seminar in New York, of all places, a very embarrassed woman had approached me. "You must forgive me," she said, "but I cannot control the impulse. I have to tell you that Frances says all is well." She had then moved away among her colleagues, and I was caught up with mine and I didn't see her again.

So I have an open mind.

I do believe that we are more than just the butcher's meat we inhabit, but where the reality of self lies, I do not know and do not think anyone else does. I don't think we are intended to know, this time round, though whether there is another one, I tend to doubt. To be so near the end of a long life and have so few answers is annoying. Not to know if we find them when we die, even more so.

"She's asleep," Maggie said and came and drew me away to take the cup of tea the nurse believes is therapeutic, but which gives me wind. She took me through to the big sitting room which, even after all these years, seems to belong to Hairy rather than to Sophie and David, settled me down in the big chair and gave me my tea.

"Drink that," she ordered. "David has just telephoned. Something has happened. There's no need to get upset. Everything is all right. Everybody is quite safe. But someone has set fire to Kate's house, and they're all up there now trying to save what they can."

I *did* get upset, of course. Who wouldn't? My cup rattled in the saucer. Poor darling Kate! How could anybody be so indescribably wicked as to do this to her!

"The police are there. And firemen from all over the area. There are so many trees that other properties are in danger. They even torched the trees down her drive to make it more difficult for the fire crews."

"Who would do a thing like that?"

"David will tell you."

It was hours before he came home. He was filthy and grey-faced, his good clothes ruined.

"How is she?"

"In shock. Tiger's taken her to Caroline's. It isn't as bad as it might have been. She's lost the studio and her bedroom, but the rest of the house is OK. Apart from water damage."

Since Tiger is not here, they would not let me climb the stepladder to the little room. The nurse made up a bed for me on the couch. "Where I can keep an eye on you," she said.

She must have been keeping an eye on me when Nell died. She went in her sleep. Alone and without causing any trouble.

It was this which made me weep.

DAVID

At the moment, Nell's death is just another situation to be dealt with. Matron, accustomed to the proceedings which follow, has advised me and everything has been arranged, quickly and efficiently.

Her body was taken to the undertaker's Chapel of Rest, where it now lies in one of their most expensive coffins. The time and date of the service and the cremation to follow have been established. Mourners will attend the service, but the undertaker will be in charge of the removal of the body to the crematorium and the subsequent cremation.

"He is *not* going to that place," Matron said fiercely.

Nell would be annoyed to think her last dramatic exit would go largely unobserved.

Sophie was buried in the earth. The procedure was quite different. The undertaker treats me as an old customer who has unaccountably changed his preferences.

I am concerned about Henry, but Matron tells me not to worry. "I will look after him," she says. So now there are just the three of us in the house.

Tiger has stayed on at Caroline's, where he is looking after both her and Kate. Nin cut her right hand badly while we were shifting rubble at Kate's place and trying to save what we could. She has her arm in a sling and is terrorising her own boys and mine into being useful. Dan has cancelled his patients and is everywhere, helping everybody. We have become a tight-knit little group. Telephones run hot.

I can no longer put off going to see Caroline. It is easier now that Kate is there. I must obviously see that poor girl, too, and do what I can for her. She needs a solicitor. And I am a good one, no matter what Nell might think.

CAROLINE

So Nell is dead. I need time to think about that, but there is none at the moment, for our hands are full with Kate. The shock of seeing her house burning and half the hillside alight has been profound. I could have wept on seeing her poor stricken face when Tiger brought her here. She has lost all her clothes — not a stitch left — and all her husband's clothes, which she had treasured and kept as the only part of him she now had. All Sophie's things are gone. At least we don't have those to worry us anymore. The basic structure of the house is still sound, and Tiger says it would mainly be a cleaning job to get the upper storeys habitable, but she shrinks at even the thought of going back to inspect the place.

The police have been here, asking questions as to who might have had a grudge against her. They must know. They know about the charges against her which have been dropped. The finger could hardly be more clearly pointed. Anybody else? they asked. The man in question is overseas and has been for the last few days. "They're wasting their time," she said, when they had gone. She appears to think that people too powerful to be brought to book have decided to teach her a lesson. She is afraid.

David has been here. He blenched when he saw my face. "Oh my dear," he said, and took me in his arms.

It was a strange moment. So much can be said without words. If we had talked for hours, we could never have communicated in the way our bodies did now. The tiredness, the confusion, the anger, the sorrow — all were there. We clung together, the familiarity sweet. We were both very near tears. We had never loved each other but I think, for one brief moment, we came near it then.

"Is Tiger looking after you?" he said at last.

"Yes. Tiger is certainly looking after me."

"What about legal help?"

"No need of it."

"That's all right then," he said.

And it was.

Kate was looking very poorly when she came down to see him. She was wearing a loose robe of mine, which I saw him recognise.

"Oh Kate!" he said, but did not take her in his arms.

He is handling everything for her, as Tiger is doing for me. We are both lucky to have someone to take the weight. I have become very tired, my strength soon ebbs.

"I'll leave you to talk," I said, and went to my bed. I needed silence in which to savour this new-found peace.

I must have slept, for I did not hear him go. "I brought him up to say goodbye," Petronella said, "but you were asleep. He stood there, just looking at you. He's got such a sad face, hasn't he? Not like Tiger."

I weep so easily these days.

I am not going to Nell's funeral. How could I? I have been in an accident and am still too unwell. The tactful hypocrisy does us all a kindness.

I am surprised to find myself wishing she had not died hating me, though since it was hardly a new emotion for her to feel

239

towards me, why the fuss? And it would be dishonest to pretend I had any time for her. But, seeing the way she was in that hospital, well, I am not inhuman.

I will send that nice old Henry some flowers or, better still, a plant in a pot, to keep in memory of her. That gets round things nicely. Tiger will drive me out to the nursery. They serve splendid lunches there, too ...

I pick carefully at the biggest scab on my face, it is coming loose ...

NIN

I get all the sticky jobs.
I rounded up the twins. "I have cut my hand very badly, someone has set fire to Mrs Hamilton's house, and your grandmother is dead," I told them.

They were fascinated by my bandages and sling. "Did you have *stitches*?"

"Seven."

"Cor!" They looked at me with respect.

"Is the house burned right down?" one of them asked.

"No."

They lost interest. "Your grandmother," I said, prompting them. They consulted each other in that quick way they have. "I don't suppose she minds," one of them said.

They are nice kids, why do they have to be so damn weird!

"Do you want us to do anything?"

You bet I did. I had them stacking the dishwasher, tidying up the newspapers, putting away clothes left lying about. "Now you can get out the vacuum cleaner," I said. I practically dared them to mention Sophie.

She didn't seem to cross their minds. "OK," they said.

"And don't bump the furniture," I said, testing them.

"I don't, he does," one of them said.

"I don't! It's you!"

241

They went off, arguing amiably, and I sat down and nursed my throbbing hand. The way things were going for us all, I would probably get tetanus.

I started to worry about Kate, She should be with us, not with Caroline Evans.

I worried about David. He is like a string drawn so tight it is bound to snap.

I worried about Henry, he is going downhill before our eyes.

The only people I did not worry about were Maggie and that brother of Sophie's.

And if I thought long enough, I could probably come up with reasons for worrying about them.

The day of the funeral has been fixed. I think my hand will become worse and I will be unable to go. I would feel Nell sneering, knowing that I was only there out of politeness.

"Of course you will go to the funeral," Dan said, "David needs our support. Funerals are for the living, not the dead."

I thought about the funeral of the little girl I killed. That had certainly been a display for the living; it was all about the grief *they* were feeling. I had been obsessed with worry about the child. Where was she now? What was *she* feeling? I had looked for answers and had found none. I am still looking. I sat and brooded. I did not wonder where Nell was or what she was feeling. I have not a big enough nature.

I wish I did not feel so lost, but how else can I feel? It only seems a short time ago that we were all leading ordinary comfortable lives. Dan and David and Kate's husband, by reason of their professions, Pillars of Society in our own little world; me, supporter of the Parents & Citizen's Association and reliable supplier of cakes for any and every function, the darling of grocer and fruit and veg man; Kate, admired and respected just because she was Kate; and

Sophie, our golden girl — God was in His Heaven, you would have thought.

Why did he have to lean down and suddenly pick us out, like the producer of a play, shoving us onstage, without scripts? I have gone off God. Not that I was particularly on him anyway. Given his record with us, I don't find him friendly. If other people do, then he has been playing favourites.

Dan has just told me that David intends to go straight back home after the funeral, so there is no need for me to make a cake.

No cake for Nell.

DAVID

On the day of the funeral we rose to find that Henry, who had apparently hurt his toe several days ago, was in acute pain, with a dangerously high temperature and infection moving up his leg. Matron was furious.

"If you knew," she accused Tiger, "Why did you not—?"

"He didn't complain, and there was so much else going on." The poor fellow was upset. He had had his hands full with Caroline and Kate.

Henry was kept in his bed with Matron to watch over him. I don't think he even noticed when I left for the church.

It all went very quickly. There were flowers from people I had never heard of. Photographers and journalists came and went. The funeral celebrant put on a wonderful performance. I had said I felt unable to give the eulogy. He obviously put that down to an excess of grief and covered for me with professional brilliance. He had never met Nell, but you would have sworn that here was a man who understood every nuance of her electrifying personality. I did not grudge her that. The empty theatricality was all part of what she was.

We did not have a funeral luncheon. The Savages took the boys back to their house, Tiger went back to Caroline and Kate, and I went home to Henry and Matron.

Matron is ropeable. Henry is far too ill to be able to keep the appointment she had made for him with some chap who would tell him about the possibilities in an operation said to be able to reverse the effects of Parkinson's.

"There are people who would give an arm and a leg to have the chance. And Kate Hamilton was going to take him!" She does not take kindly to life interfering with her schedules. Then she concentrated all her attention on me.

"Your boys," she said.

I was immediately on guard. This was a horse of a different colour.

"Things outside one's own experience are difficult to accept, I know, but that does not mean they don't exist." She is a severe woman — puts one on one's mettle. "Go on," I said.

"I worked with the dying for years," she said. "I watched and I think I learned. I grew to disbelieve that the dimension we are living in is all. Death no longer seems the end. Just a door through which we pass into the next room. And that next room is not wholly inaccessible. There are some people who find no difficulty in moving between the two."

"You mean, the boys—!"

"Maybe. Children can be psychic, and grow out of it, or it may stay with them all their lives."

"And which is it with them?"

"Who can say? Just don't make heavy weather of it."

What the hell sort of weather do you make when your children claim to talk to your dead wife? I wondered irritably.

She saw my face. "I'm sorry," she said. "I hope you can believe I have some idea of what I'm talking about. When you have experiences you can't explain, fleeting contacts as real as daylight, information suddenly given when it is vitally needed—"

"What sort of information did you get about Sophie?" I said

suddenly, feeling brutal, and was immediately sorry. She just lifted her hand and let it fall. We sat in uneasy silence.

"How well did you know her?" I managed to say at last.

"Know Sophie? Which one? I think we all had our own Sophie. She was whoever we wanted her to be."

She had certainly been what I wanted. I remembered the way she gave her affection openly, willingly, in a way I could not. I did not know how. Love was strange to me, it was something I could not handle. Her generosity overwhelmed me. I was as incompetent in handling it as a poor man suddenly coming into a fortune. But I revelled in it. I took with both hands.

For the first time, I wondered what *she* got out of our marriage. I heard myself moan.

Matron's hand was on my shoulder. "Don't agonise so," she said. "She wouldn't want—" I wasn't even sure of that.

"It's a lovely evening," the kind voice said. "Why not go for a swim before supper?"

I waded out beyond the breakers to where the silence stretched to the end of the earth.

I gave myself to the water and swam slowly. The peace of being alone was good. It was more than good.

I turned on my back and looked up into the endless blue of the sky.

I thought, they say a man does not become a man until his mother dies, but I don't know about that. What I do know is the sense of being relieved of a crippling load. I breathe free. Now she is out of my life, I must learn to put her out of my mind. Bloody David, she would say, if she knew how I feel now, just as she used to say, Bloody Henry. Life is going to be very different for him, too. It will not be my fault if he does not find some measure of ease.

Sophie.

I tried to bring her face to mind, but her smile was fleeting and the soft features blurred, the image no clearer than a reflection in water. I realised with a pang that she will be easy to forget. Her imprint had not been strong enough, nor deep enough. She had come too late. She had asked too little.

I let her go. I floated, quiet and mindless and grateful. I could not imagine what sort of future lay ahead, but it would be my own. I am now nobody else's man.

When I got back to the house, I went to see Henry.

"A window seat," he said fretfully. "She hates window seats. They didn't give her one, did they?"

His temperature was 104°C.

CAROLINE

Kate is a great worry. Although the burned-out parts of the house could be rebuilt and the rest easily refurbished, she shows no interest, just says she will never live there again. I can understand her being afraid — who would not be? You would hear the scrape of the arsonist's match every minute. But she doesn't want to see the place, or think about it, as though avoiding contact with something contaminated.

David, as her solicitor, and naturally anxious that she will not be more financially disadvantaged than she need be, is doing all he can. "Yes," she says, to whatever he suggests, but keeps her face turned away. He has dealt with the insurance assessors, taken quotes for rebuilding, packed up all the undamaged furniture, books, carpets and put them into store. You name it, he has done it. She doesn't seem to realise how much he is doing for her. Tiger says she is very near a nervous breakdown. I suppose one can understand that. What with the scheme she and Sophie were involved in, her arrest and now this, you could hardly expect her nerves to remain steady.

My face is much improved. I can wear mascara again. I asked Tiger to collect as many car catalogues as he could and we play at choosing my new vehicle.

David has now suggested that Kate should move to his place,

where she and Henry can be company for each other, and Maggie Mackenzie can look after both of them.

"Does this mean you will go, too?" I asked Tiger.

"Not if you don't want me to."

I don't. So that is settled. Not that there is anything physical between Tiger and me. I am happy because it is so like having Sophie back again and because he said, "I've just realised, you are all I have left I can call 'family'."

I don't know what makes him happy, but I believe he is. I think we both have long-term plans for seduction. But there is no hurry. If anybody had told me a few weeks ago ...

"If Sophie hadn't died, would you have come home," I asked him.

"No."

I ask myself, "Which would you choose? For Sophie to be alive still and Tiger never to have come back, or ... ?"

I cannot face the rest of the question. But I know the answer.

NIN

Christmas is impossible to ignore. One year I refused to be sucked in by the hype and sent no Christmas cards. Afterwards, I kept meeting people who said, "Are you all right? We were worried when we didn't get a card." I felt like Scrooge. I can't use my right hand, so Dan has been given the address book and a pile of UNICEF cards.

I have just realised I have not made the cake which should have been maturing in its tin for some weeks, but what with one thing and another, cakes were the last thing on my mind. I will make one anyway, but I need help.

"Aw, Ma!" and, "You can buy one with whisky in it," my pair said, but the twins were delighted with the idea. My cake has everything in it, dried fruit, crystallised fruit, brandy, nuts. It has a very thick layer of marzipan. A small slice and a liqueur and you are fast asleep. I gave the recipe to the twins and turned them loose in the kitchen to assemble the ingredients — which are now all lined up, measured and in bowls. Television can sometimes be instructive. Before we begin the big undertaking, I thought we might make parkin, which will keep well until Christmas Day.

They had never seen black treacle before.

"What's that? Ugh! You can't put that in?" (What is wrong with Australians?)

"What do you expect me to use? Vegemite?"

When we sampled the big, dark, moist result it was so delicious it was all eaten at once, and we must now make another.

Henry and his toe gave us a terrible fright. The doctor came every day and, with Tiger on tap and Maggie to look after him, they managed to keep him out of hospital. I can't damn well drive, so I have only been able to go to see him when Dan could take me.

I am glad Kate is there. I didn't see her at all while she was staying with Caroline Evans. She has lost weight she cannot afford to lose, and it disturbs me to see how dependent she is on tranquillisers. Maggie is watching her very carefully, and she is so sensible that I'm sure she wouldn't allow their use if it weren't necessary. I get touchy. Sophie helped get her into this mess.

As far as I can make out, David is handling the reconstruction of the house with a view to a sale. What she will do then is anybody's guess. She has come so near a total nervous breakdown that we are all pussyfooting around, just glad to get her from one day to the next.

In spite of this wretched hand, I have decided we should all have Christmas together. I'll manage somehow, and it will do people good to be pressured into taking part.

"Pity Zak won't be here," one of the twins said, enraging me.

"And how does your Mum feel about that?" I flared back.

"Good," they said.

I left it.

I was in a dilemma. Caroline Evans had been so unexpectedly kind to Kate, and Kate had obviously found something to like in her, and we had all stood by one another during a bad time. If I was inviting everybody else, how could I exclude her? And yet I knew that never in a million years would she and I ever have anything in common, and we were both too forthright to conceal it. I was saved by Tiger telling me they planned to pick up Caroline's new car and head North. "No real plans. Just a journey to blow away the cobwebs," he said. I had no need to worry about them.

DAVID

I don't know how Nin does it. She made Christmas for us all with one hand.

I bought her a beautiful silk scarf.

Henry is very frail, but recovering from the blood poisoning. Matron is brisk with him. She is brisk with Kate, too. She makes no allowance for self-pity.

"What are you going to do now?" she asks them both.

Henry is worried about the plants left to look after themselves in Adelaide.

"By now ..." he says, his voice full of doom.

The question is, of course, what *is* he going to do? What are we all going to do? Somebody will have to go to Adelaide. The house cannot be left unattended much longer. I cannot go. I have to see Kate's house through to a final sale. She is adamant about getting rid of it. I have sorted out the insurance money for her and find that, though she is not wealthy, the wolf will never be at her door.

I was glad when Nin went with her to buy new clothes so that she no longer had to wear Caroline's.

It was a positive step for her and relieved me of the shock of seeing on a different body clothes I had unzipped or unbuttoned in the past.

I think we are getting to the stage when it might be suggested that she and Matron and Henry all go to Adelaide together to sort things out. Matron is keen to get things dealt with; she has no patience with muddle.

I am also keen to get things sorted out. When Kate's house goes on the market, I will give the agent this house to sell, too. I have positively no wish to stay here — it is full of too much I want to forget. I have no particular wish to stay in the area either. Once the boys are safely in school, I might join Henry in Adelaide for a while.

Actually, not just "for a while". I will stay with him as long as he needs me. I shirk saying "until he dies" but that is what I mean.

Matron has come up with the brilliant idea that she should take a little holiday and escort him back home, and that Kate should go with them and stay until she feels well again, and knows what she wants to do. I can't think of anything better. Henry and Kate are fond of each other, and once Kate is herself again, she will be happy to be with him until I can make my own break from here and join him. It is a huge house; she could have her own rooms. And if she liked Adelaide and wished to stay on, well, there are many possibilities. I feel better about things than I have for quite a time.

KATE

It angers me to have fallen apart so badly. I held together in times far worse than these. They say it is the culmination of months of strain. What I feel most is the creeping horror of knowing I must have been watched for some time for somebody to know when to set the house alight with the least risk of being caught doing it. Even here, in Caroline's house, I still feel I am being watched by faceless men waiting to do me harm.

The suggestion that I should go to Adelaide with Henry and Matron is heaven-sent. Perhaps there the fear will leave me. Perhaps I will dare to feel safe now that they have done what they wished, destroyed my home and driven me away. Perhaps divine justice is at work. That dreadful man has lost all his ill-gotten money, I have been punished for what I did, but the little people who were robbed did not suffer in the end. I must hang on to that.

David is being more than kind; he is taking care of everything. "Don't worry. Just get well," he says. Nin is a rock, and Caroline Evans has proved herself other than we thought. We should have realised that Sophie would not have been so fond of her if she were only the high-handed creature we took her to be.

Sophie. It seems a long time since I have thought of her. Nin said the same thing the other day. I have given up feeling any guilt about her. Yes, she must have been under more pressure than we realised, but I have been under pressure, too, and if I had chosen to die rather than face it that would be up to me and nobody else. And I would have left a note to absolve those left behind. With the best will in the world, regard for her is being sorely tested. Weak? Selfish?

Surely not the way anyone would think about our Soph. But I am too tired to worry about it now. I have to concentrate on getting better, not only for my own sake, but to help Henry. Things are not going to be easy for him, Maggie says.

HENRY

We are preparing for the return to Adelaide. When Nell and I left, I had no inkling the return would be like this. To say that I feel odd without her is an understatement; to say that I am unhappy would be a lie. The truth is I could not have coped with her any longer, and I know it and am grateful I was not put to further test. I do not care to think of the incidents which preceded her death and which, undoubtedly, hastened it. She was being Nell. I have not spoken to David about it. There may be no need. He shows no sign that he might be worried and relations with Caroline have become free and open.

Tiger brought her to see me. I was amused. She always did remind me of Nell. She is a slightly battered Nell at the moment, but is undiminished, which I admire. It is clear that a relationship is developing between them. They ask me about Hairy, his father, whom I knew well and liked very much, and hang on every word I say. Nell was never a laugher. Caroline is — or perhaps is because Tiger is.

I very much enjoyed seeing them together. He gives her free rein to be her rather outrageous self, which he obviously admires, but I recognised the silken thread with which he pulls her in. David watches them together with some surprise, but with pleasure, I think.

If only I can keep well enough. Maggie is going to get things organised in Adelaide. She says I will need a nurse and that, later on, I may need more than one. "As long as you pick them," I told her.

Parkinson's does not take away one's mental faculties, as some illnesses do. I am lucky. Kate and I enjoy doing the cryptic crossword puzzle together, we like the same books and enjoy discussing them, and I can still climb into the car so that we can take little jaunts and have picnics. I must not mind that getting about is difficult and that I need a bib when I take food. I do not yet slur my words badly enough to make conversation difficult. This disease has taken its time. I hope it will continue to move slowly. When we reach Adelaide, I will be confronted by Nell again, full blast. I don't quite know what that will mean. I may feel, as David does, the need to get away from old memories. How quickly life slides us forward, leaving the dead behind. Nobody mentions Sophie these days. When Caroline and Tiger heard that David was planning to sell the house, I saw them exchange looks. I think he has a buyer — or buyers.

I want things to go well for David. I have had to revise my opinion of him. There was no weakness in the way he handled the nightmare situations we have all had to face. He was forthright in his dealings with Nell, and the consideration and kindness he has shown me seem to come from the heart. And now he is being a pillar of strength to poor stricken Kate.

He is obviously a good solicitor — something for which Nell would never give him credit — though I imagine clients must find him stiffer than is comfortable. He is not at ease with people, not like Tiger is. But then Tiger did not have Nell for a mother. One wonders what David would have been like if he had had Hairy for a father.

As the twig is bent, so the tree will grow. I hope the bending has stopped now. He is both old enough to recognise his faults and young enough to have years ahead in which to get things straight. I wonder if he ever will. Do people? Did I?

I have the feeling Nin has hopes about him and Kate. I don't see it. I love my Kate, but no ... That isn't the way things go. They are good for each other now, but ... Sometime — and after my time I hope it is — he will find someone who reminds him of Nell, of Caroline.

There was a hand on my shoulder. "Come on, my lad," Matron was saying. "Sit up! Nin is here with one of her cakes. A special one." I sat up at once. Nin's cakes are always worth sitting up for. It was a parkin, dark, moist and smelling strongly and deliciously of ginger.

"I cried into that when I was making it," Nin accused. "It's my goodbye cake."

"Kiss me before I get sticky," I said.

Kate came in bearing the tea tray. "Have you got his bib?" Nin asked. She had. Maggie put it on for me.

A tea party with three lovely women rates high in my litany of pleasures.

NIN

I went up to David's house to say my goodbyes to Henry, Kate and Maggie. I never go to the airport to see people off; greet them, yes, farewell them, no.

This could be my final goodbye to Henry. And Kate, whom I have come to love, will never return to live here again. I have lost that lovely day-to-day intimacy. I came home feeling low.

David's boys are still with us but will soon be going away to school. They are very excited. I still don't know what to make of them. I told both David and Maggie what they had said about Zak and Sophie. They took it very calmly, so I suppose I must. Twins are certainly different. I wonder what would happen if they were ever separated? Maggie says their gift — whatever you call it — seems quite ordinary to them. Maybe they are the ones I should have asked about my little girl.

You think such wild things when you are upset, and I am — as usual; and I am fed up with it.

Everything is in such a state of flux. David will be the next to leave. I know it. I can see him gearing up to be off as soon as he sells Kate's house.

Tiger has bought David and Sophie's house. He is not going back to England. Makes sense. After all, it was his old home. We see him from time to time, but he is mostly with Caroline Evans. She is firing on all cylinders again. She would. She and Tiger seem to have become a couple. Surprise, Surprise! Now, now, Dan says. She is all smiles when we run across each other in the village but has the good sense to leave it at that.

Dan is, as always, the firm ground beneath my feet. I am determined not to put him through any more stress on my account.

There is just one thing though. Maggie will be back. She has time for me now. One day I will drive down the country to where the strange green shapes loom over the hedges, and I will sit with her and talk. I will ask her what she has learned, as a nurse and as a medium, about what happens to people when they die. She will know why I ask. Perhaps now, when there is no Sophie to distract her, she will be willing to tell me.

MATRON MACKENZIE

As the great surge of power lifted the aircraft into the sky, Maggie Mackenzie sank back into her seat and drew a deep breath of relief. She was on her way home. Her mind ran ahead, reaching out with impatient longing for the empty rooms and the silence. No voices. No people. She was tired. Is my tiredness dative or ablative? she asked herself. Am I tired "of" people or "by" them?

Not by Henry, at least, though settling him back in his home had not been without angst. Nell seemed to have been waiting for them on the threshold. The junk mail overspilling the letterbox and littering the drive, the sagging plants in the borders had laid their immediate accusation clear as the click of her disapproving tongue. Inside the house, her strident personality was strewn around. Fortunately Kate, who had not known Nell, saw the evidence merely as things which needed clearing away. Thank heaven for Kate.

"I had forgotten," Henry had said, looking around with pleasure at tidiness and space.

Saying goodbye to him had not been a sadness, although she knew it was likely to be their last farewell. He had Kate — and would have David — to look after him for as long as needed and, when the time came for him to go, she was sure he would greet it calmly, even with lively curiosity. The thought of Henry and death was full of amused and comfortable speculation.

And no need to worry too much about Kate, she thought. Caring for Henry seemed to have given her life a purpose it had lacked and the chance to be free of the sadness and dangers of past years. The fondness she and David felt for Henry will sustain them both until they are strong enough to go their separate ways.

But Sophie. The thought of Sophie was the stone in the shoe.

So many people asking themselves in anguish and bewilderment, *was it my fault?* But they only ever saw Sophie in the light of what she meant to them. They never thought of how she might seem to herself.

I knew. *Mea culpa.* But how can anyone gauge another person's breaking point?

She kept up her façade of merriness so well. I knew that behind it was another Sophie, the one with the poor opinion of herself, the one who thought everyone else was more important than she was, the one who asked nothing and gave to those she cared about everything she thought they wanted, although it might tear her to shreds. Some people might call that doing good. I don't, but it is hard to tell those who mean well that they are doing harm. I shirked it.

She was left alone to face the growing knowledge that giving was dangerous.

The licence she gave to David and Caroline, the encouragement she gave to Kate, the abortion she had to save David stress — everything done with love, and with such dire results.

Did she, in a moment of blinding clarity, realise that she was as she was, and could not change? Did it seem better to die before she could do more harm?

I don't know. Nobody knows. Only poor desperate loving little Sophie could tell us. But life will roll on without her, we will think of her less and less. The question will become academic. But how will it be for her? What did she solve? Will she, as they say, have to come back again?

The flight was smooth, and she felt herself slipping into sleep. On the edge of oblivion, another question teased. When Nin Savage comes to see me, as I know she will, and asks the question I know she will ask, what can I tell her?

Only that I wish I knew, she thought. And slept.